I0831331

IMMORTAL PLUNDER

PIRATES OF FELICITY: BOOK ONE

KELLY ST. CLARE

Edited by Melissa Scott and Robin Schroffel
Cover illustration and design by Amalia Chitulescu Digital Art

IMMORTAL PLUNDER

Exosia

Kentro

Maltu

Pleo

Selkie's Cove

Portum

Syraness

Febribus

Charybdis

Neos

Zol

Caspian Sea

Dynami Sea

N

W

E

S

Exosian Realm

To people who lurk on beanbags in libraries

ONE

The pull of land after weeks at sea was a temptation none of *Felicity*'s crew could deny—especially not Ebba.

The wobbling feeling that lingered from life on the water would fade in a few days—just before she re-boarded their beloved ship, *Felicity*, to sail home. As much as she adored every cedarwood inch of their pirate sloop and knew every creaking nook like the back of her hand, while on land she planned to have as much fun as possible.

"Has anyone seen my silk socks?"

Ebba glanced up from the sand-encrusted wood of Maltu's Wharf, where they'd docked, and peered across at the eldest of her six fathers. Fifty-eight-year-old Barrels stood with one bare white foot propped up on the bulwark of the ship. He was the only one still aboard *Felicity*. The rest of the crew begrudgingly hovered on the wharf pier, waiting for him to finish dressing. The pull of land after weeks at sea couldn't be denied . . . and neither could the urge to dress in finery for the occasion.

"Aye, matey," said another of her fathers, Stubby. Ebba glanced over her shoulder and caught his glinting grin as he continued, "Grubby used 'em to swab the deck."

"Is that so?" Barrels replied, raising his brows.

Ebba withheld a sigh and surveyed his apparel. The buttoned doublet, knee breeches, and crisp linen shirt he wore were commonplace for him. For their Maltu trading trip, he'd added one of his best cravats, an enameled brooch, and had secured his salt-and-pepper hair in a leather tie at the base of his neck.

"Ye be lookin' fine, Barrels," she said, folding her arms. "I don't think ye need the socks and shoes at all. No one will be noticin'."

Peg-leg, another of her fathers, wiped at the sweat dripping from his bald head. Mid-day usually saw him down in the ship's hold cooking lunch, so he was unused to the sweltering tropical heat at this time. She knew that he'd be bursting to drink tea with Sherry as soon as possible, and, sure enough, his voice was edged as he spoke, "Ebba be right. How often do landlubbers look down? Hurry along, will ye?"

"As often as they look up, I suppose," Barrels mused with a ghost of a smile. Sometimes, originally being a landlubber himself, Barrels spoke fancy-like and meant something smarter underneath what he actually said. Most times, after an awkward pause, the crew just continued on with the conversation.

"Aye . . . well," Stubby grunted, the glint returning to his gray-blue eyes, "like I said, Grubby swabbed the deck with yer silk socks yest'rday."

An indignant squeak sounded. Grubby, the youngest of her fathers at forty-five, looked back at them from where he crouched on all fours, staring over the side of the wharf.

"Now, now. Don't ye be spreadin' fibs about me." He cast Peg-leg a slightly admonishing look.

Ever the peacemaker, Ebba couldn't recall seeing Grubby angry once in her seventeen years. The pirate could usually be found with a sloppy and toothless grin on his face, the result of being hit in the back of the head when he was young. Her fathers said the wooden boom hit him so hard that some of the rum in his skull had spilled out and left him a bit empty up there.

Standing, Grubby straightened his yellowed canvas shirt, tucking the ends into the top of his frayed and stained slops. He never changed into different clothes for land. Out of the seven members of their crew, he showed the least excitement when going ashore, much preferring the water.

"I haven't seen yer silk socks, matey," he said nervously. Snatching his Monmouth cap off his head, he began twisting it in both hands.

Locks, the fifth of Ebba's fathers, took mercy. Often as not, their crew ceased arguments for fear Grubby'd explode with stress. "Check in yer books, Barrels. Last I saw, ye were usin' them to mark the page."

"You're completely right, my fellow!" Barrels hurried back the way he'd come, likely going to search his cramped office below deck.

Grubby sighed, staring after him. "Well," he said, replacing his cap and patting his non-existent pockets, "that got worked out in the end. We all be happy again." He paused, scanning the rest of them. "Ain't we?"

Peg-leg snorted. "Aye, Grubs. We all be happy again." Shaking his head, he limped up the wharf, the wooden peg where his left leg used to be creating a *tap-tap-tap* as he went.

"Barrels had all mornin' to dress," Ebba muttered to her sixth father, patience finally caving. Seriously, even she was ready.

Plank smiled from the shade of the ship. "He'll be along smart-like. Don't ye worry. How about ye show me what ye're wearin' to the market, little nymph?"

He'd nicknamed her after a water creature that liked to cause trouble—one of the mythical beings that featured in his stories of old magic. His love of story-telling aside, Plank was also the most fashionable of her fathers, and the only one who understood her interest in colors, fabrics, and trinkets.

Ebba spun slowly so he didn't miss any of the small touches.

She'd tucked a billowing linen tunic into the belted waist of her full-length pants—the least frayed of her three pairs of slops. A laced, leather-brown jerkin hugged her light frame over the tunic and she'd placed black ties around her elbows on each side, so the shirtsleeves were drawn in halfway. A bright green bandana covered the top of her forehead and hairline. Her midnight dreadlocks coursed mid-way down her back and could be a pain in the hull at times, but the bandana kept the black mass out of her eyes. Not only was this helpful when the wind was high, especially considering the colorful wooden beads in her dreads liked to whip her across the face, but it allowed Ebba's single gold hoop earring to be seen. To all that, she'd added a deep-blue silk sash, with a second black leather sash on top of it, across her torso, and into *that*, she'd tucked her two pistols and three daggers. A single-edged curved cutlass swung from the belt on her left hip.

"Ye look right-fierce," Plank said seriously. "But ye'll be needin' shoes in the market. There be glass about."

Ebba crinkled her nose and stared at the dark bronze skin of her feet. She loathed shoes.

A double thud startled both of them, and Ebba stared at the leather fold-down boots now on the wharf before her. She tilted her head, eyes narrowed at Barrels.

. . . But at least he was finally ready.

She yanked on the boots and dusted her hands off, surveying the six taut lines holding their boat to the pier. *Felicity* wasn't going anywhere—especially not with the extra fee Stubby paid the dock master to keep thieves away. And if the thieves still dared, the black ship cat, Pillage, would claw their eyes out. Pillage took the protection of *Felicity* very seriously. Even against most of the crew.

"Look after the ship, Pillage." Barrels patted the overweight cat.

Their crew left the ship at long last, striding after Peg-leg toward the shore.

As she walked, Ebba ran a hand over the two strands of wooden beads in her dreadlocks. A thrill shot through her as she peered around the bustling wharf. Merchants' fluyts, chartered caravels, messenger cutters, and fishermen's rigs filled the harbor. Well, they *appeared* to. In reality, a fair number were pirate ships, but these ships blended in with the others. For good reason, too: They'd passed at least one of the King's man-o'-wars on the way in to dock. The huge navy ships floated offshore, and their crews of eight hundred navy men would be scattered around the island. Not to mention the navy crews from the cutters and sloops-o'-war bobbing in the docks.

It was the riskiest thing her fathers did, trading with the merchants of Maltu with the king's navy men about. Maltu was one of the islands closest to the mainland, Exosia, and more tightly controlled by the king who ruled over all the islands in the realm. Seeing as King Montcroix loathed pirates, not many crews chanced trading here, preferring to trade on the notorious pirate island, Febribus. But her fathers flat-out refused to take her *there*, so Maltu it was. The only other pirate crews who came here were much larger than *Felicity*, both in crew and ship.

"Ahoy, *Felicity*!" a voice boomed.

Ebba's booted feet sank into the white sand and she turned, stomach sinking fast as she recognized the pirates within the rowboat close to shore. Dressed from head to toe in black, aside from a sash the color of dried blood slung around their hips, were five of *Malice's* crew.

"Still callin' yerself pirates? Or have ye realized ye just be old merchants?" the same young man heckled. The rest of his crew snig-gered at the comment.

An introduction wasn't necessary. His name was Swindles, and he was the *Malice* captain's right-hand man. Flaming sod.

Every time her fathers docked *Felicity* they copped the same shite from this crew. *Malice* was the biggest pirate ship in the seas and *Felicity* one of the smallest, but that didn't give them an excuse to make *Felicity* the butt of endless jokes. Ebba could take a hit on the chin most times, but not about her fathers, and *not* about their ship.

Swindles snorted, not lifting a finger to help as the other crew members pulled the rowboat ashore. "Get a load o' the crazy one, lads."

He pointed to where Grubby was swilling his hands in the edges of the tide. The *Malice* crew threw their heads back, their loud, sneering laughing drawing the attention of those nearby.

White-hot heat flooded Ebba's cheeks. "He ain't crazy," she snapped at them, striding to stand next to her father. "He were hit over the head by the boom when he were young."

"Whatever ye say." Swindles smirked, vaulting over the lip of the rowboat and landing in the white sand.

Scorching anger moved swiftly into place, and Ebba opened her mouth to deliver a tongue-lashing.

"Ebba-Viva."

The soft reprimand came from Locks. He watched her with his sole emerald eye, though the brow over his eye patch was also raised, stretching the array of thin scars on his cheeks.

It was enough to give her pause. After the last fight she'd started at the docks with a pirate crew, her fathers had refused to let her return unless she minded her temper. Truthfully, *Malice* really weren't a ship to mess with, their crew being around fourteen times the size of *Felicity*'s.

Reluctantly swallowing her retort, Ebba shoved her fury down as best she could.

For lack of anything more satisfying to do, she planted her hands on her hips and scowled. They weren't even real pirates. *Felicity* may be aged, but she was reliable and manned by pirates who stuck to the old ways. The *true* ways, as Peg-leg called them.

"Those young, flashy pirates don't know anythin'," she whispered to Barrels on her other side, unable to resist saying *something*.

"No," said Barrels, his mouth twitching. "Though, you know, they're only in their twenties. Or late teens, like you."

"Would ye look at the glower on fish-lips' face?" said another of *Malice*'s crew with a snort.

Were they talking to her? They were talking to her! The white-hot anger reared up again and Ebba lunged forward.

A hand gripped the back of her sash, pulling her away from the other crew, up the beach. "*Ebba-Viva Fairisles!*"

She glared at Barrels over her shoulder, fists clenched as she stumbled backward in his wake. "Ye heard 'em. I'm goin' to shove my entire fist down Swindles' throat." She'd wipe the damn smirk off his ugly mug.

"And they'll finish it, most assuredly." Barrels continued tugging her gently in the direction of town.

Assuredly, she thought in disgust. Fancy words. What was the point of them? She let up, however, shoulders sagging as she pivoted from the jeering young men to walk beside Barrels.

"We gotta defend *Felicity*," she whispered to him.

And not just the ship. They had to defend *themselves*. Why were other pirates cruel about Grubby and the age of her fathers? Sure, her fathers were past the age of adventures and excitement. And they never chased any plunder reeking of danger these days—if anything, they ran away from it. There was no one in the entire Exosian Realm that she loved more than her fathers, but in a place filled with pirates, the reality was that their crew were perceived as weak. That rankled in several ways, but foremost was worry over her fathers' wellbeing.

Sometimes Ebba wished *Felicity* was a glossy schooner with a crew of one hundred. Blimey, even going after real plunder for a change instead of fruit and veg, might make *Malice* shut their stupid gobs.

Barrels peered down at her, his weathered face soft. "They are just words, my dear. Just words. You and I understand *Felicity*'s crew has secrets to keep close. If these pirates knew what we knew, they wouldn't be laughing at all. I know it's hard, but focus on that and ignore the rest. One day, they won't laugh at us."

She looked once more at the surrounding ships, each sleeker and larger than the next.

One day their crew might not be a laughing stock, but what happened in the meantime? What if the jeering from the other pirates turned to violence before then? *Felicity,* though aged, was still a prize for any pirate who deemed her crew too weak to defend their ship.

Ebba sighed heavily, hoping that 'one day' didn't come too late.

TWO

Leaving the white beach, they waded through the tussock grass and proceeded up the sandy pathway cleared through the pale bulbous trees. The trill of a harmonic and the high scale of an accordion blasted from the town ahead, urging her feet faster.

Her temper was quick to come and quick to go, so the wharf incident was all but forgotten, and Ebba hustled toward the bustling crowds, a small grin upon her face. She was going to get fabric for another sash, a rich color that complemented her dark skin. And maybe her fathers would gift her another bead. Every one of the beads in her dreads had been gifts from them over the years—buying beads herself would break tradition.

"Can't ye hurry a scant bit?" she pleaded with her fathers.

Grubby smiled his toothy grin. "Sure, Ebba-Viva." He lowered his head to pick up speed.

A puffing Barrels gripped Grubby's arm. "This pace is perfectly fine, thank you very much."

Grubby blanched and looked between Ebba and Barrels with wide eyes.

Smiling, Ebba tucked her hand into Grubby's. "Don't get yer sails in a twist, Grubs. I can walk at this pace. Though I'm thinkin' a fishin' rig could row through sand faster."

"More o' a run, little nymph," corrected Plank lazily. Only he and Grubby weren't puffing.

Ebba frowned and focused on the others. They were kind of . . . running. She slowed with a sheepish glance at them. "S'cuse me."

"I ain't complainin'," sang Locks in his tone-deaf voice. "I'll be seein' my light-o'-love, my star shine—"

"What's this one called?" Stubby asked, grunting as he pushed through the white sand.

Locks closed his eye, a wrinkle appearing between his brows. "Maltu harbor, see the barber, turn right . . . Delight!"

"Delight?" Ebba replied. "Are ye sure that ain't the one on Kentro?"

Doubt stuttered through the emerald shards of Locks' eye. The color was made brighter by the frayed eye patch covering the socket on the other side. "Kentro dock, chicken flock, gravy hock . . . Locks! Wait, wait. That's for r'memberin' me own name. Kentro market, has a basket, nice skin, Laylin. Aye," he said with a sigh and smile. "Delight be on Maltu."

The crew snorted, and Ebba shook her head. Served him right if Delight booted him off the limestone cliffs. A girlfriend on each island. It would come back to bite him in the tenders sooner or later. The one-eyed Locks wasn't known for his patience though—she blamed *him* for her temper. He didn't like to wait between times for just one girlfriend.

At a fork in the road, the group separated in two.

Ebba trailed after Plank and Stubby to the marketplace, jumping to watch the rest of their crew disappear into the throes of the crowd. Barrels had business to deal with in town; as the quartermaster of the ship, he looked after their investments and the trades. Locks was off to visit with Delight. And Peg-leg would head straight to Sherry to drink tea, Grubby in his wake.

She, Plank, and Stubby would meet them at the tavern later, but later never failed to feel like a long time away. Their crew splitting up always felt as odd as walking on land. Ebba rubbed her chest in an attempt to quell her nerves.

"Watch et!" Someone jostled her roughly.

She snarled at them and gripped the butt of her pistol. The person squeaked and scampered away.

"Play nice," Stubby said, pulling her to his side. Her back snapped into a straight line despite the loving gesture. It always did when Stubby used that tone. Ebba grinned impishly, not in the least sorry for doing exactly what a pirate should. Especially because Stubby taught her that particular trick at age five.

Vibrant splashes of color dotted the marketplace before her.

Bright banners hung across the square space in every direction, and through them Ebba could see drunken seamen and large-busted women waving and leaning out of the windows. A spattering of sand coated the bare ground, even after the fifteen-minute walk inland. Market stands littered the square in no particular order, and the merchants guarded their goods with eyes like hawks. Why wouldn't they, with the vagabonds and thieves skulking about? Ebba kept one hand on her cutlass and the other on a dagger. Damn thieves had nimble fingers and were nigh impossible to detect. She'd lost at least one possession from a past visit to Maltu.

The Maltu locals lived in shacks dotted across the island, but the rich lived in grand double-story wooden houses, like the houses here. Despite the wealth bordering the marketplace, she passed all manner of people at its center: merchants, servants, fishermen's wives, snot-nosed children, and other pirates—even fancy gentry men in their padded doublets. They'd be picked dry of any money before they reached their quarters. *Landlubbers.*

Soon the bustling crowd was so thick Ebba could scarcely move. She stuck close behind Stubby, whose evil look sent the inhabitants of Maltu skittering away. The same trick he'd just scolded her for.

Ebba crouched as Stubby suddenly ducked right. A navy man had to be close by. Keeping low, she weaved behind him, checking over her shoulder to make sure Plank was in tow.

After several minutes in this fashion, Stubby stopped in front of a tool merchant. As *Felicity*'s boatswain, he replenished the tools needed to upkeep the ship. But tools were the last thing she wanted to look at. She only had three days to have enough adventure to last her weeks at sea.

Grabbing Plank's hand, Ebba yanked him in the direction of a fabric merchant. She'd spent all her coin in Kentro when they were filling *Felicity*'s hold with produce. Wheedling new trinkets out of the fashion-conscious Plank was easier than Stubby. Plank wasn't the youngest of her parents, but sure looked it. His mass of coiled hair hadn't grayed from raven black, and his lean frame was as straight as *Felicity*'s mast. Ebba thought it might be because he spent half his time in a humming daydream. Not that Plank was idle. He'd just mastered the art of dreaming while working.

Ebba moved from stand to stand, picking up brooches and pins, and letting soft materials flow through her fingers. She lingered at an ancient woman's stall, staring wistfully and purposefully at the collection of beautiful beads there. Imagine having all of those. She loved her beads. Each of them was a memory and held great meaning. But there was always a tiny temptation to buy handfuls of them. A pirate with beaded hair? Landlubbers would run screaming at the sound of her rattling approach. She'd be as fearsome as Buckle O'Pigswill—the first pirate to ever live. However, the sentimental side of the beads were far more important to her, so she was willing to wait to fill her dreads one bead at a time.

She smiled to herself, reaching out to stroke a white bead.

"Which do ye favor, little nymph?" Plank asked her.

"This white one," she said. "It's like those oyster pearls we came across in Pleo."

Plank smiled, saying softly, "So it is. Trust a water nymph to pick a pearl."

He turned to the crinkled woman and began to haggle.

Another bead! Ebba withheld her smile, already thinking about where she'd start the third strand. She couldn't make the wrong choice, though luckily on *Felicity* she had nothing but time.

The sun had lowered and the crowd thinned as Maltu locals headed home for their evening meal. Her eyes passed over a vomiting navy man, who'd clearly celebrated being ashore too much, and fell on the sauntering movement of two young men, one of which they'd just left at the beach.

The ugly mug, Swindles, and his best matey, Riot, were strutting through the marketplace.

Many in the crowd watched the men's passage—though the smart ones watched from the corner of their eyes, lest they attract the wrong sort of attention. That was the effect *Malice* had. Their cruel reputation preceded them.

Ebba made sure to blend in as they strutted past, curious to see their heads were held together like Stubby's and Peg-leg's when they spoke of the brandy stash they thought her ignorant of.

As the pirates moved away, she tracked their passage, curiosity smoldering in her innards.

. . . They were the kind of people that needn't whisper unless they had something to hide.

Ebba cast a furtive glance at Plank, who was still engaged in a haggling battle with the old woman, stingy bugger. Depend upon it, he'd cheat her out of any kind of profit on the bead and would waste an hour saving a dime. Meanwhile, Stubby was yet to leave the tool merchant's stall. They'd be in exactly the same position in ten minutes' time.

She ducked between stalls and dodged through the thinning crowd. Thirty feet ahead, Swindles and Riot swaggered, their heads still close. They stopped abruptly and scanned the market.

Skidding to a halt, she picked up a brass trinket from a stand, pretending to study it closely. Ebba watched from the corner of her eye. After one last scan, the burly pair disappeared down an alley.

Anyone with sense knew nothing legal-like happened in an alley. Something was amiss, all right. And she was going to find out what it was. Abandoning the trinket, Ebba took off in pursuit once more.

Were they stealing? That wasn't *so* bad if they'd tried to get the bounty the right way first. Her crew were stole-traders—meaning they tried to trade honestly and if that didn't yield enough, they stole the rest—so Ebba could hardly judge Swindles and Riot for doing the same.

Or was a shady deal underfoot? She'd love nothing more than to wipe the smarmy grins right off *Malice*'s faces by ruining a dodgy trade. A tiny payback for their earlier comments to Grubby. A grin spread across her face; Ebba wouldn't be a real pirate if she didn't *attempt* to listen in.

At the entrance to the alley, she hesitated for the barest second before peeking into the darkness after the two pirates. There was more sand in there than the marketplace; the double-storied houses had trapped the white granules drifting in the wind. Two sets of footprints in the sand trailed down the main alley and disappeared around a corner.

Ebba touched her beads absently, noting the long shadows and littering of broken glass before her. Five minutes must have already passed, but taking a breath, she took a step into the sandy alley. Her fathers would still be exactly where she left them.

A rat scuttled across her path, and a scream lodged in her throat.

Just a rat, ye coiled eejit.

Hugging the wall made slimy by constant damp heat, Ebba skimmed across the alley to the corner at the end. Or she tried to skim, blasted clunky boots. Reaching the corner, she sank down into a crouch and pressed herself against the grimy wood of a barrel, listening hard.

"I'm tellin' ye, Pockmark has found it."

Oo, that sounded like good stuff. Staying low in her crouch, Ebba shuffled along the barrel to peek around the corner. A smaller alley branched off the one where she huddled, extending thirty-five feet or so. Swindles and Riot stood across from each other in the dark space by the far dead end. Riot played with the tip of his dagger while a wide-eyed Swindles tried to hold his attention with the gossip.

She eased back behind the safety of the wall, hunching to make herself as small as possible.

"Aye, he's *found it* afore, though, ain't he? Four years we've been searchin' for the bloody spot," said Riot dismissively.

"This time it be *real*."

"How do ye know that, Swin? He ain't told us what he be seekin'. Ever." The words were laced with bitterness. "We just search and search and search."

Four years. No plunder seemed important enough for that long a quest. It had to be something really valuable. Ebba tensed at a scuffing sound, letting out a shaking breath as she realized it was only one of the pirates kicking at the sand.

There was a long pause. "Ye swear on Davy Jones' Locker you won't say nothin'?"

"Aye," Riot answered quickly.

"Well, I don't rightly know what it be, but Pockmark told me if we plunder this one treasure, none o' us need ever work again. He said there be enough for each o' us to buy an *island*."

Ebba's jaw dropped.

The treasure had to be a whole cave full of gems and gold. *Malice* had a crew of one hundred and each of them would be able to afford an *island*? She couldn't even imagine that plunder split between a crew of seven. Her fathers wouldn't have to keep working on their secret plan anymore. They'd be able to explore the seas instead of constantly steal-trading.

"There ain't that many islands to be had," Riot said flatly. "And why did he tell ye this, and not me?"

Ebba's leg began to tingle from the cramped position. She shifted slightly and froze as her belt scraped against the barrel behind her.

"What was that?" Swindles demanded.

Her eyes sought the mouth of the alley, and her muscles coiled to dash back to the safety of the crowd. If the pirates discovered her listening to a conversation about un-plundered treasure, it'd mean a bullet lodged in her innards. She didn't dare breathe as the silence around the corner thickened and extended. Were they creeping closer?

A second rat scuttled across the alley.

"Just a rat, ye plonker." Riot snorted. The young men sniggered loudly. Ebba slowly unfroze and inhaled again, suddenly wishing her leather jerkin was looser.

"All right, Swin. I'm all ears. What be the latest?" Riot said in a resigned voice.

Swindles' voice lowered. Even with the echo caused by the narrow alley, Ebba had to lean closer to hear. "Pockmark holed up a soothsayer last night. The one down the east end of Maltu."

"The one with two heads and three arms?"

"So they say. I ain't sure. Pockmark said the soothsayer couldn't tell him where the treasure were—"

"Told ye—"

"—*But* afore he killed her, she screamed o' a secret tree. Ye eat the tree's fruit and ye can be askin' any question and get the answer. That be how we'll find the treasure."

Riot scoffed. "A magic tree. O' all the things. Ye've lost yer wick."

Swindles reply was indignant. "It be true! Pockmark told me himself. Ye doubtin' the word of our captain?"

Riot's reply was hasty. "No, course not. Never have, never will, and don't ye be tellin' lies to the otherwise." The fear in his voice echoed through the shadows and he hurried on. "So where be this magic tree then?"

They dropped their voices to barely above a whisper.

"Neos. . . ."

Ebba strained to hear the rest of their muffled conversation, startling when their voices rose once more.

"How do we be gettin' through all that jungle then? The tribespeople will fillet us one by one," Riot mused.

Swindles chuckled. "That be the easy part—we've always had the right guide for the job; we just didn't know the magic tree was there to begin with. That cocky bastard Jagger'll lead us right to it. He's from Neos, been to the mountain afore and everythin'. Pockmark will eat the magic fruit and ask where the real treasure be. Lo and behold, not long from now we'll each be havin' our own island."

With a second jolt, Ebba realized their voices were getting louder. They were moving back into the main alley.

She rose silently, ready to dash away when her gaze landed on the sand underfoot . . . the sand now imprinted with three sets of footprints, not just two. Sink her! They'd know someone had been here listening, and then they'd waste no time going for the treasure.

She wanted the treasure. For her fathers, and to put an end to the cruel comments about *Felicity* and their crew once and for all.

Working frantically, Ebba slid her cutlass free, grimacing at the slight hiss as it left the sheath.

Ignoring her rapid heartbeat, she began to smooth her trail away with the flat edge. The men's voices grew louder as they approached the main alley from around the corner.

She frantically swished the cutlass back and forth, shuffling back with tiny steps.

One of the pirates laughed, *far* too close. Halfway would have to do!

Ebba placed her boots in her old prints as though she'd just arrived and shoved her cutlass into its sheath. She may not have book smarts like Barrels, but she prided herself on being conniving when the situation demanded it. Her fathers called it 'survival smarts', but they were a scant bit bias.

Swindles and Riot rounded the corner, talking excitedly.

The two pirates didn't notice her immediately—boots in her old footprints, knees at an awkward angle to keep her balance. When they did notice her, the pirates jerked to a halt and she took another step forward.

"Didn't know the alley were oc'upied," she blurted. "I'll be leavin'." Fighting one or two of *Malice*'s crew in broad daylight with her six fathers as backup was far different from meeting two of the jeering pirates in a dark alley. Alone.

Before they could answer, Ebba spun in the direction of the marketplace, eager to tell Stubby and Plank what she'd overheard.

There was just one tiny problem.

The mouth of the alleyway was no longer empty. Planted firmly in the middle of it, the dying sunlight illuminating his burly frame, was a man everyone who wished to survive knew to avoid.

Pockmark. The captain of *Malice*.

THREE

Fear lodged in her throat and her feet slowed of their own accord. *Not good, not good, not good.*

"What do we got here?" the captain of *Malice* taunted, taking a swaggering step toward her.

Ebba made no answer. Instinct told her to keep as quiet as possible, to attempt the impossible and meld into the building if she could. In that moment, Ebba needed no help understanding that she was a seventeen-year-old pirate, and he a twenty-something hardened criminal.

The tiny scars marring his face had earned him the name, and Mercer Pockmark was as unsightly as he was reputedly brutal. There was no village he wouldn't pillage, no person he wouldn't slit from ear to ear for enough gold, or even copper. But the young man truly earned his reputation four years ago, when he gutted his own father to seize control of the black-and-crimson *Malice*. Such a misdeed was abhorrent to her every thought and sense.

Where his crew wore all black, with the single dark red sash, Pockmark dressed entirely in black with a tricorn hat embroidered with gold upon his head. So many gold jewels and chains draped across his person that determining the number of them from where Ebba stood was impossible.

A whisper of moving sand alerted her to Swindles and Riot's presence behind her. She spun and put her back to the left wall, fingering a pistol and a dagger.

Pockmark inhaled the air. "Smell that, boys? *Fear*." He smirked and his two lackeys echoed the expression.

"It be fish-lips from that wreck o' a ship," the captain said, taking one predatory step in her direction. "Whatsit called, lads?"

"*Felicity*," Swindles answered, yellowed eyes gleaming.

Riot smirked, showing his gold-plated teeth. "Aye, the one with all those old men."

Ebba licked her lips and searched the area behind *Malice's* captain. The crowd had dwindled further during her time eavesdropping. The rays of the sun were weakening in preparation of disappearing completely, and her fathers had probably gone to the town center to search for her.

Pockmark took another step forward, his black boots catching one of the last rays of sunlight. "Ye know what I think happens on that rowboat?" he whispered. "I reckon they all take turns with ye. I bet ye're a real nice whore."

Blood rushed to her face, and her temper unlocked her speech. "Don't be speakin' that way about my fathers." She glared at Pockmark.

"Wait, ye think they're all yer fathers?"

Her face burned. No, she didn't. She just didn't care about any of that. All of them were her fathers.

Pockmark threw his head back in malicious laughter, and Ebba seized her chance. She lunged for the opening of the alley.

Malice's captain stopped her movement with one outstretched arm around her waist and threw her back without noticeable effort. She staggered, wheezing to fill her chest with air again for another go—now she'd shown her intention.

"Hold her." Pockmark smiled but it didn't reach the inkiness of his almond eyes. Not even close.

Riot grabbed one of her arms and she lashed out, kicking him in the shins—boots came in handy for something, after all. He yelped, but didn't lessen his iron grip on her wrist. Ebba lifted her arm to swing a punch, and Swindles moved in to catch it.

She snarled at them, thrashing to try to break their iron hold, but like all pirates, they were strong from physical labor and larger than her. She'd bide her time. For now.

Strung out between the two lackeys like a fish on a line, Ebba scowled at Pockmark with more hatred than she'd felt in her life. If she got out of this alive, she'd break her back to steal his sodding plunder.

"Damn coward, ye are," she threw at him. "Ye gotten too soft to fight like a real pirate."

Pockmark's semblance of a smile disappeared. Her head snapped back as his fist met her face. Blood erupted from her nose and trickled down her throat. She choked on the blood as white filled her vision.

Ebba leaned forward and spat blood on the sandy ground. It took several blinks before her vision had cleared enough to straighten. Her head rang something fierce, but it was worth it to see that Pockmark's tricorn hat now sat askew.

"Knew it," she said, ignoring the warnings in her skull. "Ye *are* soft. Soft like the underbelly of a fish. Won't be long afore ye get fat and bald."

This would usually be about the time one of her fathers told her to shut her gob. The thought came too late, the words were already out.

Rage swirled in the slimy black of Pockmark's eyes. He drew a dagger from his belt and approached. "Ye've got a foul mouth for a whore. But a whore ye can still be without a tongue."

Sink her. That was more serious than a few punches. She twisted away from him, tugging uselessly to free her arms. No use. She'd have to bloody well scream. Pirates didn't scream, not the fierce ones. As the dagger neared, she decided screaming may be better than losing her tongue.

"My fathers will kill ye," she told him, never more serious in her life. They would kill him, slowly. Even for hitting her.

Pockmark stopped in his tracks and doubled over, his cruel laughter bouncing between the alley walls. Swindles and Riot hooted along with him like a personal choir. Ebba's eyes stung as they laughed at her fathers. Ebba blinked a few times, determined not to give them the satisfaction of seeing they'd gotten to her.

Pockmark straightened his hat and moved close, his rancid breath making her gag. He held the dagger to her cheek, digging the tip in until she couldn't help a sharp inhale at the pain.

"The old coots won't kill me. They couldn't kill no one," he taunted. "Face it, fish-lips, yer crew just be merchants. And if they be smart enough, they'll know to keep sailin' the other way."

Heaviness weighed in her chest, but she didn't waver in meeting the captain's eyes although she knew the kind of person to kill his own father wouldn't be scared of her. Mercer Pockmark would cut out her tongue, and he'd take pleasure in it. And it likely wouldn't be the worst thing he'd do to her before the three of them left her to die. Despite the cloying humidity, cold sweat trickled down her temple. She'd never felt fear like this in her life. But then, she'd never been alone to feel fear at all.

Or alone to feel such anger.

"Do it then," Ebba challenged, lifting her chin. "Only cut off my ears while ye're at it, so I don't have to hear yer whinin' voice."

Fresh rage erupted across his face before he mastered it. A smirk widened his lips in the wake, displaying a row of gold fillings. Pockmark took her jaw in a grip like steel, forcing her mouth open. "It'd be my pleasure to oblige."

"Captain Mercer? Oh my! *Captain Mercer*, is that you?" a shrill voice asked from the direction of the marketplace.

A trio of giggles followed.

Pockmark turned, murder in his yellowed eyes. But his expression slipped into a drawling smile at the three women standing there in low-cut dresses. His eyes dragged across their cinched frames, lingering on their rouged cheeks and fluttering lace fans.

Ebba stared at Sherry, Brandy, and Margaritta, her breath catching at the sight of her friends. She knew Sherry the very best, from a time in her life a few years back that she'd rather forget. And Peg-leg liked to drink tea with her whenever they came to Maltu.

Swindles and Riot tightened their grip on her arms, and the three women didn't spare Ebba a glance.

"Captain Mercer," purred Brandy. She sashayed into the alley, hands on hips and full silk skirts swishing. "I've missed you so."

Pockmark's eyes glittered. "Have ye now? We can't be havin' that." He cleared his throat, eyes dropping to her ample chest.

Brandy pouted, dragging her finger across the large 'V' of skin at the top of her bust. "I was beginning to think you didn't like me. I heard tell in the brothel that you arrived yesterday, but I'm yet to see you."

Swindles cleared his throat, pointedly tilting his head to Ebba, who still hung, nose dripping, between him and Riot. Pockmark flashed him an irritated glare, but raked his eyes over Brandy, saying, "I'll show ye just how much I like ye once I wrap up my bus'ness here."

The swishing of a second pair of skirts joined Brandy's. "But I have another client in two hours," Margaritta whined, tossing her golden ringlets and sweeping the back of her hand across her bare shoulder. "I wanted to join you both."

Pockmark's eyes filled with greed as he darted his gaze between the two women.

He cast another look at Ebba, who kept her expression smooth.

"We've *all* missed you, Captain Mercer." Sherry finally approached, her crimson red dress the largest of all the gowns. "If you accompany Brandy and Margaritta, I'll see you only pay for the pleasure of one. Simply because we've been so desolate without you."

Riot groaned quietly as though slipping into a hot bath. Ebba wrinkled her nose.

"I can't be sayin' nay to that." Decision clearly made, Pockmark held out his arms for Brandy and Margaritta.

He swaggered to the alley's exit, an arm around each woman. Turning back, he said, "Have fun with fish-lips without me."

Pockmark disappeared around the corner. The giggling of Brandy and Margaritta gradually receded as they moved away.

Sherry approached the spot where Ebba was still strung up between Pockmark's lackeys. Her bosom jiggled dangerously.

"Have fun with her!" she exclaimed. "I certainly mean to."

Dashing forward quicker than her skirts should allow, Sherry slapped away Swindles' hand and laced her fingers with Ebba's. "I know *several* cutthroats who'd pay handsomely, given your exotic coloring."

Riot chuckled and released Ebba's other hand. "Make sure it be a bunch of them."

"I'm the mistress of Maltu's brothel. You can be assured of that," Sherry quipped.

Remaining mute, Ebba scurried out of the alley in Sherry's swishing wake. She rubbed her bruised wrists once safely out in the main walkway, barely able to focus on the marketplace, which seemed to be blurring. Pockmark must've hit her harder than she thought. Twisting, Ebba watched as the two lackeys exited behind them and strode in the opposite direction.

Sherry squeezed her hand, dropping her act like a bucket of water. "Are you hurt, *ma cherie*?"

Ebba adjusted her weapons in her sash, staring at the ground. "I'm okay, Sherry. Thank ye for savin' me." Eavesdropping hadn't turned out as she'd expected. For a moment there, Ebba had thought she'd be a goner. Her insides were shaking and quailing from lingering fear. But aside from a bloodied face, she was in one piece.

Taking a deep breath, she straightened.

Sherry gave her a once-over, and then nodded, taking off in the direction of the marketplace center. Ebba hastened to catch up.

"*Ma cherie*, an alleyway!" the brothel matron muttered. "What were you thinking?"

Heat flushed Ebba's cheeks. "Aye, not my best notion, I'll admit. But I won't hesitate to shoot my pistols next time."

"*You won't hesitate to shoot your pistols?* I think the lesson was that you shouldn't enter an alleyway at all." Sherry threw her hands in the air in a *clink* of bracelets. "Pirates. I'll never understand your logic."

And that's why pirates didn't tend to get on with land people. "I'm right sorry Brandy and Margaritta have to be drinkin' tea with Pockmark for so long. He won't be makin' nice company."

Sherry sent her a stern look. "You know they aren't drinkin' tea."

"Aye, they are," Ebba replied. "They drink tea with their clients. And ye drink tea with Peg-leg. Ye have polite conversation. And that be all." She held her defiance steady as the mistress scanned her face.

They'd had this argument many times and Sherry likely knew how it would end—with Ebba winning.

The mistress sighed. "As you say, *ma cherie*, though one day you may be more interested in what happens between two adults. You may meet a handsome young man."

Ebba opened her mouth, but Sherry cut her off. "I know, I know. It goes against one of your precious ship laws."

"It ain't against our ship laws as such, Sherry. More my own law," she told the woman. "It just ain't what I am. There only be three types of people in this realm—males, females, and pirates. And I'm a pirate. That's all I'll ever want to be."

To be a pirate was to be free, to witness and chase the impossible. Ebba couldn't afford to be limited by the idea of what a male or female should do—or how they should live their lives. She looked at the people who dwelled on land and didn't want that existence for herself. To grow up, to marry, to get a job, to grow old, and to die. The marketplace on Maltu was only exciting because of the novelty. To go there each day for food for the rest of her life was Ebba's equivalent of a nightmare. The single time her fathers had forced her to contemplate not being a pirate had been the worst experience of her life.

Plus, the odds of meeting a 'handsome young man' weren't very good when her fathers barely went ashore. And doing so wasn't high on *her* priority list. Filling her dreads with beads, sailing with her fathers, and chasing a life of adventure far outranked that prospect.

She had serious plans.

"I be a pirate," Ebba repeated, chin jutting forward. "And yer workers drink tea with their clients."

Sherry sighed. "I would not argue with you on this issue again, my beauty, though you are nearing the age where clinging to these notions makes you appear childish."

"I'll be a child for as long as I want to be," Ebba said plainly. And she would. Childhood was working for her pretty well. If the sail wasn't torn, why would she mend it?

The matron rolled her eyes. "Spoiled by six fathers as you are, I'm not sure there's any incentive to act your age."

Huh? "I ain't spoiled."

Sherry pursed her lips, her eyes dancing. "*Ma cherie*, now that is an illusion I cannot play along with. It's normal for any father to spoil his daughter. To have six fathers is to be spoiled six times over. And. . .honestly, it's as though you've taken the worst part of each of them."

Was she referring to Locks' temper? Or maybe Peg leg's moods? "Do ye not like me, Sherry?" she asked, a small wrinkle between her brows.

"I *love* you," the mistress was quick to correct her. "If they've given you their vices, they've also given you the best parts of themselves. But it's because I love you that I say these things."

Hmm, everyone had bad and good in them. "If I have six times the bad stuff and six times the good stuff, then that seems even-like."

Ebba couldn't be sure, but she thought Sherry mouthed *pirate logic* before rolling her eyes.

Shrugging a shoulder, Ebba asked, "What are ye sayin', Sherry? Speak plain. My fathers give me too many baubles?" If that was what she meant, Ebba would stop listening and start nodding, just like Stubby showed her.

"No, my beauty. Simply that you are far too innocent and protected for a seventeen-year-old. By now, most young adults are not so . . . naïve about life. I worry that by spoiling you so, your fathers are crippling you for later life."

Phew, she didn't mean baubles. "Don't worry yer head on it," Ebba said. "I be copin' just fine as things are."

The woman shook her head. "And if you stop coping, you'll just pretend nothing is wrong because of your other pirate law. You're already pretending you're fine after what happened in the alley."

The mistress was a mite cannier than the average landlubber, Ebba would give her that. But Sherry had her ropes tangled about the ship laws. "We don't *pretend*, Sherry. It's just that when unexplain'ble things happen at sea, ye learn to stop askin' why. My nose be bunged up from the alley, and I certainly didn't enjoy it at the time, but I be right as rain now. What's the point of goin' on about things?"

"Call it what you will, my beauty. But you can only fill a bucket so much before it overflows."

When had they started talking about buckets? "Aye, true enough," Ebba hedged.

They were nearly back to where she'd left Plank and Stubby and Ebba's gut twisted with an onslaught of nerves. She'd be in serious trouble for leaving. How likely was it she could talk herself out of punishment?

"There's one of your fathers over there," Sherry said, pointing.

Ebba slowed her pace, her heart racing.

The mistress held out a lace kerchief. "Use this to clean off a few specks of blood. Though judging by Plank's expression, it won't help any."

Ebba took one peek at the furious Plank bearing down on them and turned pleading eyes on her friend.

"No, *ma cherie*. You must face the music, as they say. You insist on being treated like a child. That comes with all the drawbacks, not just those you choose. But . . . I can promise to detain Peg-leg until night falls, if that's any help?"

Through the wave of revolt at the comment, a tiny tendril of relief found Ebba. That would get rid of one angry father for a while at least. Peg-leg was a sod when he got in a mood.

"Thank ye, Sherry," she said, reaching out to squeeze the woman's hand.

Sherry swooped down to kiss her cheek. "Any time, my beauty."

The mistress swished away in a flood of red fabric and Ebba turned to Plank, her shoulders slumping.

She didn't bother to wipe the blood off her face.

Speaking of buckets, Ebba-Viva Fairisles was officially in a bucket of shite.

FOUR

"*Three moons of swabbin' the deck!*"

Ebba moaned. "Three moons? Plank, that ain't fair."

Plank hauled her down the sandy path to the town which was still visible in the dying light of day. "Ye were gone an hour, Ebba-Viva Fairisles. *One hour.* Stubby ran to get the others, we were that worried. So don't be takin' that tone o' voice with me."

Ebba narrowed her eyes.

"Tuck that lip in smart-like. Ye won't be poutin' your way out o' this. Ye returned all bloodied," he continued his rant.

She wasn't pouting. Much. And if she was, it was because usually a pout worked. She released her lip. "But I overheard—"

"Anythin' could've happened to ye."

They had to hear about Pockmark's Plunder. "Aye, but—"

Plank glanced up and smirked.

Dread filled her boots as the horde of her remaining fathers hustled toward them down the barren path. Sherry lied! The moon was yet to come out, but Peg-leg was there with the others. Ebba stole another peek at Plank's face—still furious, bugger. *Plank* wasn't even the one she was concerned about.

"Bilge-sucking Hornswaggle o' a Hempen Halter!"

Ebba's back snapped straight as Stubby cursed.

Clearly satisfied the others' anger matched his own, Plank pushed her forward and crossed his arms. She stood as stiff as a mast as the crew shouted over her head. She cringed with every clucking sound of disappointment from Locks and Peg-leg. When they clucked, she knew she'd really screwed up.

"—Is that blood?—"

"—Where be the cur who dunnit?—"

"—You know better than to wander off, Ebba-Viva.—"

She avoided Barrels' probing eyes, staring at her boots.

"I told her she'll be swabbin' the decks for three moons as punishment," Plank put in.

Ebba's mouth dropped. He was really going to make her do that? "Ye can't be serious?"

Grubby patted her on the arm, face as white as a new sail from all the shouting. "I'll swab the decks for ye."

Locks grabbed a fistful of Grubby's shirt and hauled him out of the circle surrounding her. "We're tellin' her off, Grubs."

Peg-leg tilted her chin up, scrubbing at her bloodied face with his sleeve. "Which slimy beggar did it to ye? I'll shove me wooden leg down his gullet and watch him choke to death."

The others hushed at his question.

Ebba opened her mouth, about to dive on the opportunity to tell them of Pockmark's plunder. And then shut it.

She opened her mouth again, yet Pockmark's cruel words about her fathers churned deep inside her, making her hesitate. Her fathers were on the older side. If she told them about the three hateful pirates, they'd go after *Malice* without fail. They'd do anything for her. Remembering Pockmark's horrible, vacant expression, Ebba didn't want to put her fathers at risk of being hurt by naming her attackers. She'd never wanted to go after a plunder more in her life, but her fathers *were* her life.

"I ain't recallin'," she said finally.

The three words hung in the air. Her six fathers stared down at her for a leaden second before erupting into chaos once more.

She added, "I'm sorry for goin' off—"

Her words were drowned out in the racket overhead. Ebba stamped her foot, hands on her hips. "Listen to my apology," she demanded.

Not one of them looked at her. Her temper simmered—third time today, a record even for her. She gathered all the air her breathers could hold.

"*Listen*," she bellowed.

The noise stopped.

Ebba beamed at her success. "Now," she started.

She trailed off, realizing no one paid her any attention. Something else had caught the attention of her six pirate fathers. The steels of six cutlasses rang as they were drawn from her fathers' belts.

Hunching over, she peered around Peg-leg's peg.

"Barbless stinger o' a manta ray," she whispered.

Navy men.

Ebba whirled in the middle of the circle of her fathers, staring outward. A *lot* of navy men. They were surrounded. The king's minions crowded them on both sides of the sandy path as well as the way to the market and the way to town.

"Lay down your arms, pirates," a voice boomed. "In the name of King Montcroix!"

"In the name of the king!" the other navy men boomed, taking a step closer to tighten the circle around their crew.

The man who'd spoken had the largest hat of the bunch. The dying light illuminated the harsh edges of his face.

Ebba's heartbeat thundered in her ears, and she turned to watch the silent communication between Stubby and Barrels. Hesitating briefly, Stubby glanced at her, and then shook his head.

Blast. They were going to surrender. In all their years trading on Maltu, they'd never been caught by the navy. This was her fault.

Stubby threw his cutlass down, and the rest of their crew followed suit. Ebba pushed between Peg-leg and Locks and emptied her sash of her two pistols, three daggers, and then her cutlass, tossing the weapons to the sandy ground.

Without her weapons, she felt completely vulnerable. Her mouth dried as she glanced at her fathers for a clue as to what happened next.

"Ye're all right, lass," Peg-leg whispered as the man with the big hat shouted for them to form a single line.

Two pistols were trained on her face as a young navy man locked heavy shackles about her booted ankles. Ebba grimaced at the tightness. The edges hung heavily on her ankle bones, even through her leather boots, and she knew there wouldn't be any hope of slipping the shackles off. Chains were hooked between each of their manacles, connecting the pirates of *Felicity*, making it impossible to run.

"Tonight, you will be taken to the gaol," the navy man spoke, hands clasped behind his back.

"Tomorrow, you will be shipped to Exosia to stand trial."

Ebba's ears rang. Did she hear that right?

He addressed his men briefly, dismissing their crew after the impassive announcement of their doom.

"Forward march," another navy man called.

A few shoves had the seven of them shuffling toward town in the dark, a row of the navy men cushioning them on either side. Ebba wasn't the only one in a bucket of shite any longer. Her fathers were only shouting because of her actions, allowing the navy patrol to creep up undetected. Ebba clanked between Peg-leg and Stubby, guilt weighing thick. If she hadn't followed Pockmark's lackeys and stopped to eavesdrop, none of this would've happened.

One thing was for sure. They had to escape before the gaol. Everyone knew what happened to pirates on Exosia, where the king resided. Pirates and royals were a deadly mix.

The bright colors of her onshore clothes seemed dull and lifeless in the fallen night. The bawdy singing and shouted cheers from the drunken inhabitants of the tavern called to her like a funeral song as they passed by. Soon all of Maltu would hear *Felicity*'s crew had been captured, and Sherry, Brandy, and Margaritta wouldn't be able to save them this time.

"The king's men don't raid at night," Stubby whispered. "Why were they about?"

Stubby had four younger sisters on the island and one worked in the governor's mansion. She always got word to them when the governor ordered a raid. But her father was right; the navy only raided during the day.

Locks answered from farther down the line. “Delight told me the king’s son, the Exosian prince, be visitin’ the island.”

A prince? She’d never seen one of those before.

“Ah, so Governor Da Ville be pretendin’ to do his job,” Stubby muttered.

A wiry navy man whacked Stubby with his baton. “Quiet, vagabond.”

Ebba’s face heated at Stubby’s resultant grimace. But the batons used by the onshore navy patrols didn’t hold a candle to what awaited them on the mainland.

The realm was comprised of two seas, the Caspian Sea being the main ocean where everyone lived. Since King Montcroix won the Battle for the Seas against pirate kind in Year 252 of the Reign of Kings, he’d ruled the entire realm. To uphold the law in his absence, he’d placed a governor on each of the islands. However, over the last sixteen years, the king’s hold on the islands had loosened. Today, in Year 268, the part of the Caspian Sea south of Maltu and Kentro was referred to as the *Free Seas*. In the Free Seas, there was not much a pirate had to fear. . . .

. . . On the *mainland*, they did. In Exosia, a pirate’s trial only ended one of two ways: the cages or quartering. Judging by some of Plank’s more gruesome stories of Buckle O’Pigswill’s era, she knew neither fate was pleasant. Though hanging in a cage until she starved to death and birds pecked at her body while she lay too weak to raise an arm in defense seemed a smidgen worse to her.

But they wouldn’t reach the gaol. They couldn’t. Her fathers would think of something.

Doubt clenched within her at the thought. Maybe her hesitation was a sign of the day she’d had, but Pockmark’s words rang in her ears nevertheless. Her fathers *did* sail in the opposite direction to danger, and always had. Ebba trusted her parents with all her heart and yet she couldn't help wondering why they did that. Was it to keep her safe? That's what she'd assumed. But maybe she was wrong.

She startled as a navy man shoved her to the side of the road. Whirling to glance back, Ebba spotted a white carriage careening up the hill.

The carriage slowed as it reached the front of their procession.

A woman poked her head out the carriage window. "Commander Chancey. Such a pleasure to see you again."

"Attention!" the commander called to his troop. All twenty of the navy men snapped their heels together and stood tall.

He bowed low. "Your Ladyship, I hope you fare well."

Ebba leaned out of line to stare at the woman. Lady Maybell was Governor Da Ville's much younger wife. Ebba had never seen her. Or the governor.

Lady Maybell pushed open the carriage door and accepted the hand of a footman down the step. Ebba muffled a snort at the woman's appearance. The dress hoop she wore was even larger than Sherry's, to the point of appearing the size of a small tent. The gown cinched brutally at the waist, and the front laced up so tight, the woman's bust appeared more out than in. How did she even move in that thing? Her jewels glistened in the bright moonlight, and under the powdered wig Lady Maybell wore, the peach blush of her cheeks confirmed her youth.

Lady Maybell snapped open her fan, fluttering it before her face. "You have outdone yourself, commodore. Are these all your prisoners?"

"Yes, Your Ladyship. They are pirates and headed for the gaol. They'll be shipped to Exosia for trial tomorrow morning, and executed for their pitiful life of crime."

"How barbaric!" she said, peach mouth falling open.

The commodore stood proudly. "'Tis the law."

She batted her eyelashes. "How glad I am that *I* do not have to catch such fearful-looking creatures. My, that one has an eye patch. How rustic. That one a wooden leg. . . . Do you think they understand me, commodore?"

Ebba rolled her eyes. "We be understandin' ye just fine," she called.

The blunt end of a navy man's stick dug into her gut.

"Blimey," she choked out, eyes watering.

"Today be not yer day, lass." Peg-leg observed.

"Aye," she agreed in a wheeze.

The heels of the lady's shoes clicked on an embedded stone as she moved. The governor's wife stopped in front of Ebba and gasped. "But this is just a young woman, commodore! What is the meaning of this?"

Ebba frowned. Who was she calling 'young woman'? Ebba was a pirate.

The commodore spluttered, "Not a female, Your Ladyship. A pirate—as guilty as the rest."

Ebba beamed.

"She is clearly no pirate."

Ebba frowned again.

All eyes turned to her, surveying Ebba's bright ensemble, golden hoop earring, dreadlocks and bright green bandana.

Lady Maybell snapped her fan shut. "Answer me this. If she is a pirate, why is her face bloodied? It seems to me she is merely hostage to these foul, stinking men."

They did stink, but they weren't foul. Ebba snarled, and then nearly fell on her face as Stubby pulled roughly on the chain connecting their right ankles.

Lady Maybell placed the back of one delicate hand to her temple. "To *think* what could have happened to this poor woman had I not happened upon you on my way back to the mansion."

"Your Ladyship, I do assure you this female is a pirate," Commodore Chancey said. Even he appeared to realize the argument was a hopeless one.

"Aye, I *am* a bloody pi—*oof*." The air left her as Peg-leg drove a sharp elbow into her gut.

"What'd ye do that for?" Ebba gasped.

A navy man with a key kneeled at her feet and unlocked her manacles. Her jaw dropped. They were letting her go? Just like that? All because of a stupid lady in a stupid dress?

"I will thank you not to apprehend any more women," Lady Maybell said with a sniff. "A female pirate, how preposterous."

Ebba gritted her teeth at the comment, wiping her dripping nose. It left a bloody smear on her linen shirtsleeve. She turned to stare at the rest of her crew. What about her fathers?

"You go on now, little nymph," Plank said softly when the lady moved back to the carriage. "You go with the lady."

Barrels spoke up, "If the girl is no pirate, Your Ladyship, I gather her weapons will be returned to her?"

A smile crept across Ebba's face. Genius. She'd take Maybell hostage. They'd have to make a run for it, but they could make it. Doubt crept over her as her eyes rested on Barrels' salt-and-pepper hair and Peg-leg's peg.

Lady Maybell ushered her to the carriage, surprisingly strong, considering how dainty and clean she looked. "No need for those barbaric things, miscreant."

"Lady Maybell, might I send an escort with you, just for your safety?" the commodore tried.

She sniffed. "A man in my carriage? What would Governor Da Ville say?"

As Maybell dragged her away, Ebba glanced back, frantically searching her fathers' faces. They should know better than to leave the planning to her! What was she supposed to do?

"We love ye, Ebba-Viva Fairisles," said Locks hoarsely.

Tears poured down Grubby's cheeks and he nodded sadly at her.

That sounded like they were saying goodbye. That couldn't be right. A heavy dread swept through her at their pale and drawn faces.

What was happening?

Lady Maybell shoved her into the carriage and Ebba sat in a state of shock, never more at a loss in her life. She didn't stand a chance against twenty navy men, not even with her weapons. Taking Maybell hostage was the only plausible idea she'd had. What did her fathers want her to do? Was she missing something? They couldn't be saying goodbye for real?

Numbness filled her.

"To the mansion," Lady Maybell said shrilly, knocking twice on the front of the carriage.

The mansion. . . .

"Hey, Maybell," Ebba said. "Does the mansion be havin' weapons?"

The powdered woman smiled prettily. "*Lady* Maybell, young lady."

Ebba's brows rose but she managed to quell down her hissed reply of *young pirate*. Plus, Maybell only looked a few years older than herself.

"To answer your question, yes, many, many weapons. But you don't need to touch those nasty monstrosities any longer. Poor, *poor* creature. How you must have been abused."

The governor's wife wasn't the brightest fire on the beach. Ebba needed to use that to her advantage. She had to somehow get back to the prison and free her fathers.

“Where be the weapons?” Ebba pressed.

Maybell narrowed her eyes suspiciously.

“Ye know . . . so I can avoid them.”

Maybell’s face cleared, and she flung open her fan in a grand gesture. “Of course. They are stored in the guard house where the king’s men sleep.”

That wasn’t any help. Ebba’s hands curled into fists. She didn’t have Barrels’ or Stubby’s smarts, or Plank’s charm. She didn’t have Peg-leg’s intimidation or Locks’ way with females. The seas take her, she wasn’t even as nice as Grubby.

All Ebba could say for certain was that if she didn’t free her fathers tonight, they’d be lost to the king’s mainland.

There was just one night to save them or they’d enter a place no pirate dared enter.

A place no pirate left.

FIVE

"I envy your lovely dark skin, Mistress Fairisles, but what are those atrocious black worms coming out of your head?" Lady Maybell circled Ebba slowly. "And are those . . . beads in your hair? Those will be the first to go."

Ebba growled, batting the woman's hand away. "Ye won't be touchin' my beads or my hair."

"Manners! Just how long have you been with those thugs?"

The question wasn't the type that asked for an answer. This much was clear after an hour in the frittering woman's company. She was the kind who talked for the sake of hearing herself speak.

"Your face isn't all that bad now the blood is gone, see!" Maybell brandished a hand mirror in her face, and Ebba took it to save herself from a second bloody nose. Moss-green eyes blinked back at her before flicking over the rest of her high-boned and bronzed features. The lady was a half-head gone in grog if she thought Ebba's face was all right. Already, purple bruises smudged from the bridge of her nose to the other corner of both eyes. The nose itself was twice its usual size and bright red. She shoved the mirror back at the governor's wife.

"I mean, your lips are a little big," Maybell noted. "But there's nothing you can do about that."

Ebba glared at her. Why did everyone always say that? Her lips were fine.

Lady Maybell spun around the room, yapping away.

If there was enough room in a chamber to spin around, the chamber was far too big. But Maybell spun. And if there were ten Maybells, Davy Jones forbid, each of them would have space to do the same. Even wearing tent-sized dresses. Never had she seen such poncy grandeur as when the carriage deposited them at the front entrance an hour ago. She'd lost her speech for a full thirty seconds. Columned halls with marble flooring. White statues and gilded frames of barely clad women, draped with transparent white cloth. Exotic birds in ornate cages. Silver patterned wallpaper and tinkling piano music. The place was as foreign to her as any she'd seen in her life.

Maybell's chambers were just the same, but full of pungent flowers and cushioned seats. Dresses made of yards of fabric—more than all of Ebba's clothes put together—lay tossed haphazardly over a patterned trifold screen. Her jewelry—gold, rubies, emeralds and pearls—sparkled in a tangled array across her vanity. The opulence told her the governor's wife was born into riches.

. . . So much wealth, with so little grog between her ears. And yet these people were never more dangerous. She had to get to her fathers. They had to get away from Maltu.

"Are ye the daughter of someone rich or what?" Ebba asked out of genuine curiosity.

Lady Maybell batted her eyelashes. "My father is Baronet of Pewter-shire. One of the well-to-do Baronets in Exosia, if you know what I mean."

She didn't. Ebba folded her arms, cocking a hip out. Honestly, if she came from somewhere with a name like that, she might've turned out as a Maybell, too. "That makes sense."

"You are too kind." Maybell's face turned thoughtful. "You know, you look quite savage in that getup. I am of a mind to dress you up, and, depending on how you look, I might even take you to dinner with me." Her eyebrows rose as she waited for Ebba's gleeful response. When it didn't come, Maybell said, "We have a very special guest tonight."

"The prince."

A wrinkle appeared between her brows. "Yes, how could you have guessed?"

Ebba sighed, the woman's foolishness grated on her last nerve. She didn't have time for dress-ups and a snobby dinner with the son of King Montcroix. Every pirate hated the king. She'd be more inclined to spit in the prince's eye than to rub shoulders with him. "I be tired, Lady Maybell. Is there somewhere close by to caulk?"

"Caulk?"

She looked at the ceiling and assembled the scraps of her tattered temper. "To sleep." She'd sneak out. Maybe luck would help her along the way and gift her a few weapons.

There was no answer, and Ebba locked eyes with Maybell in time to see a sudden shrewd expression there. Ebba's heart thudded as Maybell drifted closer.

"You don't fool me, Mistress Fairisles." She studied her closely. "You don't fool me for a second."

Blimey, what a time for her to be clever. She swallowed. "Lady Maybell, I—"

"You secretly want to come, but you're worried about your appearance." She clapped her hands. "Okay, okay. You pulled my arm, I'll take you along."

This woman . . . was senseless.

"I'd be worried, too, if I were meeting Prince Caspian for the first time." Maybell bopped Ebba on the nose with her fan. Ebba clutched at her injured nose in agony, eyes streaming as the lady resumed her damned spinning. Maybell arrived in that manner at the trifold screen and began sifting through her extensive wardrobe, chucking dresses of all colors over the screen. "First, we need to dress you up so you don't stand out."

The words caught Ebba's attention through the white-hot agony and she dropped her hands to look between her pirate garb and the colorful dresses on the marbled ground.

Blending in might not be such a bad idea. . . .

In fact, blending in might be the most practical thing to have come out of Maybell's mouth.

EBBA TRIED to memorize the wide branching halls as she trailed down a set of marble steps after the governor's wife. She clenched the fabric of her borrowed deep purple dress, certain she'd trip on the blasted thing and crack her skull open on the white stone.

When they reached the bottom of the stairs safely, she dropped the dress and reached up a hand to pull at her hair; the twisted updo was threatening to tear her scalp off. But at least she wasn't wearing rouge. *Nothing*, not even her plan to escape the mansion using this disguise, had been enough to allow Maybell to apply rouge to her cheeks.

After two hours in Maybell's room, there now didn't seem to be enough time to do what needed doing tonight. The temptation to bop the lady over the noggin had been hard to resist; however, busting her fathers out would be hard enough without a horde of navy men breathing down her neck. Her fathers were depending on her for the first time. Ebba couldn't let them down.

"Just through here, my exotic flower," Maybell tittered, making a flowing gesture toward ceiling-high double doors.

Ebba rolled her eyes and approached, glancing at the livery-clad servants holding the doors open. That was the problem with rich land-lubbers, perhaps. They didn't open doors for themselves any longer.

Soft music floated through the doors, and as Ebba traipsed through them, she darted her eyes to the sole harp player to her left. She inhaled and nearly choked on the cloud of floral perfume polluting the rectangular room. Finely dressed gentry and their ladies circulated around the outside of a large table that appeared to have been made to fit the room. Crystal goblets, cutlery, and silver plates glittered from where they'd been meticulously placed atop the table.

"La, now *here* he is. My husband, the governor." The lady drew herself tall and waited until Ebba let out a half-hearted sound of amazement.

Ebba lifted her gaze and found that when Maybell said he was 'here,' she meant directly in front of them.

Governor Da Ville.

Ebba wrinkled her nose at the yellow and vomit patterned padded doublet he wore. Looked like fish guts to her. Ruffles exploded out of his doublet's orifices, and a cravat erupted from the bottom of his chin like a pufferfish squeezed through a tight space. His breeches ballooned from his hips before tucking into the shiniest pair of boots she'd ever seen. Da Ville had occupied the position of governor on Maltu Island for years. Or, more accurately, the pirates had *allowed* him to keep his position. Somehow, he'd survived thus far and Ebba guessed it wasn't due to a startling intellect.

"Barnabus, my love. I have brought a guest with me tonight," Maybell announced.

Ebba stilled as the governor turned his shrewd eyes upon her. His wig was the largest she'd ever seen. The thing could probably swallow him whole at any moment, and maybe her, too. And was that a tiny crescent moon made of black fabric stuck beside the outer corner of his eye?

Blimey.

She met Da Ville's pale eyes, wondering if he was taking in her beaded dreadlocks and golden hoop earring, all of which she'd flatly refused to take off. Despite the purple dress and hairdo, surely with one look he'd know she was a pirate through and through.

He spoke as if Ebba wasn't there. "Are you sure she's quite the kind of person we want on display tonight, Maybell?" He stressed the word 'tonight.'

The sound of a dying horse came to mind when he spoke.

Lady Maybell pouted dramatically. Ebba eyed her. If that's what Ebba looked like when she pouted, she was going to stop. Immediately.

The governor sighed, shaking back his ruffles. He held himself as though the entire realm watched him, gesturing with graceful, flowing movements, which, Ebba noted as he continued his sighs and waving, never failed to display the signet ring on the forefinger of his right hand.

"Oh, very well," the governor snapped irritably. "She is to be put at the back with the prince's servants."

Lady Maybell spun twice. "You are so good to me, my love. I shall get you a rare treasure when I next go shopping."

Governor Da Ville's irritation disappeared with the magical words, and just like that, the mystery of his long reign as governor on Maltu was solved. The man enjoyed nice things, and no doubt had received a great deal of bribes from pirates over the years.

Ebba brightened. She could bribe him to free her fathers. Her skull turned directly to Pockmark's plunder. That wasn't an actual treasure she had access to, yet, but if she gave Da Ville the details to find it, he may consider her proposal.

"Are ye into nice things then?" she asked him.

He jolted, as though his body was involuntarily revolted by her voice.

"I be knowin' where some nice things are, if ye be inclined-like to do me a favor in return." Ebba wasn't entirely certain how the bribing process went.

Governor Da Ville glared at her, glancing furtively at the surrounding guests before taking two overly dramatic steps away. Maybell blanched, and grabbed Ebba's arm, dragging her with surprising strength to one of the doormen.

She towed Ebba past more than a hundred settings. Polished silverware graced the main table, and the light from hundreds of candles bounced between that and the uniformly placed crystal goblets. Such wealth boggled Ebba's mind. Money and heritage ruled Exosia and the Caspian Seas and, apparently, possessing a brain was not a prerequisite. Ebba shook her head, wondering what kind of backward world she'd fallen into.

"You nearly got yourself kicked out *and* embarrassed me," Maybell hissed in her ear, gesturing to an empty seat right at the back of the room.

The woman stomped off, and Ebba watched her go, not particularly mournful that their friendship was over.

Apparently, Ebba shouldn't make bribes in front of other people that maybe included the prince of the Exosian Realm. No problem. Ebba knew that now. For next time.

If she *got* a next time.

IT HAD to be at least ten in the evening, maybe later. Da Ville hadn't left his seat at the fancy table once. At this point, Ebba was beginning to think she wouldn't get another chance to bribe him.

Where she sat with the servants, the plates were brass—as were the goblets and the pronged devices Ebba knew to be for eating.

Using the cutlery proved another matter, and after two attempts she'd given up and now ate with her fingers.

Realizing she was trapped for the time being with absolutely no plan, Ebba had decided to look and eat her fill. She'd save her strength and the advantage of surprise for when it was needed.

Except these people didn't just eat one plateful. She'd lost count of how many dishes had appeared in front of her and been whisked away by servants once she'd finished. The sheer fact that they had servants to serve their servants was absurd.

"Fiutch!" exclaimed the governor. He talked so loudly, and everyone else sat in such a simpering silence that not listening to his every word was impossible.

"How I love fiutch," he said. "'Tis the rarest delicacy, Prince Caspian. I do think you'll rather like it." He winked at the prince, not quite managing to separate the movement of one eye from the other, though he did manage to flash his signet ring again.

Her eyes sought the young man seated to the governor's right, who had arrived in the room without fanfare. The prince was as unimpressive as Peg-leg's fish stew. That is to say, very unimpressive. Talk about disappointing. He'd sat red-faced so far, mumbling every so often in response to the governor's butt-kissery. *That* was King Montcroix's son, offspring of the man who had crushed the toughest of pirates to win the Battle for the Seas? One look at Caspian's face was enough to decide that the mainland didn't stand a chance once the current king was dead; the gaping codfish next to the governor would be overrun by pirates before he could stutter a single word.

Ebba watched as the governor put a huge dollop of the black fiutch on a cracker and placed the whole thing in his gob.

He chewed once.

Twice.

Three times, before his face paled considerably and then turned green.

For all his exclamations about the delicacy, Da Ville didn't seem to care for it. Had he even tried it before? Ebba snorted under her breath, slapping a hand on the table. "Sink me, what a friggin' eejit."

The rest of the table occupants stared at her in shock. Ebba ignored them, chuckling heartily as the governor, tears streaming down his face, swallowed the black mess, gagging twice. Funniest damn thing to happen all day.

"I take it you don't like Governor Da Ville," a quiet voice asked from her right.

She raised a brow as she took in the tall, russet-haired man beside her—probably a few years older than herself. Ebba had noticed him when she sat down, but he hadn't spoken until now. "Never met him afore in my life."

"And, pray tell, what are your first thoughts?"

Ebba fought back a smile and lost. "I be thinkin' he wears that shrewdness on his face to cover the fact he's only got half a barrel o' rum sloshin' in his skull."

The young man, someone's servant she assumed, fixed his amber eyes on her. Ebba blinked at the intensity in their depths.

"You speak . . . differently," he said. "I don't think I've ever come across your accent before."

With the way he spoke, similar to Barrels, Ebba would guess he probably hadn't. "Ye wouldn't have had much reason to speak to a pirate, I gather."

Several of the chairs surrounding the table where she sat scraped back. She relished the horrified gasps that accompanied it, safe in the knowledge that it didn't matter one jot what this table thought of her since

Maybell and the governor were so completely dense. Honestly, it was nice to actually be treated like a pirate for once.

The man's amber eyes didn't shift, though Ebba perceived from their widening that he was taken aback.

"A pirate," he said in disbelief. "Really? In the governor's home?"

Ebba picked at her teeth with the pronged tool. Not as good as a dagger. Too blunt. "Aye."

Apparently, that was all the man had to say. She turned back to continue watching the governor make an utter moron of himself, snorting at intervals. If it wasn't him, it was Maybell. Their behavior was entirely missed by the fawning people surrounding them. But the governor was the top dog on Maltu—in the absence of royalty—so it made sense people would flatter him to get as much as they could.

Ebba's smile faded from her lips and fear curled under the tight corset of her over-the-top ensemble. Here she was, sitting in a dining room laughing while her fathers were rotting in the stinking prison cell. A shot of despair ran thick through her heart and real dread pricked the corners of her eyes. If her fathers were taken, Ebba would be entirely alone. She'd been alone once and sworn it would never happen again. That her fathers could be gone from the realm if she failed to save them inspired only cold horror. She blinked, discovering Sherry might have been right after all. In this moment, Ebba felt like a child who needed her fathers to show her the way. She *did* feel crippled.

"Why are you sad?" the russet-haired man asked.

Ebba lifted a shoulder, clearing her throat of the rising lump. She glanced at the man. "My fathers are locked in the gaol. Tomorrow they'll be shipped to Exosia and put on trial to be executed."

The man's amber eyes brightened and Ebba shifted her gaze. The intensity in his look unsettled her greatly.

"They are all pirates?"

She nodded and observed the rest of the table. Her plate was scraped clear of food, but many of the plates around the table still had half left. “Ain’t any of ye hungry?”

No one answered. Their fear didn’t bring her the same joy as before.

The same man replied, “They are saving themselves for the next three courses.”

“There’s more?” She’d eaten so much her gut was starting to take up the space where her breathers usually were.

“Much more, I’m afraid.”

The surrounding plates held enough scraps to feed another five people. “And what will be happenin’ to the scraps?”

“For the animals, I gather.”

Ebba shook her head. “They chuck away food, but keep all the shiny, gilded rubbish here? There ain’t enough sense at that table to rub together.”

She glanced away again. Did the man never blink? Heat rose to her cheeks at his prolonged stare.

“You are a pirate. Forgive me, but don’t you seek shiny rubbish for a living?” he asked.

Her fathers never did anything interesting like pillage rich abodes for jewels. Ebba straightened to try to draw in a full breath without her chest spilling out the damn corset. “Nay, amber-eyes. Not me and my fathers. We mainly deal in fresh produce, which we trade for materials, tools, medicine, and food.” She left out the part where they only paid for half of it and stole the rest.

“Cosmo,” the man supplied, lifting his gaze to her face.

“Cosmo, what?”

“That’s my name.”

Huh. Ebba liked the sound of it. Cosmo could almost be a pirate name.

"How many fathers do you have?" the man pressed.

"Six. What's it to ye?" His questions got her back up in a way Maybell's hadn't. She perceived a great deal of book smarts in this man, and she knew from Barrels that quality shouldn't be underestimated, even if book smarts couldn't sail a ship.

Cosmo pursed his lips. "Don't you find it ironic you judge the governor for throwing away food when you steal and kill for a living?"

He was accusing her of being all talk? Did she need to remove her hoop earring? "My crew don't kill," she withered. "Aye, we evade the king's tax—who doesn't—but we stick to the old pirate ways. We have mercy and honor. Unlike these young pirates. . . ." She trailed off, realizing she was quoting Stubby word-for-word.

A small smile graced Cosmo's mouth. "How old are you?"

He sure sat upright for a servant. The man had a bearing she couldn't fail to notice. Nor could she fail to notice the rest of the table listened to his every word though he made no move to include them in the talk.

"Whose servant are ye?" Ebba demanded, ignoring his question.

Cosmo's eyes widened. "I'm the prince's servant."

Ebba stared at him. Drat, if she'd known that beforehand she would've given him the stink-eye and the silence of her back. It seemed hard to do, now they'd spoken a little. She made a non-committal sound.

Three more courses. . . She had to get out of here. Who knew how long it would take to finish eating, and then she'd be in Maybell's clutches again.

The waiting servants streamed in and out of the doors in a constant line. Maybe she could slip through that way. Her gaze fell to her lap, resting on her gaudy purple dress.

. . . Or not.

Ebba pursed her lips. "What're the odds of me slippin' away through that door unnoticed?" she asked Cosmo.

The servant followed the tilt of her head and his eyes fell on her dress. "Next to none in what you're wearing."

"That's what I be thinkin'."

"You will try to save your fathers then?" His deep voice was wondering.

Ebba scolded, "'Course I will. I ain't standin' by dressed in a mountain of fabric and eatin' black gunk while they're gutted or put in those cages for birds to peck their bones."

The man winced and put down his pronged eating instrument. He stared at his brass plate, which still held a large portion of the goopy fiutch. He stared for a long time with those intense eyes of his. She was surprised the plate didn't melt.

He looked up at Ebba and leaned in close. The fresh mint of his breath reached her, making her skin erupt in bumps. Blimey, Grubby could use some of that for his breath. And she couldn't help noticing how smooth and unblemished Cosmo's skin was. Probably never spent a whole day outside in his life, and yet he didn't appear weak—for a landlubber.

"I can. . . ." Cosmo frowned and cleared his throat. "I can help to free your fathers."

Ebba was struck dumb. They blinked at each other, Cosmo seemed almost as surprised by his offer as she.

"I can help to free your fathers," he repeated in a stronger voice.

She scrunched her face. "Aye, and how're ye going to do that, servant boy?"

"*Prince's* servant," he corrected.

Ebba made a derisive sound. "That red-faced prince is just goin' to go along with it? I don't reckon so."

"He will," Cosmo argued. "We've been friends since we were young. He has unwavering faith in me. I . . . saved his life once. Trust me. He'll do it."

There was that odd demanding tone again. It added a quality to his voice that Ebba nearly *did* trust. What had he done to show her that he wouldn't screw up and foil her only chance to escape? Nothing. And what had she done to convince him, a prince's servant, to help a crew of pirates?

People didn't do stuff for free—*that*, she did trust.

Ebba darted her eyes around the marble room full of people. How much time had passed? How long would this damn thing go for? She bit her lip, indecision warring within her.

"Why?" she blurted at last.

Cosmo looked at her.

"Why do ye want to help them?" she clarified.

She held her breath as he ran his amber eyes over her hair and hoop earring, lingering on her puffy nose. His expression was riddled with curiosity, yet he didn't ask about any of the things he clearly found so interesting.

"Because your crew only takes from the land," he said.

The answer didn't make sense to her head, but it made an odd kind of sense to her heart, and Plank always said she should be trusting that.

Ebba clasped Cosmo by the hand and gave it a firm shake. "Then aye, prince slave, I'll accept yer offer."

Cosmo pushed back his chair and stepped to her in one fluid movement. He held out a crooked arm with a look that said he expected her to do something with it. With a cursory glance around at the occupants of the room, who were oblivious to anything amiss, Ebba rose.

"Take my arm," he instructed softly. "Lay your hand on top."

A scan of the table behind her showed the rest of the servants studiously ignored them. She placed her hand atop Cosmo's arm with a warning glare. "Ye better not try any funny bus'ness or I'll gut you with the silver cutlery."

A laugh danced in his eyes. "Follow me, Mistress Pirate."

With measured steps, Cosmo led her to the door.

This was his plan! To slowly walk to the main door? That's why you couldn't trust a landlubber, especially a royal-servant-lubber.

"Servant boy, where are you taking Mistress Fairisles?" Maybell's high-pitched voice rang out.

Ebba winced and aimed another scowl at Cosmo. Of all the stupid plans. They should've at least lit a fire somewhere.

Cosmo bowed low. "Lady Maybell, Mistress Fairisles expressed a desire to retire. I was merely escorting her to the stairs." He shifted to glance at the red-nosed offspring of King Montcroix. "My Prince? With your leave?"

Prince Caspian startled in his chair next to Governor Da Ville. He stared at Cosmo with blank eyes and words tumbled slowly from his mouth, "Uh . . . yes, C-cosmo . . . proceed."

Maybell's mouth snapped shut at the prince's order. Hardly believing her luck, Ebba turned in a stupefied rustle of material and continued to the door with Cosmo.

The two servants swung open the entrance to grant them passage, and drew the doors shut afterward in a synchronized movement, leaving Ebba and Cosmo alone.

Ebba let go of his arm and stared at him. He grinned back.

"How did ye pull that off?" she demanded.

He shrugged. "I told you, I'm the prince's servant. He listens to me."

She considered this and nodded. "That one looks like he'd be convinced by a tiny breeze."

Cosmo frowned, and drew her arm back through his, leading her away from the stairs to the mansion entrance. "Yes, maybe you're right."

He didn't have to sound so forlorn about it. Though she was picking up another level of meaning to what he said, just like Barrels did sometimes. "So what, ye're goin' to march me right out o' here?"

Wait until she told Peg-leg. He'd bust a gut laughing. Ebba blanched, recalling it wasn't a sure thing she'd even get to tell him.

Cosmo slid her another grin. "That's the plan."

Ebba walked out of the mansion and down another few marble steps alongside the prince's servant, descending to where she'd arrived in the carriage. Her dress, while it had blending qualities, wasn't ideal for busting into and out of a prison. But at least she still had her boots on, rather than heeled shoes—if no weapons, or slops to run freely in.

A cobbled road stretched out to her left, leading away from the mansion. It seemed to be the only road, so Ebba guessed it led back to where Maybell had pulled over to talk to the commodore. She just needed to follow the road back to town, and from there, she'd find the gaol. The rest could be figured out after.

"Cosmo, I thank ye for extendin' yer help. Especially when I'm a lying, cheatin' pirate," she teased.

"One with honor and mercy. I believe they were your words," he reminded her, dropping her arm to put distance between them.

Ebba quirked a brow. "Can't be trustin' anythin' a pirate says."

He surveyed her with his amber eyes. They were riveted on her face, though it occurred to her that he was the kind of person who might be riveted by whatever he looked at.

"Aye," he said, mimicking her speech. "I be thinkin' I can."

"We'll make a pirate of ye yet. But now," she strode off toward the road, "I be off to save my fathers."

"I'll ask the prince to have them freed and returned to your ship."

The man was delusional—releasing six pirates? Ebba scoffed silently. The prince wasn't *that* daft—his father detested pirates. That was common knowledge. Even if the prince owed a life debt to his servant, he didn't seem to possess the backbone to go against the king.

"Sure, Cosmo. Ye be doin' that." Hearing the sarcasm in her voice, she spun back on the spot, the garish purple skirts swishing out wide. She smiled contritely. "I do thank ye for yer help. I'll no be forgettin'."

He lifted a hand in a stately gesture and dipped his head, a curious smile on his lips. "Until we meet again, Mistress Pirate."

SIX

"Blast this dress to the hottest part o' Davy Jones' Locker," she shouted into the night.

The parts of the dress not shredded by the wiry shrubs and three separate falls in the dark had fallen victim to Ebba's frustration.

The road *hadn't* led back to town. Only one road actually led to the mansion, of that Ebba was absolutely certain. Which meant the carriage there had turned somewhere on the way. She wished she'd paid more attention during the journey there.

Where the road *did* lead to, she'd never know because in the earliest hours of the day, more lost than ever, she'd had the great idea to scramble down a few steep slopes to reach the beach and get her bearings. The eventual sight of the water had gone a ways in calming her, dark and flat though it was.

Until. . . .

"Ye were walkin' the wrong way around the island, ye daft bugger!" Ebba spat.

The *eastern* point, where she should've been going if the cloudy night hadn't disorientated her, was all limestone cliffs. She was livid, all of her anger stemming from the cold fear in her gut. She was very much afraid of failing her fathers. Very afraid. And very exhausted. She'd nearly cried when she saw the sandy expanse of the western point.

Another long march hadn't calmed the frayed edges of her temper, but finally faint noises reached her from the town center. The nightlife in the tavern and brothel was going strong by the sounds of things. She imagined all the people on Maltu drinking grog and having fun, unaware and uncaring about what was happening to the crew of *Felicity*.

The hollow clunk of her boots as they hit the wood of the wharf was music to her ears, sweeter even than the sound of Grubby's flute, or Barrels' violin. Ebba released the hem of her purple dress and rolled her wrists around to relieve the ache from holding up the heavy garment.

Weariness piled on her. Today hadn't been the easiest day, and it wouldn't be over for another day at least, all going *well*. First, to the ship to change. She didn't have a hope of saving anyone clad in this monstrosity.

Ebba broke into a run down the wharf to *Felicity*, a spark of hope returning to her. She'd collect their spare weapons and go directly to the gaol. She *would* save her fathers or die trying.

Felicity still bobbed where they'd left her. Ebba covered the last of the distance and prepared to leap aboard.

"There ye are, Ebba-Viva," came a relieved voice.

Ebba shrieked and jerked mid-jump, bumping her shin on the bulwark and tumbling with a series of thuds across the main deck in a tangle of purple fabric. Pushing a swathe of it off her face, she stared up at the sight of her fathers' concerned faces.

All six of them.

She blamed exhaustion for the thick, hot tears that began to trickle over her cheeks.

Locks held a hand down to her, pulling her up and into his arms. Dark shadows marred the area beneath his eye. And his face was pale, nearly white like the thin scars on his cheeks. They must all be exhausted, too.

"We was just about to go out lookin' for ye," he said.

She squeezed his middle, wiping off her tears on his tunic. She swallowed the lump in her throat. "How did ye get out of the gaol? How are ye here?"

Ebba pulled back, scanning the others.

Her fathers swapped looks.

Barrels cleared his throat. He held Pillage, absently scratching the cat's chin. "We were rather hoping *you* could tell us that. The commodore released us an hour ago. Said they'd received a personal reassurance that we were merchants, and that we were to be released and returned to our ship, where we would find you."

He did it. Ebba grinned as she thought back to Cosmo's curious smile. The sod had actually done it! "The prince released ye."

"The prince?" Peg-leg stilled. "Ye spoke to the prince?"

Ebba shook her head. "No, his servant. I told him I were a pirate, and my crew were caught and I meant to free ye."

Silence followed. Ebba peered around, seeing Plank had covered his face with both hands and one of Stubby's eyes was ticking. Grubby was giving her a frantic approving nod. She smiled and walked over to pat his arm.

Locks shrugged off his weapons and placed them by the bilge door before adjusting his eye patch. "We can be considerin' ourselves very lucky, methinks. Now it be past time we were goin'."

"Did ye get yer business done?" Ebba asked.

Barrels placed Pillage on the deck. The cat immediately began winding between his legs, yowling. Barrels moved to her side and patted her shoulder. “With all the excitement, I didn’t get a chance to collect the payment, but your safety is more important.”

They’d lost an entire shipment of sugar cane? Her fathers hated coming to Maltu and she knew they’d be smarting over the loss of a shipment that would’ve gone toward their retirement. Shite, add that to her list of things she’d mucked up.

She hung her head. “I’m right sorry for all the trouble I caused.”

“Lass,” Peg-leg said, “I hope ye know how scared we were when we couldn’t find ye, but we were the ones who shouted at ye in the middle of the path. Ain’t nothin’ else but scarin’ us that be yer fault.”

They were just being nice because she was wavering on her feet, had bruises all over her face, and just cried a little. She could fall asleep standing right now. Ebba closed her eyes experimentally—one of them mostly closed already.

That felt nice. Maybe she would sleep like this. How hard could it be?

“Who was with ye in the alley?” Plank asked casually. “Was it *Malice* pirates?”

She liked his deep voice. Ebba grimaced, remembering Pockmark digging his dagger into her cheek. “Aye, Pockmark, Swindles and Riot,” she mumbled. “Talkin’ o’ a big treasure they found.” She wanted the treasure. Bet it glittered all nice, like real treasure should.

Where was the mast? Maybe she’d lean against that. Not opening her eyes, Ebba held her arms out, feeling for the massive beam in the center of the ship.

“—How many bullets have we got between us, lads?—”

“—Enough to fill the three o’ the sods with holes—”

“—Aye, we’ll need to be far away from here by mornin’—”

Her skin prickled. Ebba pivoted on the spot, suddenly wide awake. Horror doused her from head to toe. She covered her mouth, dreadfully and horribly certain she'd just mentioned the names of her attackers.

"That wasn't nice," she snapped at Plank, glaring at the others who'd undoubtedly been in on the ploy. But cold fear churned in her gut, overriding any anger.

A sinister smile crept over Plank's face. "Nay, it wasn't. But we'd already guessed. Now we're knowin' who to hurt."

That was the point though. *They'd* get hurt in the process. "Ye can't go after them. Please," she begged her fathers. "I came so close to losin' ye tonight. I don't want to go through that again just because I was rough'ned up some."

They all seemed a little nonplussed by that request.

"I ain't sure I can do that," Locks said, eye narrowed. "I might'nt always be here to protect ye. I'll bloody well be doin' it until then. Ye're our daughter. I want to wring the life from Pockmark for harmin' even a single hair on yer head."

"I'm goin' to shove my cutlass down his throat," Grubby said happily.

Her insides twisted as the rest of her fathers added their own threats to the mix. This was going all wrong. *Malice* could crush them with a single cannon, and the black ship had far more than one. She turned beseeching eyes on the most reasonable of her parents.

Barrels caught her look. "A compromise, perhaps? We really must be away from here with some haste. This treasure they spoke of, my dear. How much detail did you overhear?"

Ebba wrenched to a halt, a small burst of hope overriding her mounting panic. She could sell this. "Pockmark's been after it for *four years*," she said. "He'd be right hurt to lose it."

Peg-leg clunked forward and pulled Ebba away from the ship's edge. "Quietly with ye, lass. Ye know voices carry on water."

She lowered her voice to just above a whisper. Her fathers crowded around, leaning in. “They were sayin’ the treasure could buy each of their crew an *island*. That be one hundred islands. Mayhaps more.”

Grubby’s eyes rounded.

“It’d be enough to retire on,” she pressed, in case they needed more incentive. “Ye get revenge *and* a tidy sum o’ gold.”

All her fathers ever spoke about was their retirement plan and how, with five more years of semi-honest steal-trading, they’d be able to hang up their boots for good. If they went after this treasure, her fathers could retire in a matter of weeks.

“Retire?” Barrels repeated hopefully, taking the bait. He wasn’t even the one she had to convince.

Ebba dipped her head. “Pockmark killed the soothsayer here, and afore she died, she made whisperings o’ a tree of knowledge with magical fruit that could give ye the answer to any question ye ask. The captain plans to ask where the treasure be located and plunder it.”

Stubby snorted. “Magical fruit. Knew it was too good to be true.”

There were two laws on their ship—aside from Ebba’s personal law of males, females, and pirates. One was that life as a pirate meant accepting the unexplained. It meant not agonizing over mysterious bursts of light and sightings of unknown creatures and the damp smell of secrets in the wind. Usually, Barrels was the only one who struggled to accept the unexplainable—being of landlubber origins. But even the others appeared sceptical right now—all except Plank, who tended to believe in everything unbelievable.

“The mountain apple,” Plank said sagely.

Locks rolled his eyes. “Is this one of yer stories o’ old magic?”

“Ye know of the magic fruit?” she asked over the snickers of her other fathers.

Plank glared at Locks. "Aye, I know the story well."

"Where is this supposed mountain apple?" Barrels asked, bending to pick up the complaining Pillage again. His voice was neutral. The voice he used when they were talking of sea *superstitions*. In other terms, the voice he used when he didn't believe a word they said.

"On Neos," Ebba replied for Plank. "I heard them say it. Up the mountain."

Peg-leg grumbled, "That puts an end to that. That rainforest is nigh impos'ible to get through. And then there be the tribespeople to think o'."

"There be a guide they spoke of. On *Malice*'s crew. By the name o' Jagger. Swindles and Riot said he be from Neos and is knowin' the way."

Her fathers exchanged loaded looks. They continued doing so for long enough that a tendril of excitement joined the already-present hope. She'd dismissed pursuing the treasure yesterday. She'd almost given the details away to the governor in exchange for her fathers' freedom. But Ebba couldn't deny the pursuit of such a treasure was entirely enticing. If this somehow worked out. . . .

"It be a way to hurt them without gettin' further embroiled in trouble," Stubby began.

Peg-leg sniffed. "What better way than to hit a pirate where it hurts? By takin' their gold."

Locks growled. "Four years be a long time to search for sumpin', only to be disa'pointed at the finish line." He and Plank shared an evil look.

"I'm drawn by the additional benefits to our retirement fund," interjected Barrels, a gleam in his eyes. "However, there is still the matter of the 'magical' fruit. Which clearly, scientifically, doesn't exist. And which won't be able to tell us where the so-called treasure is."

Peg-leg dismissed the comment with a wave. "It don't matter if there be magic fruit or not. Reachin' the top o' the mountain first to leave a nice unsigned note sayin' we took it and they can go to Davy Jones will do the trick. Pockmark don't need to know if the fruit were actu-a'ly there or not. Just that someone bet him to it."

"And if there *is* a magical fruit, we can carry on and find the treasure and retire," Ebba added quickly, ignoring Plank's amused glance.

Picking up his weapon sash from outside the bilge, Locks swung it back into place across his torso. "We get to Neos Mountain, leave the note, and get out with Pockmark none the wiser it was *Felicity* who were there."

"Aye," they all chorused.

Ebba exhaled shakily. Her fathers weren't going after *Malice*. That was one less crisis to deal with on Maltu.

Barrels came to stand beside her as the others hoisted themselves out onto the wharf.

"Where're they goin'?" she asked.

With Pillage already under one arm, Barrels tucked Ebba into his side, and kissed the top of her head. The gesture should have had her ranting about how pirates should treat other pirates, but in the early hours of the morning, after the night she'd had, Ebba was nothing but grateful.

"I believe," he said in mild tones, "my co-parents are going to procure our guide."

SEVEN

The rhythmic swing of the hammock wanted to lull her back into slumber's fuzzy embrace. She might have succumbed if the swinging wasn't a sure sign *Felicity* had set sail—which meant her fathers were back from 'procuring their guide.'

She wiped the drool off her cheek, shoved Pillage off her chest, and swung her legs over the side. Pillage landed on all fours and whirled to hiss at her.

"Ye only like me when Barrels has locked ye out o' his office," she told him.

The cat slinked off into the hold, his tail bolt upright.

Their sleeping quarters in the bilge consisted of eight hammocks. All the others slept in pairs, in burlap hammocks strung high and low between two poles. Ebba didn't share a sleep space, probably because she had two trunks of belongings instead of one. An empty hammock swung above her, a guest hammock that had never been slept in and usually acted as her wardrobe. Each of her trunks was latched to one of the posts, not leaving room for anyone else to move in.

The bone supports of Maybell's corset dug into her flesh, and Ebba grimaced. She must've fallen asleep dress and all.

First things first. Ebba jumped from the hammock and kicked open one of her trunks. She grabbed her dagger and cut through the corset, casting the cursed garment over her head to be forgotten. The boots followed.

She pulled on a tunic and moaned as she tugged up her slops; she didn't care that they were on the yellow side of white or tattered around the ankles—Ebba hoped to be with her trousers forever. She tied a brown bandana around her head and tightly laced her leather jerkin over her billowing tunic. Then she remembered they had a guest onboard which had *never* happened before and wrapped a long strand of beads three times around her neck, arranging them to hang in layers. She drew out a length of brown linen and tied it over her belt, knotting it at the side and letting the ends hang.

Ebba placed her hands on her hips and swayed side to side, pleased with the result.

She bounded to the ladder and danced up the rungs to fling the bilge door open.

One squint at the blaring sun told her it was mid-day already. She'd lost *hours* of their adventure. Why didn't someone wake her?

Everyone was in his usual spot; Stubby was at the helm, which meant Locks was around doing the constant repairs that life at sea demanded.

Plank had swung the foresail wide and hoisted the square topsail for extra speed. Grubby ducked as the boom swung across deck. Probably a good thing. None of them were sure what another blow to the head would do to the happy pirate.

"Ahoy, Ebba-Viva," Stubby shouted. "Yer breakfast be below deck."

Breakfast was the least of her worries.

"How goes *Felicity*?" she hollered back.

Stubby looked after the maintenance of the boat. He forced them to careen the ship several times a year to get rid of the barnacle buildup, and directed Locks on where to make repairs, helping out with the larger jobs. Nothing stressed Stubby more than when something on *Felicity* wasn't in working order, so Ebba, like the rest of her fathers, always made a point of only asking when everything was fine.

Sure enough, Stubby gave a self-satisfied smile and tight nod. "She'll do the job," he said, his tone implying that *Felicity* could climb a mountain in her current condition.

Ebba listened to his reply with half an ear, scanning the deck. She was rewarded when her eyes fell upon a hunched form bound to the mast with his wrists behind his back. That had to be their guide. With the way the *Malice* pirate sat against the main mast, it was difficult to make out any detail—aside from the pirate's height which she'd label as oversized.

Still, he'd be the only sign of their adventure for the next week until they got to Neos, and she planned to extract every possible detail on the plunder out of him.

She snorted suddenly, calling back to Stubby, "I can't believe ye took someone hostage." She'd have given a baby albatross to see them fight the tall *Malice* pirate. A tiny part of her even wished the rest of Pockmark's crew had seen it—though the much larger part was relieved they hadn't.

"In the bilge with ye for breakfast, Ebba-Viva," Stubby called again. "There be a whole deck to swab."

She scowled. Her punishment. They hadn't forgotten.

Turning back the way she'd come, Ebba threw open the bilge door and hooked her arches around the smoothed outside of the ladder, sliding to the bottom. She spun away from the creaking hammocks and strode down the hall instead, passing by the small office where Barrels would be muttering to himself, pouring over his numbers as resident quartermaster.

Ebba jumped over Pillage's extended paw as he lingered in the shadows closer to the hold. "Get a new trick," she told him, smiling at his hiss. Spiteful bloody cat.

Peg-leg was in the small kitchen shoved in the front corner in the hold where they kept their supplies and grog.

A small kitchen bench sat against the hull, its two cupboards and three drawers stuffed with a mixture of cooking tools, carpentry tools, and any tiny knick-knacks that needed a home. Next to the bench was a sand box. A fire smoldered in the middle, underneath a heavy cauldron. Stubby had carved a small circle out of the deck overhead years ago and placed a chute over the fire, so smoke could escape the hold. He and Peg-leg got on for a whole week after the chute was installed.

"Yer breakfast be cold," Peg-leg said with a sniff, not looking at her.

Peg-leg didn't like his food to be eaten cold when he'd gone to the trouble of lighting a fire. Even with the chute, cooked meals were a treat—it wasn't always safe to light a fire onboard, especially in the wet season.

She took the plate from him without a word, holding it with the reverence her father expected. Turned out it was deserved this time: corned beef and bread, with scalloped potatoes. She beamed at the cook, and he turned away with a small smile. Even if the goopy fiutch had been on the plate, Ebba would've shown the same appreciation. If there was one thing *Felicity*'s cook wouldn't tolerate, it was negative feedback on his cooking. Every single one of them had learned that lesson the hard way.

"Lunch ain't far away," he added in a mollified voice.

A half-chewed chunk of bread lodged in her throat. She swiped up a goblet and walked to the closest grog barrel. Throwing back the top, she scooped her goblet into the dark fluid, and took several large gulps of the rum, water, and nutmeg mix.

"I won't be needin' lunch," she said. "I'm to swab the decks."

Peg-leg's belly shook as he laughed. Most likely at the bitterness in her voice.

Ebba peeked at him. "I might climb the shrouds first. Just quick-like."

His blue eyes softened. He'd been a rigger in his time, too, before losing his leg to cannon splinter. Ebba knew he missed the thrill of *Felicity*'s ropes more than he let on.

"Aye, I reckon you can go to the crow's nest afore ye start. But—"

Ebba finished for him. "I know. I'll be tellin' ye what I see." She shoved the last of the corned beef in her mouth and dusted her hands on her slops. "Were any o' ye hurt takin' the guide hostage last night?"

A curious look came over Peg-leg's eyes. "Nay, lass. He came with us as easy as a babe."

"Of course, there were five o' ye," she said.

"He be a head taller than Plank, and used to workin' by the look of him. A deal younger than us, too. He could've done some damage if he'd wished."

Ebba tilted her head, a frown on her high-boned face. "Was he drunk?"

Peg-leg winked at her, though a shadow lingered in the back of his eyes. "Ye likely be right. Now run along with ye. I be busy. Davy knows, this lunch won't cook itself."

She necked the rest of her grog and threw the goblet in the wash bucket. Up the ladder once more, Pillage successfully dodged, Ebba stared at the hunched guide tied to the mast.

"Swabbin', little nymph," Plank reminded her.

She turned to see him perched in his usual spot on the bulwark, eyes distant as he watched the sails in a semi-dream state. But he wasn't humming. When Plank hummed his old tune, they all knew he was *really* daydreaming and no amount of shouting would bring him out of it.

"Peg-leg said I can climb the shrouds first," she countered.

Plank glared in the direction of Peg-leg below deck. "Did he now?"

She tucked away a triumphant smile and returned her attention to the man tied to the mast. Circling in from a distance, she approached.

. . . *Jagger*, the two pirates had called him.

His head slumped forward in sleep, or so it appeared. He swayed with the motion of the sloop, shoulders relaxed. Flaxen hair hung in a straggly curtain to his shoulders, an odd color that sat somewhere between brown and gold. His forehead was high and, Ebba noted, the muscles she glimpsed were lean and defined from regular use. He wore the full black uniform of Pockmark's ship, the same as Swindles and Riot, with the red-brown sash slung low around his hips. The dark shirt stretched across his shoulders, and the sleeves were rolled back just below his elbow. Where the uniform had seemed to wear Swindles and Riot, for this pirate, the opposite was true.

Peg-leg was right. This man was tall and strongly built, maybe late teens or early twenties. Yet there wasn't a scratch on him or her fathers. He *could* have hurt one of her fathers if he wished. . . Why hadn't he?

Had he wanted to be taken? That seemed just as unlikely.

Ebba crept closer until she was a pace away from him, studying the high-boned plains and golden skin of his face. Three coils of rope held him to the mast from shoulder to hip. Would her fathers leave him sitting here until Neos? A whole week?

The guide lifted his head and her heart leaped into her throat as his eyes met hers. The orbs were the color of cold pistol metal. A shiver bolted up her spine—as though cold pistol metal had actually been pressed against her lower back.

In her seventeen years, she'd never had a peer on *Felicity*. For the most part, she tended to spend only a few hours at a time in the company of anyone other than her crew. Usually, it was with Sherry or one of Locks' girlfriends, or Stubby's sisters. Ebba found herself at a loss of how to proceed. On one hand, the guide was on her ship. On the other, he was a scumbag *Malice* pirate. Was he going to talk? Or should she say something? The pewter eyes were calculating and cold, and lit with much more awareness than she'd seen in Swindles' and Riot's eyes. The guide gave the impression he was entirely capable of treating her as the other *Malice* pirates had in the alley, but what it would take to make him act that way, she couldn't immediately tell, and that gave her the floundering feeling of sailing through unchartered waters. Where it was safe assuming Pockmark and most other pirates would get angry when insulted or challenged, Ebba suspected it would take something much different to bring this man to the same point.

"Little nymph, climb the shrouds and then get to yer swabbin'," Plank said softly.

Ebba was grateful to have a reason to turn away from the flaxen-haired pirate with the calculating silver eyes.

She took a steadying breath and crossed to the base of the rigging, tipping her face to the sky. With the sun directly overhead, it looked like she'd climb right into the sun itself. Her lips curved for no particular reason as she swung herself onto the ship's side and started up the rope squares. The smell of damp wood was left behind as she climbed, and the undiluted smell of sea salt took its place. The thin ropes of the rigging cut into her feet, and her arms burned, but her smile only grew at the fluttering sound of the mainsail—a happy noise, one of her favorites. She climbed higher.

Ebba would never tell anyone, but when she was younger she thought climbing through the sails took her to another place, one filled with the magical creatures in Plank's stories. At one end, she was on the ship; at the other, she sat among the stars—flying as high as a bird.

She gripped the top edge of the crow's nest and vaulted inside with ease.

. . . Then looked out over the bright blue expanse of the Free Seas.

King Montcroix reigned over Exosia, the Caspian Sea, and the islands therein. Since the end of the twenty-year Battle for the Seas in her fathers' time, the king's hold over the outer parts of the Caspian Sea had loosened, and the pirates now referred to this less-controlled part of the realm as the Free Seas.

Nowadays, the navy men only governed the waters closest to the mainland, north of Kentro and Maltu. Pirates had quickly learned that if they stopped killing the governors of the islands and instead corrupted them, the governors would report favorably to the king, and the king would leave the pirates be.

Ebba glanced back the way they'd come and her shoulders relaxed. Maltu was just a tiny dot in the distance. The shackles about her ankles and the governor's gaudy mansion could become bad memories now.

Her fathers must've pulled anchor at least five hours ago to get so far. With this head start, they would stay well ahead of *Malice*. *Felicity* may be smaller than the schooner Pockmark had killed his father to possess, but their old cedar sloop would win any race against the larger ship. *Felicity* could pick up speed four times faster, and she could anchor in bays too shallow for *Malice* to enter.

Ebba spun around to look over the bow, pushing her bandana back into position over her hairline. Below, the sea sprayed, splitting across their figurehead, a bare-chested mermaid carved by Stubby. If she took the pains to, she'd be able to spot any number of fish and ocean critters in the cobalt waters. Even at a glance Ebba could spot a huge sea turtle fifty paces from the starboard side.

But something much different occupied her mind. *Neos*. A thrill ran through her. Yesterday was terrible, nearly having her tongue cut out and all the rest. It had shown Ebba how lost she'd be without her fathers. But now that they were on the other side of it, away from alleys and the gaol and *Malice*, Ebba decided their current adventure might have been worth a smidgen of strife.

Her first quest.

Her fathers planned to get to Neos and take revenge on Pockmark for hurting her. But what if there *was* a magic fruit tree? What if the fruit could actually tell them where the treasure was? Her mind was tumultuous with the possibilities of the coming weeks. She couldn't wait to get to Neos. Ebba gripped the edge of the nest and swung her legs over, her feet finding the crosstree platform the crow's nest sat upon and then the rigging.

As she made her way down, she spied Locks crossing the deck below. His eye patch was closest to her. He wouldn't see her coming. Easy prey. She moved around the rigging so she was clinging to the inside, and hooked her knee through a rope square. Waiting.

Waiting.

With a grin, she threw herself backward. "Show a leg!" she yelled, swinging upside down in front of Locks' face.

He jumped violently, clutching at his chest. "Blow me down, Ebba-Viva! Ye scurvy wee codfish. Will ye stop doing that!"

Ebba let her arms dangle over her head, her stomach cramping with laughter as tears squeezed from her eyes. Locks had said the same thing for about a decade. Scaring her fathers only got funnier as the years went on. They just never learned.

Wiping her eyes, she found the guide staring directly up at her. Glaring, more specifically.

Taming her laughter, Ebba curled up and extracted her leg, dropping to the deck on quiet feet. She ignored the *Malice* guide but couldn't shake the feeling he judged her every move with those cold, hard eyes. Heat crept up her neck and she felt uncomfortably aware of her actions, in a way she never had before. Maybe that rigging trick was a little . . . young.

"Do ye need a change o' slops, Locks?" Plank called.

Grubby let out an uneasy laugh from where he swabbed the deck, darting a look between Plank and Locks. "Now, now," he hushed, though who he hushed wasn't clear.

Locks' gaze snapped to Grubby. "I thought Ebba be our swabbie for the next three moons." He glanced around the deck. "Did we change our mind?"

Plank stormed over. "Grubby! That be Ebba's job. Blimey, can't a single one o' ye stick to disciplinin' her?"

"Get off yer seahorse," Locks said. "Ye ain't the only one—"

"Peg-leg let her climb the shroud. . . ."

Ebba tuned out their bickering, careful not to show her glee upon seeing Grubby had nearly swabbed the whole deck. "I'll take over, Grubs," she said.

Grubby gave her a toothy smile and a consoling pat on the shoulder, and Ebba took the stiff broom from him. There was only a couple of paces left to do. Grinning right now wouldn't help her cause. . . .

"Hardly worth it," came Plank's muttered reply behind her.

Barrels emerged from below deck. "Did you already give her the beads we got her?"

Ebba froze. "Beads?" she asked them. "As in—more than one? Ye didn't get me two, did ye?" She beamed at them.

"What's the bloody point?" Plank shouted, throwing his hands in the air. He stalked away.

"What's in his grog?" Stubby called out.

Locks' emerald eye gleamed. "Ah, just the usual dis'iplinary concerns."

Barrels gave the ghost of a smile, and seeing Grubby working himself into a nervous frenzy of twisting hands and wide eyes, her fathers let the matter settle. Poor Grubs. Ebba decided to put extra effort into washing the rest of the deck for his sake. And maybe because they'd gotten her a present. If she knew Plank, he would've chosen well. *Two* beads. Where to put them? She'd really have to think about it. Eventually, she'd have a headful, but until then, it mattered where they went.

It wasn't long before Grubby, deprived of his usual job, and still fretting about Plank's state of mind, took out his blackwood flute and began to play. Music was a regular occurrence aboard the *Felicity*. Weeks spent at sea deadened to dullness very quickly, and all pirates did what they could to change the scene. There was no one she would rather be at sea with, and the sea itself was beautiful, but the *sameness* of it could make you feel closed in after too long.

Ebba appreciated Grubby's music twofold this day, considering the occurrences of yesterday were turning to bad memories but were yet to fade. Right at this moment, her fathers might have been en route to Exosia. Ebba shuddered, recalling the fearful realization she'd made last night: Without her fathers she had no one in the world. And no one to depend upon.

Her fathers clearly felt the fear of their near miss, too. Barrels went back to his office to retrieve his fiddle, and Peg-leg sat on a crate and bent his wooden leg to the deck, ready to add percussion.

The warm timbre of Grubby's flute floated over the deck—the crew of *Felicity* knew this sea shanty well. It was one of Ebba's favorites, which was no doubt why the pirate had picked it. He felt bad she'd had to swab the deck for a few minutes and wanted to cheer her up. He'd be like this for the next three moons.

Ebba stomped along with the others as the trill of the intro finished.

Soon Stubby began to bellow the lyrics from the helm.

Oh, his heart was free on the sea,
On the sea
Said the small boy, still wet behind the ears.
Aye, his heart was free on the sea.

His gut turned over on the sea,
On the sea,
His gut turned over on the sea.
The wee pirate boy was parted from his food,
Aye, his heart was free on the sea.

His hair did blow in the breeze,
In the breeze,
His hair did blow in the breeze.
Got tangled in the riggin', he was squealing like a piggin',
Aye, his heart was free on the sea.

Locks whooped loudly and grabbed Ebba's hand, dragging her to the middle of the group to dance as the others who weren't playing clapped and shouted.

What happened when he needed to pee,
Had to pee.

What happened when he needed to pee?
He pissed in the wind and wore it again.
Aye, his heart was free on the sea.

Ebba spun in circles with Locks, throwing her head back to laugh. He doubled over, wheezing as he stopped spinning, waving for her to continue.

She caught Stubby's eye and grinned as he took a deep breath to start the song again, double time. She placed her hands on both hips and spun wildly as the tempo picked up. Her feet faltered slightly as she caught the burning silver stare of their guide at the mast. But the words of the song blurred together, and the ship and sky seemed to join before her eyes as she pushed to match the beat. Faster and faster she spun in the air, her feet barely skimming the surface of the deck.

He pissed in the wind and wore it again.
Aye, his heart was free on the sea!

The flute and fiddle chorused one last decisive peal. With a gasp, Ebba fell flat on her back, breathless, her chest rapidly rising and falling beneath her leather jerkin.

She stared at the blazing sun in the azure sky, listening to her fathers' cheering.

The crew of *Felicity* was on a quest for treasure, and it was only the first day.

Could pirate life get any better?

EIGHT

Ebba sat on the deck—the freshly *swabbed* deck. Grubby had been detained in the hold while she completed it herself for the last five days. In one hand, she rolled the smooth, white bead that had caught her eye back in Maltu. In the other hand, she clutched a bead with orange and green stripes that Plank had picked out.

"I've decided where to put them," she announced to Peg-leg.

"That's good, lass. I'm sure they'll look right-fierce."

She hoped so.

Her eyes fell on Jagger. Her fathers hadn't left him tied to the mast. Taking pity a few days ago, they'd moved him into the shade by the bilge door, tying him to a barrel. When directed, the pirate from *Malice* simply stood and strode to the new spot before sitting. He hadn't spoken a word this whole trip, in *six* days. One of her fathers took food to him twice daily. The guide ate every crumb, and drank every drop of grog. . . But why didn't he speak? Ebba would think him simple if not for those shifting silver eyes that didn't seem to miss a thing. She'd wanted to pester him with questions, but something about him held her back. He had an aura of danger about him that gave her chills, but he wasn't *afraid* enough. That's what bothered her. Abducted and stolen away on another pirate ship, and not a flicker of concern on his expression.

She was becoming more certain that he wanted to be with them, but couldn't fathom why.

Peg-leg threw open the bilge door with five plates balanced on his forearms. He clunked over to her and held out two.

"Take one to Stubby, will ye?"

Ebba nodded slowly and placed her new beads in her sash, taking the plates from the cook. When Peg-leg beelined for Plank, she strode over to their silent guide instead. There were enough plates to go around, Stubby would get his plate eventually.

"Here." She placed the food at his feet and then loosened two of the ropes slightly, so he had use of his hands. He immediately began shoving the porridge with honey and sliced mango into his mouth. Ebba didn't blame him. If she matched his height, she'd eat like a sea-cow, too.

Leaning against the bulwark, she munched on her own porridge. Probably didn't pay to wander away with his hands free. She bit into a piece of fresh mango and wiped at the juice dribbling down her chin.

"Be nice to get fruit each day." His voice was low, but her interest at hearing him speak overrode her discomfort at his attention. She could even ignore the mocking undertones this one time.

"Peg-leg thinks we need a balanced and n'tritional diet," she quoted.

Keeping fruit and vegetables on board was a pain. It created the need to stop for supplies more often. But they'd learned if they went too long without, Peg-leg's temper reached epic heights. His anger in these times could be tasted in the charcoal coating the fish and in the rock-hard flatbread he cooked.

The guide fell quiet again. *Dammit.* Ebba scowled and shoved a large spoon of porridge in her mouth.

"Who's yer captain?"

Ebba swallowed her mouthful with difficulty. "Uh," she squinted, trying to remember, "Locks, this month."

He turned to face her, wiping at his mouth before asking, "The one with the scars on his cheeks?"

Her brows lifted. Just how closely was he paying attention? Did he know all of their names? She paused, and then nodded.

"This month?" he pressed.

She ran her tongue over her teeth to remove any traces of porridge. "We switch around. No one really likes bein' captain."

Jagger's brows were a few shades darker than his flaxen hair. They rose, faintly—as though he simultaneously couldn't believe her answer, and didn't care. How much should she be telling the guide? Probably not *too* much.

His plate was empty. She tightened his ropes again and swooped down to collect the empty dish, feeling a bead of sweat trickling down her back.

Today was the most humid day they'd had in the last six. It didn't help that the wind died off somewhere in the night. Without the help of a breeze, Ebba's clothing stuck to her body like some kind of saggy skin. Moisture trickled down her neck, disappearing beneath her leather jerkin. Peg-leg couldn't be coping well, not to mention. . . . "Ain't ye warm in all that black?" she asked Jagger. The only part of his uniform that wasn't black was the crimson sash tied low on his hips.

His next look asked if she was stupid. "Aye."

"Then why do *Malice*'s crew wear it? Just to match the ship?"

"Mercer's orders." His eyes fell to where her tunic was clinging to her torso.

Seemed silly to her. More from an urge to distract his attention from her body, she asked, "Why don't the crew mutiny?"

Jagger's jaw clenched and he broke off his stare. Unsure what to make of his response, she shrugged and spun to take the dishes down below. As she did there was a clattering at her feet. . . .

. . . Followed by a rolling sound.

Ebba fixed her perplexed eyes on the deck, and she seized at the sight of a small object bowling across the ship. *Her beads.*

Her beads!

Throwing the plates to the ground she gave chase, scrambling after the green-and-orange-striped bead. Grubby and Peg-leg rushed from the helm, drawn by the racket. On hands and knees, she dove for the bead, head resting on her arms when she trapped it close to the mast.

She gripped it tight in her fist and rose to her feet, patting her sash and frantically searching for the white one.

"Ebba."

She lifted her head at the odd quality in Locks' voice.

His eyes fixed behind her and Ebba followed his gaze, smiling in relief as she spotted her white bead trapped against Jagger's extended foot. He'd shifted to keep it from rolling through the scupper and out to sea.

She took three steps in his direction, a "thank you" on her lips when, without warning, he bent his knee.

The bead's roll was slow at first, and Ebba's reactions sluggish because of her disbelief at Jagger's cruelty. The bead picked up pace and she jolted to life, sprinting across the deck with a cry.

She stumbled to a halt as the bead disappeared through the hole and out to sea. She blinked at the scupper in a daze, but soon felt heat flooding her cheeks. Her rage boiled over at the wolfish smile on Jagger's lips. "Ye—"

His eyes fixed on something behind her. She whirled just in time to see Grubby jumping over *Felicity*'s side into the ocean.

Ebba turned on Jagger once more, fists clenched, a burning anger rising hard and fast inside her.

"He jumped into the sea," Jagger blurted. He scanned the crew, his lips pressed firmly together—displaying something other than boredom for the first time. "Is he crazy?"

No one answered. In truth, Grubby was slightly crazy, but he was a great swimmer. He often leaped off the ship, even when they were traveling at eleven knots. He skimmed through water as quick as any dolphin.

"Why'd ye do that?" Ebba demanded, ignoring the pirate's gaping expression.

Jagger's mouth closed, and his gaze cooled, though she saw him glance again to where Grubby had disappeared. "Why not? Stupid, the way ye fawn over those things."

She curled her hand into a fist, ready to deliver it into his stupid gob.

Locks wrapped an arm around her shoulders. "Aye, he's a right mean bastard, ain't he? Did ye expect anythin' else from a pirate o' *Malice*?"

Jagger's eyes flashed.

Sensing the comment hurt him more than her fist would, she let Locks lead her away.

Plank threw a rope out to Grubby, who soon appeared over the ship's side and flopped onto the deck. It always took him a good minute to stand after a swim. When she defied pirate law two to ask him once, he said he needed to remember how to breathe on land after being in the water. That wasn't so hard to accept when compared to his tales about family feuds between the octopi.

Ebba waited patiently and eventually Grubby got to his feet and held out a hand to her.

In the center of his palm sat her white bead.

"Ye got it." Ebba threw her arms around his neck, the water soaking her clothes as she hugged him close. Aside from her six fathers, her beads were the most important thing to her. While her fathers had not always been by her side, the beads had—the trinkets were a reminder of them, that they'd always come for her. And a reminder of the fearsome pirate she wanted to be. "Thank ye, Grubs."

Grubby patted her gently and grinned. "There were a couple of interestin' fish down, too, so I'm glad I went."

Ebba clutched both beads and hurried for the bilge to put them in her hair. As she passed close to Jagger, she glared at him. Their guide wasn't looking at her, though; he was too busy drilling Grubby with those silver eyes, his mouth ajar. His bottom lip was fuller than his top lip. But it didn't matter what the Neos guide looked like—he was rotten inside, and she didn't like the feeling he gave her.

Checking none of her fathers were paying attention, she kicked the *Malice* pirate in the thigh as hard as her bare feet would allow.

She smiled at his grunt of pain and ducked below deck with her new bead additions.

EBBA CLIMBED THE KNOTTED ROPE, ocean water pouring off her as she scaled *Felicity*'s side to the deck. She reached back to check the two new beads were still in place in the dread behind her right ear after her bath. The linen shirt she wore clung to the dark skin of her stomach and thighs. Normally, she didn't bother wearing anything when going for a dip, but Stubby was adamant about her wearing the shirt that morning, so she'd let up, too happy to have arrived at Neos.

At Barrels' suggestion, they'd circled *Felicity* to the shallow west side of the island. If *Malice* arrived behind them, they'd have to drop anchor at the deeper, eastern coves.

Ebba swung over the bulwark and picked up the drying cloth Barrels had left out for her, wrapping it around her lithe body. She turned back to stare at Neos; it was the smallest populated island in the Caspian Sea and sat as far south as most pirates would dare to go. They stopped here a few times a year to trade with the locals before stealing from neighboring islands. A mountain sat at the island's center, the peak visible from here, distant and gray. Ebba dried herself absently, watching the mountain with unfocused eyes, squeezing the water from her dreads.

They were searching for *real* plunder today. Ebba's lips curved and she pushed away from the side and made for the bilge. She scowled in Jagger's direction—as she'd taken to doing since the bead incident the day before. Her scowl had no effect this morning, with the blanket Peg-leg had chucked over his head while Ebba bathed.

It had to be boiling hot under there, but the pirate didn't make a peep.

Opening the bilge door, she called, "I'm done," and slid down the ladder. As soon as she reached the depths of the sleeping quarters, she heard her fathers filing to the ladder and back up to the main deck to work.

Ebba threw on her clothes, emerging not two minutes later. Slotting her pistols into her sash, Ebba rushed over to help Plank lower the rowboat over the side. They'd leave *Felicity* here with Barrels to stand watch. Barrels wasn't really the mountain-climbing type, but he was a good shot, should anyone come looking to pilfer their ship. Peg-leg wasn't the mountain-climbing sort either, but none of their crew would make the mistake of telling him so, and he was too stubborn to remain behind.

Locks untied their guide and Peg-leg pointed his pistol at Jagger's belly, his meaning crystal clear.

The young pirate rose painfully, not immediately straightening. A week sitting down on hard wood would do that to anyone.

She gathered up the rope ladder coiled on the ground at her feet, and tossed it over the bulwark.

Once all were aboard the rowboat, Locks and Peg-leg grabbed the oars and began to heave to shore. Ebba smiled at Barrels, who waved them goodbye from *Felicity*'s deck, Pillage scooped up under one arm.

"Byyyye, Barreeeels," she bellowed.

He smiled and looked around, before yelling, "Byyyeee, Ebbbaaaa."

She snorted. Nothing better than when Barrels forgot his dignity for a few seconds.

"How old are ye?" Jagger asked, the jeer in his voice unmistakable.

His words stung where Sherry's comment about Ebba's naivety hadn't. In comparison to the *Malice* pirates she did feel . . . untested somehow, but that hadn't bothered her until she'd found herself alone on Maltu. Or maybe since Jagger had been on the ship—she recalled his face when she'd scared Locks the other day. Clearly the guide thought she should grow up. Was clinging to childhood really such a terrible thing? Everyone else seemed to think so.

"Old enough to not feel shame in showin' my fathers I love them," she quipped, a bite in her voice. "What about ye, Jagger?" she asked. "How old? Or do ye just feel ye need to act older than ye are?"

Her fathers tensed but didn't move to interrupt.

"Old enough to know ye need to be able to stand on yer own two feet," he replied shortly.

She stared at him, heat entering her cheeks. Jagger couldn't possibly know how incompetent she'd felt when trying to save her fathers, could he?

Ebba was saved from answering as the bottom of the rowboat slid into the black sand of Neos. She leaped out to guide the boat ashore, trying to avoid the jellyfish floating about. Already, sweat beaded on her forearms and neck. They hadn't even entered the rainforest, yet water filled the air and made each breath thick and unsatisfying.

Ebba stared into the forest, fidgeting as her fathers hunkered out of the rowboat, taking their sweet time.

Jagger stood off to one side, a few paces away. He'd been brought here to lead them up the mountain, but he wasn't looking at the tip of the mountain, just visible above the rainforest canopy. He was staring off to the far right.

"What're ye lookin' at?" she demanded, crossing her arms. "What's over that way?"

He ignored her, turning from whatever he'd been gazing at. His eyes fell on her bare feet. Ebba resisted the urge to wriggle her toes in the sand.

"Ye'll be wantin' yer boots," he said curtly.

Her nose scrunched. He was avoiding her question. Not happening. "Why—"

"He's right, little nymph. Boots on." Plank dropped the boots at her feet and continued up to the trees. Sod it, she'd hidden them this morning. How did her fathers always find them?

She scowled and brushed the black sand from her feet, pulling the boots on as her fathers passed her, one by one. "Wait for me."

Peg-leg waved his pistol in the air. "Hold on, mateys. I'd like a word with our *guide*."

Jagger returned his look, seemingly unfazed.

"I may not know me way through that maze o' a rainforest. But I do know that compass tells me the mountain be northwest." He jerked his head at Locks, who held a brass compass. "And I will surely be knowin' my way back to the ship. Lead us to the top and ye'll remain free of bullets, aye?"

Jagger gave a wary nod. "Aye, I'll get ye there in one piece."

"Aye, laddie, I know ye will. My pistol will be ensurin' it. I also know that ye be agreein' a smidgen too easy for my likin', and that ye left Maltu with us easy-like as well. Whatever thoughts ye've got in that head, get rid o' them smart-like."

It hardly mattered if Jagger had other thoughts, in her opinion—he was their hostage. Ebba fidgeted with impatience. "Let's go. There be treasure ahead."

She moved to the head of the line, Jagger's eyes following her as she did so.

"Back here with me, lassie," Stubby called. "We'll protect the rear. And then our guide's eyes won't stray to places *they don't belong*."

She spun and flushed, encountering Jagger's silver gaze as it rose to her face. She returned to the back, surprised to see Stubby had removed his dagger and stood smiling at the guide.

Ebba glanced from the impassive Jagger to her father. "Ye all right, Stubby?"

He slid the dagger back into his sash, saying calmly, "Never better."

The village where they usually steal-traded sat at the east end of the island. Ebba had entered the village on occasion, but never the rainforest. From her father's comments and those of Swindles and Riot, she gathered the rainforest wasn't the kind of place most people went, if they had a choice. Ebba peered into the trees, her heart racing. She wondered if they'd see a real, live tribesperson here. The tribes on most of the islands valued their privacy and did not welcome strangers.

Her fathers said they were very protective of their lands, and no one stood a chance against them on their home ground. King Montcroix had beaten pirates in the sea, but he'd tried to clear the islands of tribespeople and lost.

A centipede scuttled across the ground as they stooped and wove through the knitted tree vines and thick canopy. The trees were as tall as *Felicity*'s mast, maybe bigger. In years gone by, it seemed dead trees had tried to fall, but only achieved an angled lean due to the thick growth surrounding them. It was as though water seeped into every pore and recess of the trees and undergrowth. The dirt was a step away from mud, the plant leaves were so bloated that one touch might pop them, and the tree trunks had grown gigantic in size from the constant heat and moisture. Vibrant blue butterflies fluttered from leaf to leaf. Lizards froze in place on exposed rocks as she passed by. Chattering animals whistled through the towering, dark-green canopy high above.

She inhaled deeply; the forest combined so many new scents, discerning one was impossible. Ebba smelled only dampness and the deep scent of tree bark, punctured by the occasional sweet aroma of exotic flowers.

Unfortunately, the novelty of the forest could only hold her attention for so long before she began to notice how slow their progress was. From the shore, the path to the mountain seemed obvious, but as they wound further through the rainforest, Ebba began to grudgingly appreciate Jagger's sure step through the dense labyrinth of vines and leafy debris.

Her eyes widened at the sight of a huge black-and-green snake readjusting its death grip around a thick tree trunk. Shite, wouldn't want to meet that one on a dark night.

A curious roaring filled her ears and Ebba sent Stubby a frantic look, but he just swung his tricorn hat atop his gray, curling hair and winked at her.

Seconds later, buckets of rain poured down through the trees so thick she could only see Grubby before her.

Ebba blinked through the torrent of the tropical storm, holding a hand over her mouth so she didn't choke on the wall of water. The others had the foresight to bring hats. Why hadn't Plank brought her a hat, too? He'd remembered the damn boots. Ebba watched as Jagger tore off a large flat leaf and held it over his head. Too bad she'd lose face copying a *Malice* pirate.

By the end of the downpour, Ebba was as wet as she'd been after her ocean swim, but a whole lot *less* refreshed.

She slugged through the now muddy ground and squeezed extra moisture from her dreads.

"My compass be tellin' me we're headin' northeast, not northwest, *guide*," growled Locks. "I hope ye're not leadin' us astray."

"To the river," came Jagger's low reply. "It will lead us to the mountain."

TRUE TO JAGGER'S untrustworthy word, arrive at the river they did. The tepid water did little to refresh Ebba, but she ripped off her bandana and dipped it in the rushing surge, her fathers seeking the same relief on the bank next to her.

"Don't linger at the river edge," Jagger said to them. "Crocodiles have been known to come inland this far."

What? Ebba quickly backed away from the water.

Up the river a ways, Jagger took off his black tunic, slinging it over his back and tying the sleeves loosely around his neck. He stood in profile to her, and his muscles were defined as she'd initially suspected. He obviously knew how to work. Her cheeks warmed as she took in the way his torso tapered to narrow hips.

Peg-leg stood in front of her. She stared down to where her nose almost touched his sweat-soaked tunic.

"Ye doin' okay, Peg-leg?" she whispered, referring to his wooden leg.

He lifted the leg back and knocked at her ankles.

"Hey." She laughed.

His belly pushed out with his answering laughter. "I be just fine, lass. Don't worry yer head."

In comparison to the dense vines and trees, the river rocks allowed a pace three times faster, and only a couple of hours later the ground began to slope upward.

"Ye know," stated Plank from the front, "they say the tree of knowledge fruits once every hundred years, and that the tree itself is guarded by Ladon, a huge serpent-ridden lizard."

Ebba grinned as the others let out a heartfelt groan. According to them, Plank's stories took forever, and she had to agree that he always spoke them in an ominous, posh voice that made it hard to focus on what he was actually saying. But Ebba had always loved his tales.

"Legend has it—"

"Stop, stop!" interrupted Stubby. "We're in air so thick I can scarce breathe, and we're clamberin' over rocks like young folk. One o' yer stories will just suck up what's left o' the breathin' air."

Plank's expression turned flinty and he faced the front. Ebba was probably the only one left disappointed. She loved hearing about the time when magic apparently ruled the realm, according to her father's tales anyway. She'd never witnessed magic firsthand, yet sometimes when she looked out from the crow's nest, a trick of the light in the water or the sky had her questioning if such a thing existed. Odd things happened at sea.

"Legend has it," Plank started again in his ominous and posh story voice, overriding her fathers' groans this time, "that ten thousand years ago, when mythical creatures weren't myth, and magic ruled the realm, a lizard-like beast ex'sted. His name was Ladon, and for each soul he devoured, he gained a new serpent around his neck."

"Pleasant pastime." Stubby fell silent under Plank's quelling glare.

"Ladon was a powerful being of great compa'sion, but on the darkest night—"

Peg-leg snorted. "How could they be knowin' that? Ye can't see dark."

"Maybe they could see less that night than usual and that's how they knew," Locks offered.

"*—On the darkest night of the coldest winter*," Plank half-shouted, scowling at them, "a hooded witch stole into Ladon's crevice abode and drained his soul of all light and goodness, leavin' only black evil—the same inky shade as that very night—or so sources say—"

Stubby rolled his eyes.

"—The soul-thief left Ladon for dead and emptied the goodness of his soul into the core of a tree atop the highest mountain. The witch was desp'rate to eat the fruit the tree would produce, you see, to learn how she'd bring her infant child back from death. But she hadn't expected Ladon to survive the ordeal and become a creature of horror. He ate the witch whole and gained the first of the serpents around his neck. Yet eatin' her did not satisfy him because now his evil half-soul screamed always for its light. With the passing of each century, Ladon now waits for the tree of knowledge, which encases his light, to bear fruit. That the fruit has never, upon eatin' it, filled the void inside him only serves to fuel his ire. And to this very day, Ladon continues to eat it, driven by his thirst for what he had. His light. *That* is why he'll never wil'ingly allow anyone to eat from the tree of knowledge and why he devours any soul that crosses his path. Always searchin' for his stolen light. The cruel irony being that he can only devour a soul that has black in it, too, ensuring he'll never again find the goodness the witch stole."

His voice rang out over the river water and had hardly dispersed before. . . .

"That be an utter load of fish guts," Peg-leg whooped loudly.

The rest of her fathers snorted and hooted along with him, but Ebba didn't join in, feeling unaccountably sad for the lizard-beast who'd spent eons searching for his light.

Plank, used to such treatment from her fathers, sighed and ignored them.

Despite the derisive reaction, the tale itself, or perhaps the general cloying feel of the rainforest, pushed their group into silence as they wandered on and on. Their crew trudged up the rocky slope after Jagger, and Ebba's shoulders tightened in a similar way to when she climbed the riggings all day. The tension affected the others, too—even Jagger, who sunk into predatory, stalking quiet.

They moved deeper into wilderness and the animal sounds lessened with each step.

"Walk on tiptoes here, Ebba-Viva," whispered Locks.

She nodded and softened her tread.

Jagger stopped, and they closed around him. It was the first time she'd seen his front. Ebba frowned at the markings on his chest.

Tattoos.

They covered the top of his chest from the tip of each shoulder, up to his collarbone and halfway down his breastbone. They looked . . . tribal. The tattoos were made up of swirls and semi-circles, of masked faces and daggers and animals. Some of the shapes were filled solid black while others were lightly shaded. In some, his golden skin shone through. Someone had spent a lot of time on intertwining the patterns into an endless weave, into a story.

. . . They were *beautiful*. Awe spread through her chest as she studied them.

Back in the alley, Swindles and Riot had said Jagger was from Neos. Upon first seeing him, Ebba assumed he was from the village. If not for his tattoos, she'd *still* be inclined to think him a villager. Many fishermen turned to the pirate life when times got tough, or when greed turned them toward plundering for a living. But the villagers didn't have tattoos. Not like his. Maybe the fishermen had a mermaid, or turtle—or their wife's name on their butts, but one glance at Jagger's chest and Ebba could tell his markings were meaningful in a cultural way and had taken months, if not years to complete.

"We be enterin' tribal grounds; stay silent if ye wish to live," Jagger said.

Ebba ripped her eyes away from his bare torso, clearing her throat and ignoring the heated look the *Malice* pirate aimed at her. He opened his mouth as if about to add something, but then resolutely pressed his lips together.

An icy shiver ran down her spine, and she glanced at the rainforest, which ran thick on either side. If someone, or several someones, hid there, their crew might never realize it until they were attacked.

Jagger jerked his head. "Come on. We still have a few hours to the top."

EBBA PEERED down over the mountain edge.

Locks pulled her back by her belt. "Yer givin' me a damn heart attack, Ebba-Viva. Will ye stop that?"

They'd climbed for the last two hours, using a winding path that circled the mountain in large rings. The sun beat down upon their backs relentlessly, the shelter of the canopy long gone. None of her fathers had stopped to rest, though Stubby's and Peg-leg's pace had slowed. Plank and Grubby, the fittest of the crew after her, poured with sweat, breathing hard.

Ebba's calves burned something fierce, but she pushed on, refusing to let Jagger see weakness. If anyone found him marooned on an island after all this, she wanted him to tell stories of how *Felicity*'s crew never stopped. In fact, she took savage pleasure in the surprise on his face each time he turned back and saw that her fathers still trooped up the grassy mountain behind him.

Lost in her focus to push on, Ebba passed the others until she trailed directly in Jagger's wake. Her breath moved in and out in a steady rhythm. She concentrated on the steep ground under her feet, and as the minutes whittled away, the grass and plant life became patchier. Steamy tendrils began to rise from the now bare rocky ground—the moisture escaping into the sky, powerless to resist the sun's heat.

The ascending rings around the mountain drew tighter as the top coned into a peak, the paths flattening and narrowing.

She glanced over her shoulder. Plank was just behind her, then Grubby—Locks rounding the bend. Hopefully the other two followed close after.

"Two more rings."

Ebba faced forward at Jagger's low words.

Two more rings? She craned her neck. He was right; the top was in sight. Swindles and Riot were right, Jagger really had been here before.

Another glance over her shoulder told her Plank and Grubby had fallen farther behind. One of them needed to be there to make sure Jagger didn't get to the magic fruit first. She picked up her pace to match his long stride.

Last ring.

With silent hands, Ebba drew one of her pistols from her sash. She'd blast him to Exosia if he made the wrong move. As if sensing a change in the air, he glanced back, searching her with his silver eyes until they landed on the weapon in her hand. Her defiant look faded when he simply shrugged and turned back.

They walked through a triangular space between two leaning slabs of bulky gray rock. Paintings and markings occupied every inch of the inside of the tunnel—stick figures of humans and animals. Jagger slowed, hovering his fingers over the tribal markings without actually touching them. Reverent, as if afraid to damage the paintings in any way.

Ebba squeezed past him, fresh energy in her legs.

She ran out the other side of the tunnel onto a rocky clearing, chest tight with excitement.

The mountaintop was circular and had no barriers to prevent her from falling over the side to her death. The ground was uneven, made of huge stone plates that had risen and sunk against each other over the years. Nothing grew over the rocks to add a splash of color; the gray stone itself was only given a brown tinge by a collection of dust, debris, and dirt.

The only bit of life on the plateau was a knotted and twisted tree on the opposite side, extending out over the cliff edge.

. . . From the tree, glistening in the beating sunlight, hung a single golden fruit.

"The mountain apple," she said on an exhale, her skin crawling at the sight. "It's real."

She turned back to shout to her fathers just as an inhuman screech split the air.

NINE

Ebba's body was beyond her control—immobilized by terror's iron grasp. The hairs on the back of her arms stood on end. Her mouth felt like she'd spent three days at sea without water. Her mind accepted a tree of knowledge with a golden fruit might exist. But it could not process this. . . .

. . . *beast.*

Serpents knotted around the reptilian creature's neck in a writhing mass. Distinguishing where one began and ended was impossible. The beast's face was a snake's features pulled taut over a flattened skull. The powerful, muscled body of a lizard extended five paces behind it.

"Don't move," Jagger whispered from behind, low in her ear.

If taking her gaze from the serpent-like creature were an option, she'd consider telling him she could look after herself. As it was, she just shut her mouth and took his advice.

"What is it?" she mumbled, already knowing the answer, even if her mind was also chanting that none of this was possible. *Ladon.*

Jagger's reply was barely above a whisper. "I have . . . no idea."

Seemed like Jagger was in denial, too, and he'd heard Plank's story just as clearly.

Red slits formed the creature's eyes. And the red eyes were fixed on her and Jagger as the beast's pet snakes continued to slither and rub against each other.

Footsteps pounded behind her, the *tap, tap, tap* of Peg-leg's wooden pin hitting the ground in rapid staccato. Ebba cursed under her breath, hearing Jagger do the same as the five men erupted from the passage behind them, shouting at the top of their lungs.

One by one, her fathers gasped in shock. . . .

Except Plank.

"Ladon," he said grimly.

She had to do something. This beast wouldn't let them get to the mountain apple without a fight, and she didn't want her fathers to be hurt. Ebba cocked her pistol and the creature spoke.

"The puny pebbles shot from your weapons will see you killed sooner rather than later, mortal," the beast hissed, his forked tongue flicking out to taste the air.

She jerked. The lizard-snakey-man talked. She was out of her depth. Ebba lowered her pistol, uncocking the weapon as she did so.

The beast's forked tongue lashed again, the slits of his eyes on her. "Wise choice."

The creature was making tiny, disjointed movements as though shivering. It made his outline appear blurry. Ebba blinked and looked again, trying to focus on the beast before her.

No. . . Not disjointed movements. She squinted. The beast flickered—so fast her eyes could barely see. He was disappearing and reappearing on the same spot nearly faster than her sight could register. Invisible one moment, here the next, but so fast it looked as though he was trembling.

The lizard reared on hind legs. “You mean to steal my mountain apple. Mortals, ever seeking more than they have. In ten millennia, my fruit has been stolen but once, and from those much more powerful than yourself. You are fools to try, and fools you shall die.” He roared.

Ebba screamed from the force of his bellow. It echoed in her ear. In her mind. In a deep place she knew had to be her soul.

A hand dragged her back, and arms clutched her tight.

Gasping for air as the roaring receded, she lowered her hands and stared at them. Blood stained her palms. Her ears had bled? Numbly, she glanced up at Plank, who held her, then at the others. None seemed to be affected.

Whatever sadness she’d felt after Plank’s story was long gone. Ladon might’ve had a soul once, but it wasn’t there any longer.

The creature laughed manically, his eye slits glowing red. “Only one innocent among you,” it hissed. “And one with so much delectable black inside.” Ladon’s eyes flickered to Jagger. “My pretties, we shall feast tonight!”

The snakes around his neck thrashed in ecstasy.

Plank gripped her by the shoulders, talking low in a rapid whisper, “Ebba, ye need to leave. *Now*. Back down the mountain to Barrels.”

“W-what,” she mumbled in confusion, looking at the blood on her palms again.

“Ye’re the only one who can be leavin’. Ladon can only feast on those with black in their souls.”

Rushing filled her ears. “What are ye talkin’ about? Let’s just go back through the tunnel. He won’t fit through the rocks. . . .”

She trailed off as her eyes finally saw the rest of Ladon's trap. The archway behind them no longer existed. Solid rock filled the space.

"Only ye can get through," Plank pressed.

Panic surged within her. "Nay—"

"Ye must!"

Locks leaned in. "Ebba, if ye don't return, Barrels will never know what befell us."

Barrels. Her face fell, and indecision warred within her for the briefest second before she stood back from the pair and withdrew both her pistols, cocking the weapons and aiming them at Ladon.

"Nay," she said through gritted teeth. Barrels was currently safe, the other five of her fathers weren't.

"Your intent to kill is as scattered ash in your soul, young mortal," Ladon gloated, tongue flicking and tasting. "*Delectable* gray. Close enough to black, don't you think, my pretties? The way is barred to all."

Ebba swallowed back her queasiness at the sight of the snakes' rapture around the lizard's neck. He had to be bluffing about the way being barred now. A mere thought couldn't have made her soul gray. What did that even mean? That she was evil or something? Checking whether she could still leave was tempting, but Ebba resisted. She wasn't leaving without her fathers.

The creature took a single step forward, but then flickered out of existence for a full two seconds. Ladon reappeared back in the previous spot.

"What be goin' on with him?" whispered Peg-leg to Plank.

Jagger answered, "He seems weak-like. He be there one moment and gone the next, but so quick it looks like he's blurrin'."

That's what she'd thought, too.

"If he can't move, we may have a chance, but how do we find out if he can?" Stubby asked in a hushed voice.

Only one way Ebba could think of. She spoke to the beast, "Oi, can ye move, or are ye stuck there? Ye seem weak."

Ladon's response was a roar as ear-splitting as the first. His snakes reared back and spat their venom toward the group, but the droplets landed several yards away. Ebba wasn't compelled to cover her ears this time, and her heart jumped into her mouth. Was her soul actually gray? Why didn't his roar hurt anymore?

"I think that be a no," Stubby said drily.

"It's of no matter if he can move or not," growled Locks. "The way off this clearin' be blocked, and there only be sheer cliffs around us."

"Can I just say I told ye so?" Plank said. "But no, none of ye wanted to listen to me story—"

Peg-leg growled at him. "Not the time."

"Er, right." Plank cleared his throat and slid closer to the beast. "Ladon." The beast's red slits fell upon Plank, who swept his raven curls from his forehead in a quick, nervous gesture. "Ladon, we are at an impasse. Ye can't move—"

"And none of you may leave," hissed the creature. "You will not eat my beloved apple."

Plank opened his mouth, but the creature continued. "A test," Ladon declared. "A game. A *bargain*." The word echoed, eliciting another violent shiver from Ebba.

She slid closer to Peg-leg.

"What kind o' bargain?" Plank asked.

Two of the snakes unfurled on either side of Ladon's head and drew close to where Ebba guessed the creature's ears to be.

The beast's lipless mouth stretched into a smile. "Yes."

The two snakes returned to the throbbing mass, and Ladon lifted his great, horrific head. "Three correct answers to three riddles for your freedom."

"The riddles will be about things we know?" Plank asked suspiciously.

Irritation shuddered over Ladon's face and into the surrounding rock. "Of course. Answer correctly, and I will clear the way so all may pass. Answer any of the three incorrectly and I will feast on your innards while you still live."

She swallowed. That seemed . . . unfair.

They gathered together. Her fathers looked devastated, but Peg-leg rounded on the grim-faced Jagger.

"Ye led us to him, ye traitorous bastard! Ye knew Ladon was here." Peg-leg accused.

Jagger's face tightened and he stepped toward her father. "I'm in this trap, too, ye fool."

The *Malice* pirate did seem as concerned about being trapped here as they did. Whatever he'd come with them to Neos for, apparently it hadn't been to trap them up here with Ladon.

"Enough," Plank said tightly. "There's no time for this." His glinting eyes rested on Jagger, however. It might be best for the younger pirate if they *didn't* make it out of here.

With a muttered curse, Peg-leg spun away from Jagger, who watched his retreat, jaw clenched.

"We need Barrels," Locks said with a sigh.

Everyone turned to him.

"I reckon that sounds fair," a voice rang out.

They froze.

“And I like games. We’ll play,” the pleasant voice continued.

Ebba wasn’t the only one who dove to stop Grubby from speaking, but as she did so a heavy golden ring snapped into place around her neck. She coughed and tugged on the solid band, frantically seeking a crack she could use to pry the collar off.

She turned to the others with wide eyes, trying not to panic. All seven of them had a golden ring about their necks, too.

“Grubby!” Plank moaned.

Grubby jerked, staring at the rest of the crew. “What?”

“Too late,” Ladon said gleefully, stretching his neck to full height. “The golden ring has sealed your fate.”

Everyone, including Jagger, glared at Grubby, who shrank to the back of their group.

“And where be yer gold band?” croaked Ebba with a scowl. “How can we be sure ye’ll stick to yer word, beast?”

Ladon roared in fury, stamping his clawed limbs, but his red eyes flared as a golden ring snapped around one of his snakes.

Plank squeezed her hand. “Good thinkin’, little nymph.”

She only nodded in response, eyes focused on Ladon.

Nostrils flaring, the beast spoke again, “Let us begin.”

Shite, Locks was right. They really needed Barrels for this. He was the smartest.

The beast flickered in and out again before speaking in an echoing voice, “I grow harder to conceal with each attempt to hide me. I am festering, born of fear and humiliation. . . What am I?”

Ebba shared a nonplussed glance with Peg-leg. Sounded like a boil to her, but that didn’t quite fit.

Her fathers began to gather in a group, but Jagger moved away, not looking at any of them. His silver eyes darkened and he swallowed hard. “A secret,” he called to Ladon.

Her heart pounded in her chest as she and the crew waited to hear of their imminent doom.

Ladon’s thin nostrils flared. “Correct,” the beast said, in barely concealed rage. He flickered out of sight for three full seconds before coming back.

Felicity’s crew stared at Jagger.

“How’d ye know that?” Locks asked.

Jagger shrugged a shoulder in reply, not removing his ever-watchful silver eyes from the beast.

Another snake untangled itself and hissed at length in Ladon’s ear.

This was wrong, she shuddered. All of this was wrong. Snakes didn’t *talk*. Giant lizard-men didn’t wear hundreds of snakes as a scarf. Because that meant magic was real. But how had they never seen anything like Ladon before? A magic fruit was one thing, but a mythical *creature*?

Ladon’s thick tail lashed as his snake-minion finished.

“Listen closely, mortals: What do I spell? Contentment’s sound before the twenty-six’s leader. Yeo’s missing lover and a selfish man’s repetition. For all of this, you will not succeed, not unless you remember the sea.”

Ebba wasn’t alone in turning to Jagger, but Plank began to pace, tapping his mouth. “Yeo’s missing lover is named Gee.”

“Contentment’s sound. . . .” said Peg-leg. “Yum?”

Jagger turned to stare at the rocky ground.

He then glanced at Locks. “Dagger.”

Without batting an eyelash, Locks passed the weapon over.

Jagger whirled to the beast. "Repeat the riddle." He crouched as Ladon recited the riddle again.

Ebba leaned forward to watch Jagger, studying his high-boned profile as he scratched letters in the smooth stone. He could spell? A pirate of *Malice* knew his letters? Even she didn't know her letters—well, she knew the *letters*, but not how to put them together. First he'd come aboard their ship without a fight, then the tattoos, and now he knew how to spell? Ebba couldn't make anything of the pirate, including that he'd seemed so cold a week before, but was acting with some human decency right now.

He scratched a line for each part of the riddle, and added Plank and Grubby's contributions.

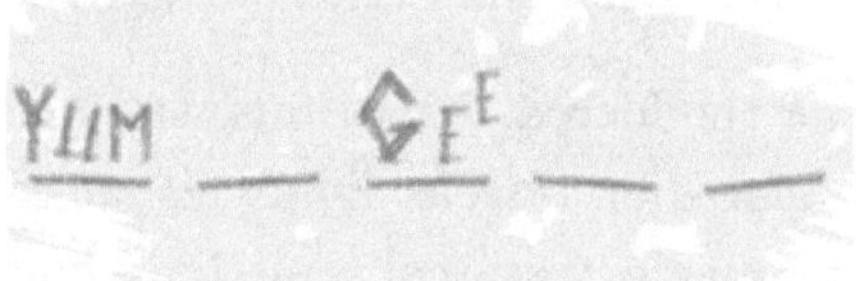

"A selfish man's repetition." Stubby rubbed a hand over his forehead, glancing at Peg-leg. "Me, I guess. Or I?"

Peg-leg glowered. "Why are ye lookin' at me when ye say that?"

Jagger's eyes gleamed, and he scratched in Stubby's guess.

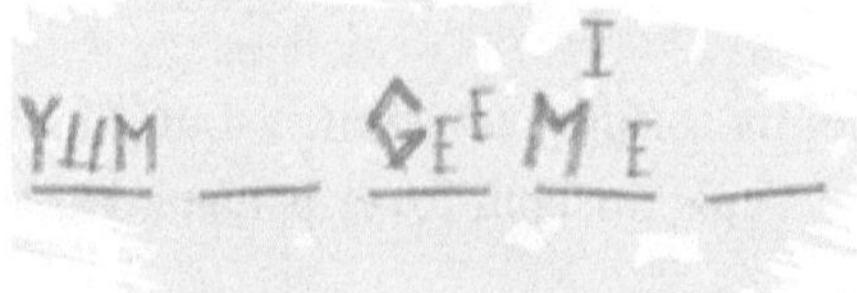

Ebba's mind whirled so fast it hurt. She could only remember the second clue.

Locks gestured wildly, his eye blazing. "What be the twenty-sixth leader?"

"No, that ain't what he said," Ebba interrupted, happy she remembered something. "He said twenty-six's leader."

Everyone stared at Jagger's markings on the ground. No one offered an answer.

"Yumgeeme," Plank tried. "Yummgee-I."

She sighed. This was hopeless. "The last clue. What did he say?"

"For all o' this, ye will not succeed, not unless ye remember the sea," Plank recited.

"The sea." Stubby lifted his head from his hands. "He gave it to us. C. We can't forget the C!"

Locks slapped him on the back and Stubby nearly face-planted.

"They be indiv'dual letters, mateys," Locks exclaimed, eyes scanning the ground. "Not small words, one single word. Let's look again."

She leaned closer over Jagger's shoulder as he scratched a 'C' into the ground on the end.

"The fourth one would have to be 'I', not 'me', if we be goin' with single letters," Peg-leg offered hesitantly.

She heard the hitch of Jagger's breath as he swept the 'me' and 'I' away and redrew the 'I' in the same spot.

Plank leaned down and carefully brushed away the two 'E's' after 'G'. "Yum. Gic," he said, in the nonplussed silence.

Ebba frowned, annoyed at herself. For once, she wished she knew her letters better. Barrels had attempted to teach her more times than she could count. But he'd given up. Truly, she held no interest in the alphabet. Not until now when it might save their lives.

Jagger held the dagger in a relaxed grip. His other hand clawed around the ring circling his neck, almost as if he wanted to pull despite knowing the futility of it. "The first clue. Would it be 'Y'?"

'Y' was the second to last letter in the alphabet. That much she knew. Though she'd always thought the realm could get by with half so many letters. Who really needed—

Her mouth dropped open. "Twenty-six," she whispered.

The others looked at her.

"Twenty-six's leader!" she jumped. "It's 'A'. There are twenty-six letters in the alphabet."

Jagger shot her a triumphant look, which she returned before thinking better of it. He whipped back to his sketch in the dirt, scratching in the letter 'A'.

"The first one ain't 'Y'," Plank said, his voice strained. "Mmm. *Mmm* is the sound of contentment."

Jagger didn't glance up, but his cheeks lifted as a grin spread across his face. He wiped away the 'Y'.

"*Magic,*" Plank breathed.

Ladon's outraged screech shook the mountain and Ebba fell to the ground, unable to stand with the sheer force his anger radiated.

Peg-leg collapsed next to her and they watched, powerless as Ladon threw his head back and sank his exposed fangs into the knot of snakes around his neck. He pulled viciously, and a snake tore free—the same tiger-striped snake that had whispered the riddle in his ear. Ladon tossed the snake up and opened his reptilian jaws wide, stretching and disfiguring the jaw until it was as big as a third of his body. The small snake twisted as it began its downward fall. Ebba felt its fear, could almost imagine it screaming.

She shut her eyes tightly as it fell into Ladon's mouth.

His jaws snapped closed with a pop of displaced air and his forked tongue swiped across his lips. "Very good, mortals. You surprise me. Time for the third."

None of the snakes rose to offer him advice this time. Instead, Ladon's head dipped and swayed as he stared at each pirate in their group in turn.

Stubby whispered to Plank, "He can't do anythin' funny with those red eyes, can he?"

Plank shook of his head. "Not in the story. But—"

He didn't have to finish the sentence. No story could've prepared them for this.

Ladon's talons gouged the stone as he roared. His red eyes throbbed and pulsed as he stared into each of their eyes in turn. Slowly, the glowing faded, accompanied by a curving of his lipless mouth.

"Your third riddle," he hissed quietly. His menace rolled over the edges of the plateau and down the cliffs of the mountain.

He faced Peg-leg. "He'll take your dignity and pride."

His eyes sought Plank. "He will slaughter your wife, and . . ." his tongue lashed in Stubby's direction, ". . . your father."

Ebba looked at her three fathers. Plank's face had lost all color. The three of them didn't react, their faces frozen, eyes wide and fixed on the beast.

Ladon wasn't done. He turned to Grubby. "He'll destroy your mind."

Next was Locks. "He will control cowards and half-men," the beast stated.

The snakes around Ladon's neck unfurled and the grotesque creature hissed his laughter as he faced Jagger. "His grandson has taken everything you once were. You are a shell. And soon all you hold dear will be dead and gone."

Ladon's voice was victorious and swelled high until it more closely resembled a scream. "He is the name you swore to never say. He is gone, but with you always. Still you hate him, *still* you fear him. This is my final riddle. Who is he?"

Ebba waited for one of the others to answer. Jagger seemed to be the only one who hadn't seized during Ladon's riddle, though he looked pale and drawn, like he'd been socked in the gut too many times.

"Who is it?" she asked him.

He shook his head, fists clenched. "He r'ferred to Mercer Pockmark as the grandson, but I ain't be knowin' the name of his grandfather."

She turned to her fathers. *They* clearly knew who Ladon spoke of.

That stuff couldn't be true, could it? . . . The beast hadn't meant Plank's actual wife, or Stubby's actual father, had he? She didn't even know Plank used to have a wife. He would've told her that.

Ebba's chest tightened; her fathers didn't like to talk about their pasts and she'd never thought to pressure them, only because she'd never dreamed they were concealing anything important. All they ever said was they'd been an honorless bunch of pirates until the day they found her. They'd always say it with a bit of a grin on their faces, like their pasts were no big deal.

If Ladon was right, and from their reactions, she guessed he spoke at least *some* truth, then they'd lied to her. Her entire life.

Who was the man who did this to them?

Ebba strode forward and took the cook's hand. "Peg-leg, who does Ladon mean?"

Grubby turned a tear-streaked face her way. Her breath caught at his vacant look and a lump rose hard and fast in her throat. *He'll destroy your mind.* She gripped Grubby's hand with her free one. Her fathers had told her Grubby was hit by a boom by accident. Was that even true? Or had Pockmark's grandfather done it to Grubby on purpose?

"They're keeping things from you, child," sneered Ladon. "They've lied to you."

"Shut yer ugly gob!" Ebba marched in front of her fathers, picked up a stone and threw it at the beast. It hit one of the snakes and the snake fell forward, dead.

"Shite," she whispered.

Ladon screamed and stamped. The force spread out in a wave, throwing Ebba back into Stubby's stocky arms. His roar was shaking the entire mountain, and the sound of loosened rocks careening down the cliff face below them was deafening.

Ignoring the crashing around them, Ebba turned and placed her hand over Stubby's heart. "Did this man kill yer father, Stubby?"

Mouth pulled down, he nodded.

Ebba gasped. It *was* all true. How could this be? How had she never known any of these things?

"Who?" she pressed. "Ye need to tell Ladon. He's goin' to bring down the mountain!"

Stubby shook his head and placed her back on her feet. She wobbled and fell on her butt, staring up at her fathers from the ground.

Jagger staggered forward to Locks and Plank.

"Yer daughter will die if ye don't name him," he shouted over the roaring and crashing of rocks.

His words seemed to rouse Locks and Stubby somewhat. Plank's eyes remained empty, nearly lifeless. Pockmark's grandfather slaughtered his wife? Ebba felt numb with disbelief.

Locks whispered, and yet the soft sound echoed to Ebba on the ground. "We made a solemn vow never to speak his name on the day we locked up the people we'd become. The day we decided to be the people we needed for our child."

Peg-leg stared at Ebba, who struggled to her feet again.

"Yer daughter," Jagger repeated, "Ebba-Viva will be slaughtered, if ye don't recover yer wits."

Ebba wondered if he chose the word 'slaughter' on purpose. Plank's eyes faltered, before searching for her.

"*He is the name you swore to never say. He is history, but he is with you always,*" recited Stubby. The five men shared a look so expressive of shattered hearts that Ebba felt tears slide down her cheeks. She knew nothing of what they'd gone through to break so badly. How had they hidden this from her?

They hadn't sheltered her from others, they'd sheltered her from *themselves*.

Jagger gripped her shoulders and shook her roughly. "Do ye see what ye're doin' to her? Ye can stop her tears. Ye can save her now. Speak the name."

Ebba pushed his hands off her arms and stepped away, too shocked to do more.

Jagger's pewter eyes were burning. "Stop Ladon now," he thundered.

With a soul-weary groan, Peg-leg looked at Ladon, and spoke.

TEN

"*Mutinous Cannon.*"

The whispered name seemed to bounce against the rock faces surrounding them, repeating over and over again like some cruel joke.

Beside her, Jagger repeated Peg-leg's words, "Mutinous Cannon." His eyes widened. "That be Pockmark's grandfather?"

The golden bands disappeared from their necks in wisps of golden smoke.

Ladon began to laugh manically as the flickering of his outline intensified. Though he'd lost their game, his cackle held more glee than at the start. Ladon and his snakes blinked out of existence and didn't return after a full minute. He was gone. At least for now.

But Ebba stared at her five fathers, mouth dry, and wondered if the lizard had won after all.

"Who's Mutinous Cannon?" she asked Jagger in undertones.

He raised his brows. "The most notorious captain to ever live. His crew were merc'less, feared through the seas. He was the last pirate left standin' during the Battle for the Seas against Montcroix."

Ebba threw a worried glance at her fathers, but they weren't listening. Each of them appeared lost in his own world, drowning in memories of this pirate. Had this man been their captain once? She knew they'd all sailed together. That's how her fathers had all met, so he had to have been their captain. The timing matched as well. The Battle for the Seas ended around two years after she was born.

"How did ye not know that was Mercer's grandfather?" she asked.

"Why do people gen'rally not know stuff?" Jagger asked darkly.

"Because they ain't told, or they don't ask, I guess." Should she have asked her fathers more questions?

Jagger didn't respond. Whatever his deep thoughts, he didn't share them.

"What happened to Mutinous Cannon in the end?" she asked him, hating that she knew less than him about matters pertaining to her fathers.

Jagger's mouth twisted into a bitter smile. "King Forge Montcroix did what he does so well. He killed him and ended the war. Cannon's entire crew were hung in the gibbet cages."

That confirmed her theory. If her fathers were part of his crew, they left before the end of the war to care for her. They'd then stowed away their pasts under lock and key. For a couple of years now, Ebba had seen the difference between herself and other people her age. She hadn't needed Sherry to tell her as much. She also hadn't cared one jot about that difference. After the alley with Pockmark, her confidence was shaken. Bad things could happen to her. And when her fathers were taken to the gaol, she'd seen how easily they could be torn from her side. She was unprepared for life without their guidance. Her fathers had protected her from a lot of things—maybe concealed was a better word, but Ebba had encouraged the way they spoiled her, content to remain in her youth. If they'd stowed away their pasts, she'd enabled them to do so. Ebba had thought she knew everything about her parents.

Not only that, *magic existed*.

The limitations of the small world she'd known had been shattered. Broken. Gone.

She stared past her fathers to the golden fruit. The reason they'd all come up here. The reason her world had just shattered. Unable to resist scanning the circular plateau for Ladon one last time, Ebba pushed away the tumult in her mind and jogged across the uneven stone plates to the opposite side.

The twisting tree extended over the cliff edge, and the golden fruit dangled off the tip of the farthest branch. Sink her. She couldn't reach it from the ground.

Swiping a dagger from her sash, she placed it between her teeth and shimmied halfway up the tree.

"Ebba-Viva!"

She ignored her fathers' cries as they woke up enough to realize what she intended to do.

"Get down," bellowed Locks. "Right now."

No, she wasn't going to do that. Ebba worked her way around the trunk and stood atop a limb twice the width of her foot. *This is no different than walking along the spar*, she told herself silently.

. . . The bushy treetops that appeared to be the size of copper coins from up here said otherwise.

Perhaps she wouldn't walk out. Ebba carefully crouched and lay atop the tree branch. The rivets of the bark scratched her stomach as she shuffled out to the end of the limb. She clutched on for dear life as a breeze caught the tree and swayed the branch side to side.

Swallowing hard, knowing that one peek down would snap the last of her tenuous courage, she inched forward until the limb narrowed and began to bend.

Her stomach lurched with the branch. There was no choice now but to look down, the blasted fruit sparkled below. Just out of reach. Ebba's head spun as her eyes moved past the fruit to the tiny trees far, far beneath her.

Breathing fast, she squeezed her eyes shut. "Ye're on the riggin'. This be a boom. Nothing ye ain't done afore."

Opening her eyes, she gripped the limb with both legs and swung underneath, entirely focused on the fruit. Ebba removed one hand and took hold of the dagger between her teeth.

The golden fruit glinted an arm's length away.

Releasing a shaking breath, Ebba removed her other hand, legs clamped around the branch. She took hold of the fruit in one hand, sawing through the stem with the dagger in her other hand.

"Come free, ye bastard," she growled.

With a final saw, the stem was broken. Gripping the golden apple tight, she placed the dagger back between her teeth, and crunched up to right herself atop the branch. She shuffled all the way back to the trunk, not trusting herself to stand with such precious cargo.

She half slid back down to the ground and sat against the trunk, shaking with relief.

Locks dragged her to her feet. "Ye shouldn't have done that."

"Why not?" she challenged. "I climb the shroud to the crow's nest every day."

A gratifying silence fell over her fathers.

Ebba held up the sparkling fruit.

"If ever a fruit be able to give ye knowledge, methinks it'd be this one," whispered Plank.

The mountain apple was shaped like any normal apple, but there the normalcy stopped. It was entirely golden in hue, yet its surface swirled as she gazed upon it. A pearly iridescence sat just beneath the golden skin.

Peg-leg broke the quiet. "I'm not thinkin' it wise to take this fruit for a long walk."

"More chance for it to be taken." Locks agreed in a rumbling voice.

Ebba pursed her lips. "Who's gonna eat it? Stubby is most smart after Barrels, and Barrels ain't here."

Peg-leg's mouth clicked shut, and he glowered at the smirking Stubby.

"Now, now," Grubby said kindly. "Ye're both as smart as each other."

"Aye, Stubby should do it," Locks spoke over Grubby.

She passed Stubby the fruit. Wasting no time, he bit into it. She'd been right about the pearly substance underneath. Liquid pearls dribbled over his scratchy, white-and-gray stubble to disappear into his dirt-streaked tunic.

His eyes widened briefly, and he stared at the crew in panic.

"Ye want to know where the treasure that *Malice*'s captain seeks be hidden," Plank reminded him drily.

Stubby's eyes lit with relief.

He swallowed the fruit, and asked, "What be the location of the treasure that *Malice*'s captain seeks?"

His gray-blue eyes rolled back in his head. The crew gasped, and Ebba shifted to his side, clutching his arm to support him. The fruit tumbled from his fingers, rotting and blackening before it hit the ground at their feet.

Stubby jerked forward, clutching his stomach for several long seconds.

Slowly, he straightened—panting. His mouth bobbed ajar for a time. "There be an island. Portum."

"Never heard o' it." Locks screwed up his face.

"I have," Grubby said. "I used to go to the western point o' Kentro sometimes. Portum be on other side o' Syraness. In Selkie's Cove."

"The cliffs beside Charybdis?" Ebba asked. Charybdis was a huge whirlpool that would suck ships down into the darkness of oblivion. No seaman or pirate entered the whirlpool or the cliffs beside it. When her crew sailed *Felicity* to Kentro, they took a wide berth east around both.

"Big whirlpool and razor rocks," Plank said in a wooden voice.

"Nay," Peg-leg said. "If we pursue the plunder, we'd be better to go round the coastline of Kentro and enter through the top of Selkie's Cove. It'll smack on four days, but be safer by far than goin' through the cliff passage."

If they pursued the treasure? That her fathers might not want to hadn't occurred to Ebba.

"What else did the apple tell ye?" she asked Stubby, brows furrowed.

Stubby took a breath. "The voices were clamorin', Ebba. Ain't ever heard anythin' like it—as though a thousand voices spoke at once." He shuddered. "There be a cave on Portum, at the northern side of the island. The treasure is there."

"What *is* the plunder?" Locks asked. "Did it tell ye that?"

Peg-leg hobbled forward. "Does anythin' guard it?"

Stubby shook his head, shuddering again. "Nay, nothin' else. Just the location. And I'll no be eatin' any more o' it. That stuff ain't natural-like."

They stared at the shriveled apple, now black and covered with green mold.

“Don’t blame ye,” Ebba said. “That’s a stomach-ache, if I ever saw one.”

Turning from the rotten fruit, their group walked back to the archway, the way clear since Ladon’s cackling departure.

She sighed. “I guess we’ll be findin’ out the rest when we get to the cave.”

“Continue to the treasure? Out o’ the question,” Stubby interjected as they passed through the rocky arch. “It’s only brought us harm.”

They all turned at the click of a pistol hammer being drawn back.

Plank had his weapon aimed at Jagger’s head. The guide was yet to pass through the arch. She’d forgotten he was there at all, he’d stood so quietly during their discussion.

Jagger was staring across the island of Neos, but turned to face Plank, strands of flaxen hair falling forward in a wave either side of his high-boned face.

“Ye led us into danger, guide,” Plank snarled.

Jagger met his gaze with a level one of his own. “I led ye to the mountaintop, as promised.”

Peg-leg rounded on him, too. “We told ye what we’d do if ye betrayed us.”

Jagger shrugged. “I’ve been here at least ten times in my life. To this very spot. Ladon has never been here. And the tree has never born fruit. In my lifetime.”

Plank’s eyes narrowed. “Then why did Ladon show?”

Ebba blinked as the unbelievable events that just occurred hit her again: a mythical creature with . . . with *snakes* on it. Snakes that whispered riddles in his ears.

Her heart pounded.

A trap door slammed shut as her mind threatened to become overwhelmed with the possibilities of a whole other world to the one she knew. The idea of magic had long drawn her imagination, but the reality, if all magic was like the evil Ladon, was much different to the magic in her head.

"Maybe Ladon were here because the fruit were here," Stubby mused. "Ye said yerself the mountain apple only fruits every one hundred years."

Stubby could be right, yet that still didn't give Ebba an explanation for the mythical creature *existing* in the first place.

"There be time for wonderings and musings later, my hearties. We be needin' to get back to the ship and away afore *Malice* catches up," Peg-leg said.

They began to file back down the mountain, Plank tucking his pistol away and gesturing Jagger to go ahead of him.

"And if we be lucky," Peg-leg continued. "They'll hike up here lookin' for the fruit and Ladon will come back and eat the lot o' them."

THEY TREKKED in a weary line across the river rocks, still hours from *Felicity* as the sun began to sink in the sky.

Ebba stumbled and scrubbed both hands over her face in an attempt to brush away her weariness. Her legs ached. Even the tips of her toes were raw, telling her to stop, to rest.

"Nobody think it fishy we ain't seen no tribespeople?" Peg-leg asked.

"Oi, guide," Stubby said, turning to Jagger. "Where be all the tribes-people? I was o' the understandin' they ruled the heart o' this island."

Ebba watched Jagger stiffen. She wished she could see his face through the growing shadows of the rainforest.

"They do," he replied. "Or at least they did. I suspect Ladon's presence be havin' somethin' to do with their . . . absence."

"They're prob'ly all dead," she said in a ghostly voice. "Ladon likely ate their bones." Jagger blanched at her words, and the action tickled her memory. She turned to Plank. "Do ye really think there be ash in my soul now?"

Plank bumped her shoulder and tugged on a strand of her beads. "Nay, little nymph. That ain't true for a second."

"Ye heard Ladon, though," said Jagger in a harsh tone. "Intent to kill is as ash in yer soul. Ye be tainted with evil now."

The words stung. He'd been nearly okay up on the mountain. "I'd rather be tainted than have black in my soul. Ye couldn't have gotten out right from the start."

A faint red crept up his jaw. "Aye, and neither could the rest of yer crew."

Ebba turned forward, anger giving her new energy. "Ladon was wrong about my fathers. They have souls as golden and beautiful as that fruit."

"The fruit that turned to black and rot?"

Her blood boiled.

"I've seen a lot o' impos'ible things in my time. But I ain't never seen magic," Peg-leg interrupted, his voice a low whisper.

A chorus of 'ayes' met his words.

"Plank," Ebba started, throwing a last glare at Jagger. "Where did that beast come from?"

They reached the part of the river where they'd exited from the rainforest. Stubby led them back into the thick canopy as darkness began to settle in. Ebba swallowed, remembering the massive snake they'd passed on the way in.

"Old magic ruled the realm afore the Age o' Prosperity, Ebba. Which was five hundred years afore the Reign o' Kings," he replied.

"Aye, but we ain't seen nothin' like that afore," she countered. "Why is it showin' up now? Or did we never venture into the right places?"

He shook his head. "I have no answer to that, little nymph. Accordin' to the stories, magic left sudden-like more than seven hundred and fifty years ago."

Ebba remembered the flickering Ladon. "Maybe it never left. Maybe it were just weak." She turned back in time to catch Plank's serious expression.

"Mayhaps ye're right. And that's why we need to keep goin'," he said. "To find out why."

Finding out why. That had never occurred to her. Finding out why didn't seem like their business.

"Nay, matey. I say that findin' out why be breakin' *both* our ship laws," Locks said. "We don't need to know why, and we surely can't put the crew in harm's way."

Ebba stopped in her tracks, glancing around. "Where's Jagger?" He wasn't in front of them, and neither was he behind Plank—the last in their single-file line.

Plank whirled. "He was here when we turned out from the river."

The ruckus attracted the others' attention.

"What's wrong?" Grubby asked anxiously.

"The guide ran off. I didn't hear him leave," Plank said.

Stubby groaned. "Ye were s'posed to be watchin' him!"

Ebba stared between them. "Why does it matter? We don't need him anymore."

Locks answered grimly, "He knows *Felicity*'s crew be poachin' Pockmark's plunder, lass. If he runs back to *Malice,* that doesn't bode well for us."

She gasped. That was exactly what she'd hoped to avoid in the first place. "We've got to find him."

Her fathers were several steps ahead of her, already split into two groups.

"He'll make for the eastern beach to board *Malice*. That be the only place the ship could've dropped anchor," Stubby blurted. "Grubby and Peg-leg, get back to the ship and ready her. The rest o' us will try to corner Jagger afore the damage be done."

Peg-leg shook his head. "Ebba ain't goin'."

"Ye've seen the size o' him." Stubby disagreed. "If he gets hold o' a weapon, he'll be a force to be reckoned with. And there's sumpin' not quite right with him. Sumpin' dark. I don't trust him as far as I can spit."

"Yet ye'd let—"

"We don't have time for ye two to squabble!" Locks said.

Ebba swallowed before announcing, "I want to go, Peg-leg."

He stared at her before giving a tight nod. "All right then. We'll be seein' ye at the ship then. More than half a day and we'll come lookin' for ye."

Without another word, he hobbled away. Grubby hugged Ebba before turning to follow.

She inhaled a shaky breath, watching their backs. She hated when their crew split in two, and now they were split in *three*. At least Barrels waited safely on the ship and Peg-leg and Grubby would be back with him soon. But anything could happen to two pirates in the rainforest between here and the ship.

Unease spreading through her chest, Ebba wrenched her gaze away from their retreating forms.

With the others, she jogged back to the river and turned right toward the ocean instead of left to the mountain. They stayed as quiet as they could, silent but for their jagged breath, an occasional scrape of a boot on stone, or splash in a pool of water. Fear gave her new energy. She kept her eyes trained on the shadowy rocks under her feet. The moonlight made the river surface gleam—and their route a little easier to see—but an eerie sensation filled the black silence of the rainforest, and in her mind every tree hid a tribal warrior who sought to ambush their group should she lose focus for a single second.

Eventually, the rocks turned to sand under her feet. Ebba raised her head at the quiet roar of the crashing waves over the other side of the sand dune.

Locks rested his hands on his knees, panting hard. "This be the eastern beach."

Stubby sniffed the air. "Get a load o' that, lads."

Ebba did the same. "Smells like gun pow—"

An explosion rocketed through the air. She threw herself to the ground behind the dune, covering her head.

Lying beside her, Locks shouted over the din, "What is it?"

She shook her head, trying to rid herself of the ringing in her ears.

Plank crawled to the top of the dune and pointed out to sea. "Sumpin' to do with that, methinks."

Ebba pushed at the sand, scrambling up beside him to peer over the top. Her jaw dropped.

A ship, a hundred yards from shore, was on fire. Flames licked its sails, curling the material into embers that flew high into the air. The screams of the crew were easy to hear over the churning rumble of the ocean.

"What ship is it?" Her voice trembled. She knew pirates did this, of course. But she'd never witnessed the sight firsthand.

"A navy ship," Locks said grimly.

What was a navy ship doing all the way out here? They always stuck to the routes closest to the mainland. For one to be south of Maltu was unprecedented.

"Look." She pointed.

Locks, Stubby, and Plank followed the direction of her finger. The flaming ship illuminated the beach, and with the help of the moonlight, it was easy to see the sandy shore for several hundred yards.

There, waving a burning torch in the air, was Jagger.

"Bastard!" Stubby shouted, ripping a pistol from his sash.

Plank pulled him down by the belt as he made to give chase. "I wouldn't be doin' that, matey." He jerked his head. "Who d'ye think set the navy ship ablaze?"

Ebba hadn't seen it before, hidden as the ship was by the fiery beacon of the navy wreckage.

Malice sat anchored in the sea not far behind the flaming ruin.

"Look smartly, they be sendin' a boat for him." Locks dashed a hand through the sand in front of him.

Sure enough, Ebba spotted the torch of a rowboat as it made its way to shore. "Could we still snatch him?" she wondered aloud.

Stubby shook his head. "Nay, lass, they be too close now. They'd see us."

The rowboat bobbed just beyond the breaking waves.

"They'll know it was us if they get Jagger, too. What's there to lose?" she demanded. At least then they wouldn't know the location of the treasure.

Her three fathers slid back down the dune the way they'd come. "There be our lives to lose, little nymph," said Plank. "We're not knowin' how many pirates be in that rowboat. We don't know what weapons they carry. We show ourselves and *Malice*'s crew will hunt us across the island—with their younger and fresher legs."

"With Jagger, who knows Neos like the back o' his hand," Locks added.

"Jagger, who knows where the plunder be," she said through gritted teeth. *They* were the ones who'd defeated Ladon to get the fruit. And now Pockmark would get the answer after they'd done the hard work? Instead of revenge, they'd ended up helping him. Still, she couldn't focus on that. Her fathers were right, they couldn't outrun the *Malice* pirates if it came to a race.

"All we can do now is return to *Felicity* and make for safety." Stubby's next words were low. "And figure out what the hell we're goin' to do with this mess we be in."

ELEVEN

Ebba dragged herself up the ladder, arms shaking with fatigue. It seemed like days since she'd last stood on *Felicity*, yet they'd only left for Neos Mountain sometime in the early hours of the previous morning.

Barrels squeezed her shoulder and leaned over the side to help Stubby over.

She stepped out of the way and immediately sank down against the bulwark. They were screwed.

". . . They escaped the navy boat together. But the prince caught a bullet," Barrels murmured.

Ebba yawned, her jaw cracking. A nice, cozy hammock summoned her from below deck. If only she could get to it without using her legs. Maybe if she fell asleep here, someone would carry her. That sounded like a plan.

The murmur continued. "He died a few hours ago."

She frowned, her foggy mind perplexed at some small detail. She rolled her head to check on her fathers. All six were there, alive and well. She let out a sigh; their crew was together again and they would find a way out of this trouble. Everything would be okay.

There was a hammock at her fathers' feet, she realized. Ebba studied the hammock through bleary eyes. It looked like it had something inside.

Curiosity overcoming her sleepiness and sore muscles, she clambered to her feet and shuffled toward the parcel. "What is it?" she mumbled.

Her fathers fell silent, but her mind wasn't working quickly enough to perceive what that meant.

She stilled. The outline of a human body was clear within the hammock with the rope tied around the person's ankles, hips, and shoulders. Ebba's moss-green eyes were drawn against her will to the blood staining the hemp fibers of the rope around the shoulders.

"Come away, lass." Peg-leg wrapped an arm around her.

The others fell into a frantic whispered debate. "What about the other one?"

Ebba shrugged off Peg-leg's arm, now fully awake. "What other one?"

Grubby pointed to the mast.

Ebba pushed through her fathers to where the moonlight shone on a slumped form. The man lifted his head and amber eyes glistened through the dark.

"Cosmo!" she exclaimed, staring at the servant she'd left on Maltu and never expected to see again.

The young man jerked upright. ". . . Mistress Fairisles. Is that you?"

How did he know her name? Ebba had a moment of confusion before recalling he'd overheard Maybell saying it.

Her fathers crowded around the mast, their eyes darting between her and the servant.

"You recognize this young man, Ebba-Viva?" Barrels asked.

Ebba nodded slowly. "Aye, he's the prince's servant. The one who saved ye from the prison." Her eyes fell on the body again. If Cosmo was here. . . .

Locks erupted, throwing his hands in the air. "We need to get rid o' the prince's body afore Montcroix comes lookin'."

Barrels dipped his head. "Yes, but what to do with his servant? Leaving him here seemed like the best option before. . . ."

Before Ebba recognized him?

"But. . ." Barrels straightened his cravat. "If we do leave him, it's certain he will be taken, either by the crew of *Malice* or tribespeople. It was due to his kindness that we escaped the Maltu gaol. . . ."

"Aye," Plank muttered. "We can't be ignorin' that."

"Well, that's sorted." Stubby leaned down and untied Cosmo, who sat in silence, though his amber eyes were wide and blood-streaked.

Ebba spoke. "What be sorted?"

Plank clapped Cosmo on the back. "He'll come with us. Probably to certain death."

The remaining color faded from the servant's face.

"Peg-leg," Plank called. "Get the poor lad some food. He be lookin' a tad peaky."

Peg-leg grabbed Cosmo by the scruff of the neck and Ebba noted the dried blood staining the servant's shirt. Cosmo's eyes fell on Peg-leg's wooden leg, and he shot Ebba a panicked look. She attempted a reassuring nod which didn't help any, judging by his white face as he disappeared into the bilge.

Her fathers hunkered down.

Ebba sank to her haunches with them. She didn't know what kind of internal grog was helping her to stay awake—maybe seeing a dead body did that to a person. Or maybe she'd gone through the tiredness and come out the other side.

"From what I understand," started Barrels, "we are now in a position where Mercer Pockmark is aware of our involvement in pursuing his treasure." He waited for a few grunts of affirmation before continuing. "Then we have but two options I can think of."

"Yer fancy words will make my head explode one day," Locks said grouchily.

Barrels smiled. "I apologize, dear fellow. The captain and crew of *Malice* rule the Free Seas, in absence of the navy's presence south of Kentro and Maltu, so we are certainly in a pickle. Continuing our regular trade without harassment from *Malice* is unlikely, considering he's searched for this treasure for four years."

They constantly traded. *Malice* would put out the order for their heads. There was no way they'd be able to trade as they had.

"Aye, but we can just go to Zol for a while," said Grubby, twisting his cap.

Barrels shook his head. "We could go there for a time, yes. Our retirement plan still requires five more years of trade until it is financially viable long-term. Simply put: we don't have the material to survive there for long. After several months of hiding, we'd be required to emerge and return to trade."

Peg-leg folded his arms. "Which takes us back to square one."

"Indeed," he answered. "I see but one option."

"Aye?" she asked, leaning forward.

Barrels opened his mouth, but Stubby interjected with a heavy sigh. "We go after the treasure."

"Be that wise when *Malice* will be doin' the same?" Ebba asked. Sure, after hearing the treasure's location, not pursuing the plunder would be a bitter tonic to swallow. Very bitter. But she'd rather her first quest be cut off short than for her fathers to go up against Pockmark's cannons.

"From what Ebba overheard, the treasure is worth enough to finance our retirement plan, and much more," Barrels said. "Instead of years of trading with the threat of *Malice* overhead, we would take this plunder and trade for everything we'll need in one burst to survive in Zol."

Ebba withheld her sigh. Her fathers were fixed on this retirement plan, all of them ready to part ways with the sea as soon as could be. She wanted them safe but didn't want to achieve that by spending the rest of her life on Zol. Weren't there other adventures to be had? Places to see? She was seventeen. Retirement plans were for people over thirty.

Plank added, "We saw magic up on that mountain. If somethin' is changin' in this realm, we need to get to the bottom o' it."

Stubby exclaimed, "Bah, matey. Not our problem. If magic the likes of Ladon be returnin', the sooner we plunder the treasure and get back to Zol, the better. Let the king's territory fall apart. It ain't our mess to fix."

"Will it be our mess when it comes to Zol?" Plank challenged.

Their crew fell silent. They were rarely at true odds with each other, and the tension didn't sit right with Ebba. Or poor Grubs.

Barrels pressed back a strand of his peppered hair into the leather tie. "I propose this: Our ship is both faster and smaller than *Malice*." He turned to Stubby, Locks, and Plank. "Is it possible we'll be able to navigate the cliff passage south of Kentro and get to the treasure before *Malice*?"

The three looked at each other, grunting and pulling faces without actually speaking a word.

"There are those who've made it through the Syraness," said Plank finally. Dubiously.

Stubby nodded. "Aye, it's been done. Not my path o' choice, as ye know."

Barrels smiled. "This is good news. *Malice*—a larger ship than ours—will be forced to follow the coastline of Kentro, to enter Selkie's Cove from top. The whirlpool and Syraness form a wall that prevents them entering anywhere else. Is this correct?"

"Aye," Locks answered after a pause.

"How long would following the Kentro coastline take?"

"Thirteen or fourteen days," Locks replied, looking to Stubby and Plank for confirmation. They nodded.

"And how long would it take us to navigate the Syraness to exit far closer to Portum?" Barrels asked.

"Nine or ten days, thereabout."

Barrels stared around their circle. "Accounting for a day restocking the ship at Zol, we can reach Portum at least three days before *Malice*. We can retrieve the treasure, return through Syraness, trade as much of the treasure as we can, and successfully retire in Zol," he said, adding, "*Malice* will be unaware we've beaten them there until they enter the cave and discover the treasure gone. By the time they get back to these waters, we'll be hidden away."

Ebba's mouth dried. They were really continuing the quest. That a magical fruit existed had been a huge *if*. Then the apple was real but too dangerous to pursue. Yet Barrels' plan made sense. In fact, despite the slight twinge in her gut, his plan seemed like the only safe path forward. Most of her other fathers were nodding with him, too. Could they race *Malice* there and snatch the riches from under Pockmark's very nose? If they didn't, they'd be stuck trading under constant danger for the rest of their, most likely, short lives. Ebba thought of the dagger Pockmark had dug into her cheek, and her fists curled. Nothing would give her more pleasure than thwarting him.

"I dunno," Grubby hedged. He twisted his Monmouth cap in both hands. "I'm thinkin' we should just go hide."

"We'd have to come out sometime, Grubs," Locks reminded him.

Stubby gripped Grubby's shoulder. "I understand yer misgivings. I do. But we be involved in this. The only way out o' the mess is to head deeper in."

Plank scratched at his stubble. He dropped his hand. "Ye know I think we should be goin' anyway. Not just to secure the plunder, to figure out why a creature like Ladon be back in the realm. I say aye."

"Aye," added Locks.

Ebba forced back her eagerness with difficulty. "Aye," she said casually.

Barrels cast her a wry look. "At least someone is looking forward to this."

She battled a grin. And lost.

Stubby looked east. "Unless Pockmark be stupid, he'll have left already and will be makin' for Portum like Davy Jones himself is whippin' his back."

"And if he ain't, we'd best be far from here," added Locks.

Plank stood, making for the sheets to ready the sails. "If Pockmark be that stupid, Jagger is certa'nly not. They'll be makin' for Portum already, no doubt about it."

Locks groaned, and Ebba hurried to help him up.

"Who be on first shift?" he asked.

Ebba glanced toward the bilge door and slid one foot in the direction of their sleeping quarters. A whole day's caulk in her hammock cuddling Pillage sounded about perfect.

Barrels raised a brow at her and she froze. "I think it's only fair for

Peg-leg, myself, and Grubby to give the rest of you a few hours of rest," he said.

Ebba smiled, shoulders sagging.

He continued. ". . . Except for Ebba here, who is probably too excited by our venture to sleep right now. To the helm, my dear. There are those with older bones needing their rest."

The others cackled. Evil buggers.

Muttering under her breath, she changed her trajectory mid-stride and placed her foot in the direction of the stern instead of the bilge.

Once there, Ebba gripped the spoked wheel tight.

"Weigh anchor," she called across the night to her crew of fathers. Grubby and Barrels circled in the heavy anchor, and soon the mainsail was inching up the mast, directed by Peg-leg.

Ebba looked over her shoulder at Neos, unable to see the mountain peak in the night, but in the shadows and the dark, recalling the terror when she first saw Ladon was all too easy.

The choppy waves slapped at the sides of *Felicity* as the ship shifted. Feeling the tug as the mainsail filled, Ebba directed the ship to face south, releasing an uneven breath—the more space between her crew and Ladon, the better.

Despite her misgivings about retirement, there was nowhere safer in all the seas than Zol.

TWELVE

Ebba stood beside Cosmo as, lacking a cannon ball, two sandbags were tied to Prince Caspian's feet. Locks gave him a pirate's farewell, sewing the hammock ends together with four looping rope stitches, one stitch each for north, south, east, and west. That way, his soul wouldn't be torn into pieces as he journeyed to the oblivion to face judgment. At Cosmo's insistence, Locks didn't make the final stitch through the prince's chin to make sure he was dead.

"Aye, well if he still be alive, that'd wake him up smartly," Locks grumbled at Cosmo. "Always good to check these things."

"A shot through the heart, master pirate. I believe he is gone." Cosmo's voice cracked. "He should have had a proper burial."

Ebba would much rather sink to the bottom of the ocean than be burned or put in the ground, but she supposed Cosmo's comment had more to do with the deceased being a prince. Should she hold Cosmo's hand? Or say something? Some of her fathers didn't mind affection when they were sad, but the others liked to be alone. Ebba wasn't sure which group to put Cosmo in.

Without ceremony, Locks and Plank hefted the prince overboard. Cosmo winced at the splash, but made no move to look over the side as his master sank to the depths.

"Many would be still alive if not for the prince," he whispered bitterly.

Bitterness sat oddly on the man with the amber eyes, like he didn't wear the emotion often.

Ebba reached out and took his hand, deciding she'd try. "I'd say," she said quietly, "many would be alive if *Malice*'s captain weren't so cruel."

Cosmo stared at her, unspeaking, as though searching for something.

"And," she said, "Prince Caspian's soul will be caught by a bird, did ye know?" Ebba flicked her eyes up, and Cosmo did the same.

A fish eagle soared high above in looping, swooping circles.

"Yer master will fly high above the clouds, free and at peace forever."

A tear fell from the corner of Cosmo's eye. He tried to speak, but his voice failed him. Pulling his hand free of hers, he made for the bilge. Ebba watched him cross the deck, her heart squeezing. She wished there was some way to make him feel better. He'd saved her fathers, after all. If freeing them from the gaol had been left to her, they'd probably all be hanging in cages on Exosia right now.

"He lost his master and all the navy men on the ship, little nymph. He might've had many friends onboard." Plank sat at the back of the stern perched atop a barrel. "Ye just give him time to himself. He'll soon recover."

It seemed odd someone might have navy friends. They were a pirate's natural enemy. They meant certain death to Ebba. Cosmo was probably raised believing they were good, though.

"How long to Zol?" she asked, more from a need to distract herself than to hear the answer.

Plank gazed at the full sails. The wind had steadily risen in the last day. The blue water was darker than the aqua seas they'd traveled between Maltu and Neos, the smooth surface broken into one hundred thousand smaller pieces by the stirring air currents. "I'd say six days, if this wind keeps up," he answered.

"And if it doesn't?" she asked.

He shrugged. "Then we better be thinkin' of another plan because if what ye say be right and Pockmark has searched for this treasure for four years, he won't rest until we be dead."

"THE DOLPHINS SAY the storm will be hittin' in an hour, Stubs. Will we make it?" Grubby asked, standing slowly after climbing the rope. He'd been swimming again.

Ebba's brows lifted. Grubby was making comments like that more and more lately. After Barrels questioned what he meant without success, the crew had decided to do their best to accept the harmless statements. Especially since the comments were proving entirely accurate.

A wall of torrential rain fell in the distance, and they were sailing straight at it. Combined with the rolling waves that began an hour ago, the storm promised to be a large one—not the 'dump your water and move on' type of tropical weather Ebba preferred.

"Guess we'll wait and see," was Stubby's neutral reply.

Cosmo joined her at the bulwark, a little green around the gills. His appearance was a far cry from the first time they'd met. He wore an old, yellowed set of slops and shirt from their spare clothing chest. He'd put his buckled shoes back on, and his doublet.

Despite his changed appearance, he stood erect, both hands clasped behind his back as though about to conduct a lesson, or inspect the seaworthiness of their ship.

"We need to get ye a golden hoop," Ebba declared.

He darted his eyes to her earring before hastily glancing over his shoulder at her fathers.

"They won't hurt ye. If they wanted to do that, ye'd be back on Neos, bein' roasted over a fire for the tribespeople's meal." She cut off when Cosmo's green color deepened—his sea sickness clashed horribly with his russet hair.

Cosmo squeezed his eyes shut and breathed deeply. "What does the golden hoop do?" he forced between clamped lips.

Ebba flicked her own earring, making it *ping*. "Helps with the sea chunders, o' course. And makes ye see better," she added.

She turned and leaned her back against the ship side, tilting her head to peer up the mast.

"Seriously?"

She met Cosmo's eyes. "Huh? Oh, the eyesight? Aye, it helps. Why d'ye think so many pirates have them?"

Barrels teetered past, lashing down the crates, ropes, and buckets on deck. No good to have those flying around in a storm.

"Pirates have many suspicions and theories, Cosmo," Barrels said. "I'm not certain the majority of them are accurate or based in science. Whatsoever."

Cosmo smiled tentatively at Barrels.

"Methinks ye've been with us long enough to have learnt all our suspicions be true," Plank called over the gusts from where he furled the topsail with Grubby's help.

"Ye know people from Exosia can only be believin' what they see, Plank," Ebba replied.

Barrels laughed lightly and sent Cosmo a pointed look.

“What you said the other day,” the servant said after Barrels moved away.

Ebba peered up at the taller man. “Mmm?”

“About the birds and the prince’s soul. . . .” he supplied.

“What o’ it?”

A shadow passed over his smooth face. “Thank you, Mistress Fairisles,” he said shortly.

Ebba smiled at him, unsure what to say in reply. She inhaled the scent of damp rain instead. Grubby was right again, or the dolphins perhaps—the storm was coming at them fast.

Cosmo cleared his throat. “Where are we going? Where. . . . What do your fathers mean to do with me?”

Ebba shrugged. “We be on a tight schedule or we’d drop ye as close to home as we could. I’m sure that after we finish our quest, we’ll drop ye somewhere—”

“Kentro,” Cosmo blurted.

“I be guessin’ ye’d like to go to Kentro.” Her lips curved.

He smiled sheepishly. “I apologize. I do not wish to appear ungrateful for your crew’s hospitality.”

Ebba snorted. “Ye’re a prince’s servant on a pirate ship. I ain’t daft enough te think ye’d want to stay.”

Cosmo laughed, a rich sound that made her want to smile with him.

“Every child wonders what life as a pirate would be like. To explore the freedom of the seas,” he admitted.

The wind caught one of her beaded dreads and whipped it across her face. “Sod it,” she cursed, rubbing her smarting cheek. She rolled off one of the leather ties around her shirtsleeve and tied back her black hair.

"You didn't answer my other question," he said.

"Nay," she answered, folding her arms. "I'm afraid ye won't be gettin' one. But we will need to blindfold ye just now. The place we're headin' is a secret, and not one we'll be sharin'." Covering his amber eyes would be a shame, but he'd only be blindfolded for a day, tops.

Cosmo's eyes widened. "What?"

He spun and jumped, yelling at the sight of Peg-leg, Locks, and Stubby behind him.

"Just for a little bit," Ebba said reasonably.

Zol.

Ebba sighed, a deep contentment spreading through her. Even the seas knew *Felicity*'s crew had arrived home. Their sloop slid through the calm waters of their secret cove, hauling to the wooden wharf jutting out from the few scattered shacks they'd erected over the years.

The circular cove was half a mile in diameter with sheer white cliffs rising one hundred yards into the sky, bordering the cove entirely. The high cliffs ensured the small tribe in residence on the island would never be able to climb down into the cove from above. The only other way to reach the cove was via the ocean.

From the outside of the cove, it appeared as though a cave sat in the southern cliffs of Zol. This was no cave, but a tunnel that led all the way inside from the Caspian Sea.

The ceiling of the cave wouldn't allow a masted ship to enter—the reason no pirate had ever found it—and the rolling waters inside the tunnel depths made navigating it via rowboat treacherous.

A ship Stubby and Locks had crafted was another matter. With their design, the mast could be de-constructed into three parts, allowing

Felicity to easily fit through the low cave into the hidden bay. Only *Felicity* could enter and exit, and only their crew knew of this secret place. The hidden inlet was her fathers' retirement plan. Their crew's sanctuary. A plunder they kept from all the realm.

Barrels called the inlet security. And he was probably right, though Ebba didn't quite understand what he meant. Or didn't care to understand, at least.

Birds squawked overhead. The sun was back out and shining far above. They'd tied the blindfolded Cosmo down in the bilge so he wouldn't turn as red as a lobster.

"It be good to be back." Locks sighed heavily. "Ain't it, Ebba?"

"Aye," she replied. For a few days. . . .

Their crew furled the sails as Stubby maneuvered *Felicity* around his hobby ship—the only other ship in the inlet, and one that could never get out because it was too large—through the crowded harbor to dock.

The ship's stern bumped gently against the wharf.

"Lines!" Stubby bellowed.

Ebba leaped from the sloop and turned in a graceful spin. She caught the line Barrels tossed her from the bow and wrapped it once around the top of the piling. She heaved on the line with all her might, knowing Locks and Plank did the same from further down. Securing the line, she turned to catch another from Stubby at mid-deck. A pirate could never be too safe in these seas; tropical storms erupted smart-like, and with little warning. That's what Stubby said anyway. Truth was, they were pretty protected in their Zol inlet and Stubby fussed over *Felicity* too much. But it was better to humor him than listen to his woeful fretting for the next day.

Ebba caught the final line from Grubby at the stern.

"Right," shouted Stubby from the wheel. "We have a day to stock up *Felicity* for six weeks."

“It will take us three weeks at most to return,” said Barrels as he disembarked *Felicity*. Pillage leaped down after him. Somehow the cat never seemed to trip Barrels. The rest of them weren’t so lucky. . . .

“Yer plans be great, Barrels. But I like to be prepared.”

Barrels contemplated him with a mild expression. “I do believe I’ve garnered that much about you in twenty years or so.” The two shared a grin.

Ebba looked around the seven rustic shacks that made up their sanctuary.

Locks said that when the time came to move here permanently—when they all *retired*—he’d build them something stronger. The shacks didn’t hold much, but the secret stores underneath them did: materials, preserved food, tools, and medicines. There was even a garden Barrels and Grubby tended to when they visited between trade runs.

Zol was what she was supposed to keep in mind when other pirates ridiculed *Felicity* and her fathers. She was supposed to remember the joke was on them because they’d plunder and fight for the rest of their days; *Felicity*’s small appearance and the semi-honest living they did their best to uphold was all to “disguise their true cunning, and their secret pr’sperity”—according to Peg-leg.

As her fathers went through the motions of trading and selling, gathering and stocking, each of them focused on retiring here, Ebba felt the brush of wind on her face, the rolling water underneath the ship, and the fierce excitement of the sea in her veins. And she knew she was a pirate. *Felicity* felt real to her. Yet sometimes she did feel caught between the life of a pirate and a common merchant. She was finding it harder and harder to shrug off the mean comments from others, though she knew better. And part of her felt guilty about that because all of this *should* be enough. If her fathers were happy, Ebba should be happy. Yet being a *pirate* made her happy, not their retirement plan.

Sometimes, she felt trapped.

“Can ye help Peg-leg restock the fruit and veggies, Ebba?” Plank asked.

His eyes pleaded with her as she shot him a surly look.

“Ye know he’s the nicest to ye, little nymph. And he’s sulkin’ that we won’t be able to dock and refill our stocks for a few weeks durin’ our trip.”

Ebba groaned.

“Come now, little nymph. Do this for yer favorite father.” He wrapped an arm around her shoulders and marched her down the pier. “Isn’t it good to be back? Not long now till we’ll be retired and wakin’ on the white beaches to eat coconut for breakfast each mornin’.”

Ebba smiled until her cheeks hurt. “I can’t wait.”

THIRTEEN

Ebba sat back on her haunches, and ripped off Cosmo's blindfold with one hand.

He squinted at the sudden light. It probably hurt his eyes after a day and night under the dark cloth, but his face softened when he saw her sitting before him. The prince's servant seemed awfully worried about her fathers—especially the one-legged Peg-leg and the one-eyed Locks. He watched the pair like they were fish flopping around on deck. Ebba guessed she'd look at King Montcroix the same way.

"We've been moving for a while. Where are we going now? Why did we stop? Are you going to untie me?" he blurted.

How different Cosmo was to Jagger. They were the only young males she'd spent any length of time with, and both were around her age. Cosmo had honor, for starters, and probably an education, but Ebba wouldn't say he was smarter than Jagger. In fact, she'd say if both were marooned on an island, Jagger might be the only one left standing after a month. Cosmo's smarts were like Barrels' smarts. Not the kind that really helped you survive. Still, Ebba thought back to how he'd behaved at the governor's party; Cosmo was kind-hearted and must have a measure of bravery to have done what he did that night. And maybe honor was worth more than survival smarts.

Ebba ran her eyes over the servant's face, the rich colors of his eyes and hair. She liked Cosmo. He'd given her a good feeling from the start. When they dropped him in Kentro, she hoped he wouldn't forget her, and that he'd leave their ship no longer afraid of her fathers.

"We're out at sea again, off on an adventure to plunder a great booty," she answered before wondering if she should be telling Cosmo that detail. Perhaps that hadn't been wise.

"Oh?" said Cosmo, his amber eyes fixed on her with the intensity of their first meeting. "Where?"

Ebba waved vaguely, feeling the roll of the moving ship beneath her. "Through some razor-sharp rocks not many people've survived, after avoidin' the whirlpool that sucks most ships into the oblivion. But that shouldn't be a problem. We do it all the time on the way to Kentro. The whirlpool part anyway."

Cosmo smiled indulgently. "Your imagination is something to be envied. Why did we stop?" He trailed off as he looked at the bilge around him, which was now three-quarters full. "To restock," he answered himself. "Where are we now, then?" he asked.

Ebba brought her face close to his before leaning across to untie the rope holding him to the mast. She didn't shift her gaze from his face. "That be a secret I can't be sharin' with ye."

He scanned her face and she dropped her eyes as the knot came away.

"There," she said, straightening. "Ye be free at last."

He winced, bending his knees before pulling himself up from the deck, gripping the hammock post until he was steady. He took a lot longer to get up than Jagger when they'd tied him up on main deck—and Cosmo'd been tied up for much less time.

"Ye're a bit soft, aren't ye?" she observed, looking him up and down.

"Excuse me?" Cosmo said around a laugh. "I've never been called soft in my life. I hunt and fish, and ride and fence."

Ebba picked at her teeth, shrugging. "Maybe all the people ye be doin' that with are soft, too, and none o' ye recognize the softness no more."

Cosmo paused. "You know, in a bizarre way that makes sense."

Ebba grabbed his warm, soft hand and pulled his hobbling form to the ladder. "Well, don't worry. Ye'll have muscle on ye afore long. Though I don't think ye'll be buildin' any fences aboard this ship."

A puzzled look met her words before it cleared. "No, Mistress Fairisles, not that kind of fencing. Fencing, like . . . swordplay. That kind."

"Why call it fencin' if ye ain't buildin' a fence? Why not call it swordin'?"

His warm eyes filled with mirth. "I daresay you are right about that, too."

Ebba studied him. "I'm glad to see ye ain't wholly useless. Up the ladder with ye." She jerked her head.

They emerged from the bilge.

"Stubs," Ebba bellowed. "I was lookin' at Cosmo and thinkin' he'd do well with some more muscle on him. What'd'ye think?"

Stubby bent a leg up on the stern step. "Lookin' at him, were ye?" he asked slowly. He turned his flat gaze to Cosmo.

Ebba looked at Cosmo as the green color returned to his face. "Ye sick again? The sooner we get ye a golden hoop, the better."

Stubby smiled—manically, like the time with Jagger a week before—showing the three gaps in his teeth. "Aye, Ebba. I'd be happy to help Cosmo gain some muscle."

She pushed him toward Stubby and, satisfied he was in safe hands, she took a few bounding steps to the rigging and scampered to the top, swinging into the crow's nest.

Ebba looked about.

In the stern, Pillage was stalking prey through the large coils of rope. Probably a mouse. Or his shadow. Idiot cat. To the east, a mere dot on the horizon now, was Zol. Directly west, before them and too far to see, was Charybdis. Stubby would steer them well clear of the whirlpool. Its pull spread for hundreds of yards from its black eye, and those caught in its current did not come out again.

Immediately north of the whirlpool was Syraness, the cliff passage. Together, the whirlpool and cliffs formed a barrier to Selkie's Cove for larger ships, which sat on the other side.

If the wind remained high as they headed northwest, *Felicity* would arrive at the cliff passage in four days. And from there, it would be another four days through the passage, and then only part of a day on the other side to reach the treasure on Portum. Her chest rose and fell, her moss-green eyes set in the direction of Syraness. They'd never ventured into the cliff passage before.

"All clear up there, Wobbles?" Stubby hollered up.

Ebba swung over the edge of the crow's nest and skimmed down the ropes. Her shirt and slops plastered against her with the rush of her descent.

"All clear," she answered, landing on the deck. "Nearly out o' sight o' the . . . place we left."

"Why do you call her Wobbles?" Cosmo called from where he swabbed the decks.

Ebba grinned at the sight. She knew the fathers would forget her three-moon punishment. But she picked up a broom to help the servant anyway. Perhaps she deserved to swab the decks for a while for worrying her fathers on Maltu.

Grubby chuckled. “Because she were a bit wobbly up there when she were two.”

The others chuckled.

Ebba snorted, though slightly embarrassed her fathers were telling Cosmo such things.

“You let her climb up there when she was two?” Cosmo had stopped swabbing, and looked between her fathers with wide eyes.

Stubby wiped a tear away. “Aye, prince slave, we did. Right cute she were, totterin’ around up there in naught but her diaper and the wee eye patch she liked to wear.”

“Wanted to be just like me,” Locks said proudly, emerald eye blazing.

“Only until she were three,” Peg-leg spoke. “Then it was me.”

“I rather think it was me at three.” Barrels frowned. “She liked my quill and ink.”

Ebba knew where this talk led to. A whole heap of loud voices and angry fathers. Grubby knew it too; he darted his eyes between Locks and Peg-leg, hands twisting.

Cosmo interceded. “It sounds like all six of you were an integral and loved part of her childhood. It must have been something, to raise her together as you have.”

“Aye, Cosmo. If ye’re sayin’ what I think ye be, it were at that. Co-parentin’ ain’t always smooth sailin’, but we didn’t do too shabby a job,” Locks said in a mollified voice.

Barrels passed Ebba some grog, hiding a smile. “A very diplomatic response, Cosmo.”

The two Exosians shared a grin.

She was happy to see Cosmo getting on with someone aboard the ship. They’d be together for at least a few weeks. Hopefully, he’d come to see the others weren't bad either, if a little rougher around the edges than Barrels at first glance.

"We're heading to find a treasure, I've been told," Cosmo said haltingly.

Several pairs of eyes slid toward Ebba.

"I didn't tell him where," she said sheepishly.

Cosmo chuckled. "No, you said we were heading through razor-sharp rocks, past a giant whirlpool that could suck us to our death."

The silence following his comment was lengthy.

Cosmo licked his lips several times before turning to Barrels. "You cannot be serious," he said, aghast.

Barrels cleared his throat, ears turning pink. "Ebba's answer was quite true, if containing highly graphic details for someone unused to this life." He shot her a reproving look.

Ebba snickered and busied herself washing the deck. Wasn't her fault Cosmo was soft.

"We head for Syraness," Plank said, plonking down by the mast.

Cosmo frowned. "The rock formations south of Kentro?"

Grubby clapped his hands, and cast Cosmo an approving nod.

"And we can't go around because. . . ?" the prince's servant pressed.

"Because *Malice* is headin' that way and we need to beat them," Ebba supplied.

"Who is *Malice*?" Cosmo asked.

"*Malice* be a ship, lad," said Locks. His voice softened. "The ship that burned the boat ye were on, and killed yer prince."

Cosmo's face firmed. "And . . . you plan to thwart this ship, *Malice*, by reaching the treasure first?"

A chorus of 'aye's' answered him. That wasn't strictly true. Initially they'd only been after the magical fruit. Now, they'd been forced to chase the treasure because Jagger spilled his guts to Pockmark. That was left unsaid—and that the treasure would fund their retirement plan. Their answer was mostly true, and that's all a pirate owed anyone.

Cosmo smiled tightly. "Then I heartily approve of this quest."

Ebba didn't blame him for wanting revenge. Out of all of them, Cosmo had the most reason to want Pockmark to suffer. Revenge started the whole quest in the first place, after all. Well, not *exactly*. Her foolish slip of the tongue had started it, really. Ebba frowned at the thought.

"Ye know," started Plank, "Syraness orig'nally came from the term siren's nest. And—"

Peg-leg groaned. "Here we go."

Ebba dug her elbow into his rotund gut. She wanted to hear.

"I'd have thought ye'd all be a sight more inter'sted after what happened on Neos Mountain." Plank sniffed.

The other men grumbled, but didn't retort.

Cosmo watched the exchange with fascination. Was he fascinated by everything? "What about Syraness?" he asked, perching on a barrel.

Plank retied his pale green bandana over the front of his raven curls. "It was said that one day a warrior out fishing with his young daughter caught sight of a magn'ficent bird. Its song was so beautiful, he knew he had to have it for his own, so he wounded the great bird with his harpoon."

Ebba gasped. Shooting a bird was a sure ticket to Davy Jones's Locker. To do so was to kill the soul of someone passed from this life.

"But his harpoon missed its mark." Plank's eyes flared dramatically. "Instead of the wing, the arrow pierced the bird through the side. The warrior caught the bird as it fell, lamenting as it sang its dying song.

The song wrenched at the warrior's heart so, he called upon the old magic and wished the bird's spirit into his daughter's body and mind. The beautiful bird was savagely ripped from its body as it drew its last breath, and thrust into that of the warrior's daughter."

Spray hit them as a larger wave split over *Felicity*'s bow.

The only sound was the rhythmic drop of the ship over each wave.

"The bird's spirit was too powerful for the girl. Her soul fled to the bird's empty carcass and she died instantly. The warrior drew his bow and arrow, seeing all semblance of his daughter had disappeared and a voluptuous woman rivaling the beauty of the dead bird now perched in his daughter's place." Plank paused. "But as he did so the woman opened her silken lips, and such sound poured from her, the warrior lowered his weapon, forgetting why he'd raised it to begin with. The bird-turned-woman, realizing her new power and enraged by the loss of her wings, vowed she would kill any man who dared cross her path from that moment forward. Spotting jagged rocks close by, she sang to the warrior:

Handsome warrior, to the rocks I bid thee,
For you are weary, and there you can rest your weary head.
Come with me, mighty warrior to the rocks, I bid,
Together we will rest, together we will be.

EBBA CROAKED, "But . . . surely he didn't go to the rocks."

Plank turned his solemn gaze upon her. "Aye, Ebba-Viva. That he did. And happily, too. Even as his body dashed over the rocks as sharp as daggers and blood poured from a hundred different punctures in his body, he smiled."

Plank had told stories before, but never this good. Or maybe, after

Ladon, *knowing* that magic truly existed, Ebba listened a little harder. They all did; even Cosmo's eyes shone with sadness.

Plank lowered his voice and they leaned forward. "The siren claimed her first victim that day, and made her nest in those very rocks." He looked ahead. "The rocks we know today as Syraness."

The ship rolled side to side and no one spoke until Locks laughed nervously, eye patch lifting with his cheeks. "Aye, Plank. Ye tell the story well. But Ladon was a one-off magical creature; there ain't nothin' in the cliffs to be sweatin' about."

"Plank and his stories." Peg-leg slapped his thigh, though it lacked its usual gusto.

Ebba peered at the tense set to her fathers' shoulders and their dark eyes, and was unable to brush away the foreboding creeping up her spine.

They'd entered Neos and found Ladon.

Was something waiting for them in the hazardous Syraness?

FOURTEEN

"Rocks ahoy!"

The distant call startled Ebba from her swinging slumber.

"Rocks ahoy!" the watch repeated.

Ebba scrambled out of bed, fully dressed, only stopping to secure her bandana and weapons.

"Where're we?" mumbled Cosmo from the opposite end of the sleeping quarters, lifting Pillage from his chest.

Peg-leg, who slept in the middle of the room, answered, "We've reached Syraness, lad."

Ebba dashed for the ladder, flinging the bilge door open and racing to the bulwark to look over the side.

A thick fog surrounded *Felicity.* Ebba could only see ten yards from the side. Grubby and Locks perched at the bow of the ship, shouting back directions to Stubby at the helm.

Plank had them sailing at a creeping pace.

"I'm o' half a mind to take everything down but the foresail," he said as she crossed to him. "The current is pushin' us along just fine, and too much speed be our worst enemy here."

She glanced up as a shadow crept over the deck. *Felicity* was passing between two towering rock faces. Plank had hoisted the small foresail windward to help them maneuver the ship. No wonder—the rocks peeking just above the surface of the water would only allow them a couple of yards' error. Not to mention the cliffs to each side. "No problem to have the others down—unless the current be movin' us where we don't wish to go later on."

"That's what I be worried about," Plank said softly.

The morning passed gratingly slow, the fog not abating in the slightest. Early into the afternoon, the open water and rocks lurking nearly unseen in the dim light began to increase in number.

Felicity inched through the water, bobbing side to side.

Ebba kept her chin tilted up as the crow's nest drew within a breath's whisper of another jutting rock face. The top of their mast was getting too close to the cliffs either side for her comfort.

Stubby waved her over, not shifting his eyes from the devices in front of him as he spoke. One showed the water's depth beneath them. Ebba squinted at the device. *Felicity*'s hull was shallow; she only needed a few yards, and the depth on the device showed the number six.

"Take the helm, Ebba," he instructed. "Listen out for Grubby and Locks, mind. Ye be keepin' yer focus."

"Aye, Stubs." She straightened and took the closest spoke on the wheel tight in hand. She stepped in front of the wheel's pedestal as Stubby moved away to check on whatever plagued him. He wouldn't be worth talking to for weeks after this adventure if *Felicity* got damaged.

"Ten starboard!" Locks hollered.

Ebba adjusted the wheel without delay. The water ahead sprayed high over whatever rocky obstacle lay in its path.

She winced as the crow's nest just inched past a jutting rock. She released her breath as they swung by the spraying water, indicating a hidden rock.

Ebba completed three more maneuvers before Stubby returned with a pile of oars in his hands.

"I've a feelin' we'll be needin' these afore long." He passed her one. "Off with ye up to the crow's nest. Use it to push off the cliffs."

Ebba nodded and made for the mast.

Cosmo was up on deck, his russet hair disheveled from sleep. She found hammocks as comfortable as a cloud looked. Clearly, the same wasn't true for the servant.

"Syraness doesn't seem so bad." Cosmo said the words tentatively, like a question.

Peg-leg slapped him upside the head, scowling. "Don't be temptin' fate, boy. That's ship law one."

Intrigue lit Cosmo's eyes. "Pirates have rules?"

"Aye, but every ship be dif'erent."

Cosmo glanced around the ship. "What are the rules of *Felicity*? I'd hate to overstep the boundaries."

Their rules? Ebba bit back a grin. "Our two main laws be simple, don't put the crew in harm's way, and don't fuss about what ye can't understand."

"And what about tempting fate?" Cosmo still rubbed the back of his head where Peg-leg had hit him.

"That be a subclause o' ship law one." Ebba rolled her eyes. Was he daft?

Peg-leg rubbed his right knee. It tended to ache when the temperature dropped. "All I be knowin' is we could do with an albatross right about now," he remarked.

Ebba hummed in agreement.

Cosmo looked between them, his brown brows raised in bafflement. "Will it violate any subclauses if I ask what an albatross would do?"

Peg-leg and Ebba shared a look before shaking their heads in unison.

"Sightin' an albatross would mean the end o' the fog," Ebba explained.

If she didn't know how Barrels struggled with all these things, she'd think Cosmo had been hit across the head with a boom, like Grubby. Such things were basic sea survival knowledge.

Cosmo's face remained smooth. His gaze flicked between them as if waiting for one of them to dissolve into laughter. He cleared his throat. "Oh, I see. Right."

Peg-leg shook his head again and Ebba shrugged at him. Cosmo's ignorance didn't make sense to her either.

Slinging the oar under the sash across her back, she shimmied up the rigging, keeping an eye on the cliffs either side. Kicking into the crow's nest, Ebba pulled the oar free.

It had been difficult to see from the main deck, but from the crow's nest, visibility was almost zero. As the ship leaned to one side, Ebba readied the oar. The cliff faces came into view a few seconds before nearly impacting with the ship. She dug the end into the cliff and pushed with all her might, her feet spread as far apart as the nest would allow.

She kept this up until her arms began to shake and then called for a replacement.

Grubby ascended the shrouds for a shift with the oar in the crow's nest and Ebba slid down, taking a plate of meat and bread from Peg-leg.

She shoved the crusty bread in her mouth without ceremony, wiping away the crumbs on her lips with her sleeve.

The only sign the afternoon had passed while she was up in the nest was the disappearance of what little light had been filtering through the fog. Locks and Barrels shouted back orders to Stubby from the bow while Plank likely rested below.

Cosmo sat beside her, passing over a goblet of grog.

"I feel a little useless," he said with a self-deprecating laugh.

Ebba shrugged, stuffing another slice of salted pork in her mouth. "Don't see how ye'd be knowin' how to sail a ship after a week."

"But is there anything I can do to help?"

Ebba handed him her plate. "Ye can take that to the wash bucket for me."

He took it with a wry smile.

"And," she added, "I'm sure everyone would appreciate ye doing the rounds with some grog to keep the thirst at bay. Aside from that, ye be knowin' how to swab the decks."

Cosmo tilted his head. "I did that yesterday."

"We do it every day." She arched a brow. "Sometimes more than once." She glanced down at Cosmo's hands. The palms faced up and several large blisters were forming on them. "I thought ye used a sword with fencin'. Why're yer palms torn?"

His voice was amused. "Another sign of my softness, I'm afraid, Mistress Fairisles."

"Just Ebba."

"You seem to have several names," Cosmo noted. "I've heard you called Wobbles, little nymph, Ebba, and Ebba-Viva."

Heat rose to her cheek, and she broke eye contact with him to look at the cliffs. "Aye, the first just be a childhood name. And Plank has always called me little nymph. He says that the cheeky water nymphs must've handed me over to the pelicans."

"The pelicans?" he asked.

"The ones who dropped me off," she said, an edge to her voice.

"A . . . pelican dropped you to your fathers?" Cosmo said carefully.

She'd certainly believed that to be the case for a long time, though she'd long since outgrown the notion. To admit that out loud meant that she'd have to look for another reason for having six adoptive fathers, though, and that wasn't something Ebba was willing to do, yet, no matter what Cosmo thought of her. Ebba nodded curtly. "That's what I said. Near on seventeen years ago. Pelicans."

Cosmo's silence dragged on too long. She glanced at him, but his expression was closed off.

Ebba cleared her throat, growing nervous in the silence. "Anyway, my full name be Ebba-Viva Fairisles. They voted on my name; half wanted Ebba, and half wanted Viva. So I got both. For a long time, I got called Viva or Ebba, dependin' on what name they'd voted for at the start. But in time, they all began to call me Ebba."

"What does it mean, your name?"

Ebba scrunched up her face. "Hey, Barrels, what does my name mean again?"

He called back, "Ebba means strength. Viva means alive. Five port!"

"There ye go," she said to Cosmos. Ebba stood and brushed the crumbs from her frayed slops.

"Strong and alive," Cosmo mused. He got to his feet with a graceful movement, picking up her goblet and plate. His eyes settled on her. "It suits you."

Ebba's cheeks burned. She thumped on her chest and belched behind her hand to cover her reaction. "Thank ye."

She rushed to join Stubby at the helm, and he spoke to her in a low voice, "The waters be calm, and we'd do well to take adv'ntage of them while they hold. There be no knowin' when a storm may hit."

Ebba stared ahead. The thinnest stream of light remained, and soon that would also be gone. "Aye, but the rocks are no joke. What if we hit somethin' in the night?"

Stubby slid his eyes to her. "How do ye feel about a wee shimmy down the bowsprit to hang a few torches?"

Ebba grinned despite the tweak of apprehension in her gut. "Aye, I can be doin' that."

. . . Ten minutes later, she clung to the pointed stick protruding from the bow of the ship that was the bowsprit. In truth, sometimes in calmer waters Ebba would shuffle out onto the bowsprit to feel the sea's spray on her face. She liked to pretend she was like the mermaid figurehead located just underneath it.

But falling off and dashing against rocks wasn't usually a risk. The thought of ending like the warrior who trapped the bird's soul in his daughter didn't appeal to Ebba.

She held an oil lantern in one hand and shuffled out using her legs and her remaining arm, in a similar way she'd done with the tree on Neos.

"As close to the tip of the bowsprit as ye can, little nymph," Plank called.

Ebba's stomach lurched as the ship swung without warning to the port side. The cliffs were near impossible to see now, coated as they were in the darkness of the lapping water.

She reached the tip. If *Felicity* crashed into the rocks right now, her guts would be the first of the crew to paint the walls of Syraness.

She gripped the wooden beam with her legs and held the lantern between her thighs, thankful her trousers made the hot metal painful but bearable to touch. Unwinding the end of the rope slung across her torso, she tied a loop knot, tugging it firmly to check its hold. She passed this through the lantern's handle and held both ends of the rope as she dropped the lantern down into place. She then fed the other end of the rope through the loop twice before pulling it tight against the bowsprit she sat upon.

She shuffled backward, feeding out the rope.

Plank held out another lantern for her to place.

She repeated the process twice more before swinging off the bowsprit and onto the deck again.

The lanterns shone light a full ten paces in front of the ship. More than enough for those giving directions back to the helm.

Just as Plank clapped her on the shoulder, an eerie keening sound echoed through the rocks. The crew froze—as did Cosmo, who'd come to watch her hang the lanterns.

"What was that?" Stubby said from the stern.

None of them answered, each straining to catch the sound again.

Ebba let out a sigh when the breathy shriek didn't come again. "Probably just a—"

The high scream ripped through the rocks again, louder this time. The sound bounced between the cliffs, seeming to come from everywhere at once. Ebba gripped onto Plank with one hand, her insides frozen by the pure menace the call held.

"Plank, is that the siren?" she whispered.

Plank stared into the water ahead, pressing his lips together as the scream echoed for the third time. "I be thinkin' we need to take some pr'cautions."

"Against what?" Locks asked, then rolled his eye. "Not yer blimin' siren?"

"Aye, *my blimin' siren.* That sound like anythin' ye've ever heard? Magic be back in the realm," Plank snapped. "I don't know how or why, but it is. We saw Ladon with our own eyes. If he was back on Neos Mountain, who's to say the siren hasn't returned here?"

Uncertainty crossed Locks' face. "But ships've made it through these channels afore. They had no tales o' sirens. . . ."

"You said Jagger had never seen Ladon on the mountain of Neos before, despite being there several times," Barrels said. "Clearly something has happened for him to return. I don't think we should discount there being more magical creatures around."

"Twenty starboard!" shouted Peg-leg to Stubby.

The ship tilted and Cosmo stumbled into the bulwark.

Plank lifted his hands. "There ain't no harm done if we tie ourselves to the ship—just in case, ye savvy? If the way be clear o' the siren, we'll laugh about it on the other side. If the siren is around, we stand a chance of makin' it through with Ebba at the helm."

Ebba inhaled sharply. "Why me at the helm?"

A pregnant pause followed.

"Someone else can explain. I need to, uh, trim the sails," Plank said, hurrying away.

"Ye just did that." Ebba frowned at his back.

Locks blurted, "I'm busy watchin' for rocks. Can't talk."

"Aye, same here," Peg-leg echoed, avoiding her gaze.

Ebba turned to face Barrels, the last father left in front of her.

He scrubbed at the salty grime covering his face.

Ebba glanced over her shoulder. All of them were hiding, except Cosmo. Locks and Peg-leg were in plain sight, but looked to be pressing themselves into the deck as though hoping to merge into it. She could see Plank's hand sticking out behind the mast, and Stubby's head peeping over the helm.

"What did he mean, I can be at the helm?" she demanded.

"You see, Ebba-Viva," began Barrels hesitantly, "legend says the siren's call affects *men*."

Ebba glanced over her hiding fathers again, her stomach tightening. She hated this topic with a vengeance. It was a particularly raw point between her and her fathers and one they *always* avoided. She was a pirate. A *pirate*.

"Why?" she said, playing dumb in the hopes he'd run away like the others.

Plank threw ropes to Locks at the bow, and then retreated so quickly his feet tangled together. He hit the deck, but jumped up and hid behind the mast once more.

"Because," Barrels said, "I guess if the siren's call affected women, then the siren herself would succumb to her song. And you are . . . not a man." He stared at the others, who were fastening the ropes Plank chucked to them around their waists.

"Tie those knots tight, lads. Two or three of them," Stubby shouted, peeking out and hitting his head in his haste to backpedal when he saw Ebba watching.

They were really doing this. Her fathers were really defying her personal pirate law. "Well her song still might affect me because I'm a pirate," Ebba said, lifting her chin, eyes burning as a lump rose in her throat.

Cosmo interrupted. "Wait. Mistress Fairisles doesn't know she's female?" His voice showed his disbelief.

Barrels fidgeted on the spot. "We didn't mess things up that badly. Ebba just doesn't think being female or male is relevant to how someone should be treated. She identifies as a pirate. *Which is fine*," he blurted, seeing her thunderous expression. "Though I'm afraid her reason for making the shift from female to pirate came on the backend of a grievous error of our own."

Blood pumped into Ebba's face. "I'm a pirate," she said, her voice louder as fear pounded through her. At fifteen, her fathers had abandoned her to Sherry on Maltu. They'd left Ebba there and run off for months without explanation. In the end, she'd figured out why. Hard not to when her body began changing into adulthood two weeks prior to being abandoned. Ebba had thought they were never coming back, and all because they couldn't ignore that she was female any longer. When they did return, she swore they'd never see her as a weakness to be discarded. On that day, she became a pirate. For good.

The rest of the realm just had trouble getting that fact through their thick skulls.

"She wears a corset," Cosmo noted.

Ebba rounded on him, jaw clenched. "It ain't a corset. It's a *jerkin*."

He dropped his gaze to her chest. "Awfully tight jerkin," he muttered.

Her skin heated under his intense look. Ebba scowled darkly at him. She had female parts, sure. She even liked a lot of female things. And she found some men attractive, but. . . . "I'm a pirate," she growled. "Don't ye or any other sod be forgettin' it."

Cosmo flushed a deep red. "My sincerest apologies, Mistress Fairisles."

Barrels kicked Locks in the side. "You two could help, you know."

Locks' and Peg-leg's response was to flatten themselves further into the deck.

Her eldest father sighed. "How about a compromise? That you're a pirate is of no doubt. But . . . let's just say you are a different kind of pirate. One which can, uh, *resist* the siren's lament?"

Beside her, Cosmo smothered a cough with his hand.

The pressure on Ebba's breathers eased. "Aye, I can go with that." As long as her fathers never felt they had to leave her again.

Cosmo opened his mouth. "But—"

Peg-leg kicked his wooden leg out and swept the servant's feet from under him. The air whooshed from Cosmo's lungs and he hit the deck, flat on his back.

"Best leave it at that, boy," Peg-leg said.

Cosmo wheezed for air. "Why don't you talk? You're all just pretending." He trailed off in response to a glare from Locks.

Pretending. That word was cropping up an awful lot lately.

"We don't fuss over why on this ship, boy. And ye'd do well to mind that," Locks snapped.

Ebba paced the deck, her lips pursed. The issue of pirates, males, and females aside, if the siren was real, they could be sailing into danger. And they knew very little of the siren's power. A rope was only a slight inconvenience against potential death on the rocks.

"I'll still be tyin' myself to the ship, just in case," she told them. "We've never really tested this element o' my pirate nature. Better safe than dead. And we should keep Pillage below deck. He's a lad, too."

The words froze on her lips as she saw Barrels was gone and now mimicked Locks and Peg-leg's posture, flattened against the deck.

Cosmo clambered to his feet with a grimace. His amber eyes glittered as he scanned her fathers, and if Ebba had to guess, she'd say he was unhappy with her fathers. Aye, well, he could get in line. She'd cried every day when they left her. For more than a year after they returned, she'd been near-speechless with fear for a week either side of docking in Maltu. But slowly she'd seen proof that her theory was right. As a pirate, she was safe; safe from the scripted life of an existence on land. Safe, and sailing with the six fathers who were her world, even if they'd shown that they could do without her.

Sherry blamed *her* for being childish and spoiled, but sometimes, when Ebba couldn't pretend otherwise, she blamed her fathers for the same. This was the ship dynamic that worked. Being a dependent pirate were the unspoken terms of compromise whereby Ebba remained on *Felicity*.

It would take a braver pirate than her to risk changing that.

"I think we can be pretty sure you'll be okay, Mistress Fairisles," Cosmo said softly, his eyes lingering on her face. "But how about you tie yourself down, just in case?"

FIFTEEN

Ebba slept out by the helm, tied to the wheel's pedestal, while Stubby continued to direct the ship in response to the crew's calls from the bow. He was tied to the wheel also.

The rocky spires extended high above now. So high that even with the fog lessening on the second day, scant sunlight made it down to them.

"How much longer, Stubby?" She yawned, jaw cracking. Sleeping through the echoing shrieks bouncing through the overhangs proved a challenge. Especially as the screams became more frequent the farther into Syraness the current took them.

He passed a hand over his drawn face. "We're only a day and night in. Thrice that distance to go." His soft, reflective eyes squinted up to the heights either side of the ship. "I ain't likin' that those shrieks have fallen silent just now."

Ebba sat up, circling her shoulders to alleviate the stiffness in them. "They have?" She listened for a moment. Silence. He was right—the siren had finally shut her gob. Thank the sea for small mercies.

Stubby hummed, spinning the wheel to port side at a call from Barrels, who was taking a shift at the bow.

“Grubby up top?” she asked. Stubby nodded.

“I’ll go get ye some food and grog and then take over for a shift.”

“That’d be nice.”

She loosened her rope and made haste for the bilge, noting Cosmo resting in his hammock, tied to the far post. No one else was below deck, except the ship cat, all hands helping above.

She grabbed two plates of tropical fruit and balanced two goblets of grog on them. Then, she returned to the main deck, shoving the bilge door open with her hip.

“Here ye go.” She shoved the plate and grog at Stubby and began to shovel food into her mouth. She slurped at her grog. Being constantly on edge gave her an appetite.

Stubby’s plate clattered to the deck.

Ebba picked it up. “Stubby, what—?”

The ship careened to port side. The wheel spun wildly and Ebba threw the plates away, lunging forward to grab a spoke. She pulled back on the wheel with all her weight.

The bowsprit at the front scraped along the rocks, and *Felicity* groaned at the demanding change.

They’d nearly crashed into the cliffs. “Stubby,” she shouted. Damn pirate fell asleep at the wheel.

She spared a quick glance at him and gasped.

Her father’s face was blank, his mouth slightly ajar and eyes empty—their usual reflective quality gone as though he’d fallen asleep standing . . . with his eyes open . . . mid-meal.

“Stubby?” she said, keeping one eye on the water ahead. “Yoo-hoooo.”

He didn't show any sign of hearing her.

Ebba let out a shaking breath. "Shite."

Up at the bow, Locks and Barrels stood in the same way as Stubby, staring at the cliffs with vacant expressions.

She peered to the bulwark where Peg-leg had been pushing off the rocks with an oar. He was the same. As was Plank at the mast, and Grubby in the crow's nest.

Fear nestled into her gut. This wasn't good.

Spray flew high in front of the ship. Ebba wrenched left on the wheel, the spokes spinning wildly on their axel. There was no way to know if she'd avoid the rock causing the spray.

The crow's nest scraped against the jutting spires high above

"Grubby," she screamed.

The toothless pirate swayed on the spot, oblivious to the peril inches away from him.

This couldn't be happening. Was the siren here? It was the only explanation she had.

Spray erupted to the port side, and she pulled down hard to the right. Ebba needed the directions called from the front. She might miss a smaller rock. How long would her fathers be out of it?

A high-pitched giggle resonated through the channel. The childish sound sent a shiver of terror through her body and a shriek lodged in Ebba's throat.

The giggle came again. Closer.

It sounded in her right ear, turning into an inhuman screech at the last second. Ebba drew her cutlass, swiping at the thin air, her eyes searching the shadows by the cliffs.

Stubby groaned and began to push Ebba aside to get to the sound.

"No, Stubby," she cried. "It be the siren." Her eyes fell on the rope around his waist.

Did they all have their ropes secured?

She quickly searched out those of the crew she could see. Relief poured through her as she saw the tight fastenings around their waists.

She guided the ship to the starboard side.

Tension coiled tight within her until *Felicity* passed around another rocky hazard without harm. Stubby stepped forward until his rope grew taut, and Ebba shifted to the other side of him to get a better hold on the wheel.

The giggling came again, but this time the sound held a sultry quality to it. A huskiness Ebba associated with Sherry, Brandy, and Margaritta back on Maltu.

Handsome warrior, to the rocks I bid thee.

THE HAIRS at the back of her neck prickled. Ebba stilled as something, *someone* blew on the back of her neck.

There was nothing there when she whirled around.

Stubby strained against his rope, grunting. "Comin', sugar plum."

Ebba scrunched her nose, heaving to the starboard and then to port in short succession.

"Barrels! Locks!" she shouted, knowing deep down her cries were futile. The sirens hold on them was unshakeable.

The wind howled and despair knotted in a noose around her neck. If the wind was rising, so would the swell.

Come with me, mighty warrior to the rocks, I bid.

STUBBY AND PLANK pulled against their restraints, reaching blindly for the cliffs. Both were wildly joyful in response to the siren's throaty call.

Ebba tightened her grip on the helm, trying to think. It was three days to the other side of Syraness. The curving spires had finally blotted out all trace of natural light overhead.

Three days without hitting the cliffs, or a single rock. . . .

She was in a bucket of steaming shite.

Together we will rest, together we will be.

EBBA SHIVERED, doing her best to focus through the siren's call. She couldn't rely on her fathers—not until they were free of the siren's spell.

She was alone. She listened to the grunts and yearning shouts of her fathers, dread immobilizing her as she stared into the darkness ahead, the swinging lanterns her only beacons into the black unknown.

THE WINDS HAD RISEN, and the current had quickened, adding a rolling swell that oscillated sideways through the channel, slapping against the rock interfaces.

Ebba was powerless to slow *Felicity's* new speed.

Her grip upon the wheel's spokes was like iron. Her eyes and ears focused entirely on the path ahead. She'd shoved the siren's song into the back of her mind, ignoring the feathery brushes across her skin and light breath on the back of her neck as best as she could.

She had no way of knowing how much time had passed.

The cries and laughter of her fathers had turned to mourning screams and tearful pleading. They clawed at the night.

Ebba did her best to ignore them as well. But there was one thing she couldn't ignore.

. . . The lanterns' lights were dwindling.

She'd denied it at first, unwilling to let despair overwhelm her, but the length of their beacon had steadily lost ground and now shone light a mere four yards in front of *Felicity*. To leave the helm and refill the lanterns with more fat was out of the question. Yet Ebba had no idea what she'd do when the lanterns ran out of fuel.

A gale ripped through the darkness, and *Felicity* surged forward.

Ebba's eyes widened as she worked to keep her footing.

The siren—as though sensing how close the crew were to meeting their doom—began to shriek her song, abandoning any pretense of grace and elegance.

The creature had remained hidden, but now the magical being rose before Ebba.

Blonde hair flowed to her waist, ruby red lips pulled back in a snarl. Ebba gazed upon the beautiful woman, who had skin of white feathers and the most captivating—

A fist smashed across the right side of her face. Ebba cried out and stumbled to one knee, the pain blinding her.

Did Stubby just hit her? She lifted a hand to clutch her jaw, and the siren giggled a high-pitched musical sound that did not belong in this realm.

The hiss of spray sounded up ahead.

Shite, the ship. Lurching to her feet, Ebba shoved a snarling Stubby aside.

Seawater erupted high into the air in front of the bowsprit.

Ignoring her throbbing jaw and the siren floating in front of her, she pulled right on the wheel with all her might, a harsh cry leaving her lips. *Felicity* groaned, tossing erratically with the sudden shift. The wheel spun faster and faster; Ebba followed it, her hands blurring before her.

The ship dropped into a swell, and she clung to the wheel for dear life, too deathly afraid to make a sound.

A terrible scraping noise came from the starboard side. Eyes round, Ebba could only listen in cold despair as the rocks tore at *Felicity*'s side.

Stubby snapped at her, incoherently. She shoved him away again, but that wasn't going to fix the issue when he was tied to the wheel she had to use. His face twisted into a snarl. His eyes were flooded with black. Had she not been standing next to him this entire time, she might not recognize her own father.

Ebba evaded the erratic swing of his fist, spinning the wheel the other way as spray slapped her in the face.

She couldn't risk Stubby hitting her again. If she lost consciousness, they'd all be victims to the siren's nest.

Ebba ducked down to pick up an oar and stepped closer to Stubby, bringing the flattened end down atop his head.

His eyes rolled back, and he crumpled to the deck in a heap.

She swayed on the spot for a moment, wiping at the blood oozing down her temple. Ebba blinked away the blurriness in her right eye.

At least the siren was gone—though her screaming song still echoed from all directions.

Ebba rested against the wheel, staring at the swell and erupting seawater ahead. Burning hopelessness filled her as her tired green eyes fell upon the weak six-foot shine of light from the lanterns.

She watched, weary beyond measure as the light shrank to three feet.

Then half. . . .

"Someone please wake up." Her voice broke as she called to her fathers.

Tears trickled slowly from her eyes, and horror washed over her like a wave, splitting across her dread like the water on the rocks.

The lanterns flickered.

The flames inside shrank and surged pitifully. And weakened.

And with a final sputter. . . .

The lights went out.

SIXTEEN

Ebba stared into the pitch-black darkness where light had been only seconds before.

Her hands shook so hard she could barely grip the spokes of the wheel.

The light was gone. She didn't know what to do.

The siren's lament rose to a feverish chant, beating at her and disorienting her sense of where the cliff faces were. The cruel bird-like beauty rose before her once more. Ebba's breath coming fast, she grabbed the oar at her feet and swiped it at the siren, screaming. The wood passed through her.

"Bugger off, bird-lady," she snapped, furious. "No one gives a shite a warrior pissed ye off."

The siren screamed and flew at her, jaws wide. Ebba flung up an arm, crying out as talons ripped across her forearm.

She clutched at her arm, searching wildly for the siren, but the creature had disappeared for the moment. Blood seeped between her fingers, and she reached for her tunic to tear off a strip, but a rushing noise had her dropping both arms to her side.

What was that sound?

Stubby reared to her left, his eyes a soulless black and a dagger in his hand.

"Stubby!" she shouted. Where was the damn oar?

The rushing noise grew louder, but Ebba couldn't take her eyes off her possessed father.

There was a loud pinging sound behind Stubby, and her eyes rounded as the boom—broken free of its restraints—careened toward them. Ebba winced as it smacked into the back of his head. He fell to his knees and Ebba ducked as the boom bowled past to the port side.

Stubby swayed, his black eyes closing as he slumped unconscious against the deck.

How did the boom get free?

The rushing noise had grown to overwhelming levels, overriding even the siren's song.

Abandoning the helm, she raced to the bulwark and stared over. So far, the ocean's current had pushed *Felicity* through the cliff passage littered with jagged rocks.

Not anymore.

Time seemed to stop as *Felicity*'s bow jutted off the edge of a waterfall into thin air. *A waterfall!* Ebba couldn't see the bottom of the black drop, but could hear the water pounding far below. How was it possible for a waterfall to be in the middle of the ocean? Her fathers would have mentioned it to her if they'd known. So where had the drop come from? Was this magic, too?

Felicity groaned and Ebba sprinted for the port rigging and weaved her arms and legs through the squares, clinging on for dear life, hoping her fathers were secure enough.

The ship hovered for an age at the precipice of the waterfall, before—with a deep groan from *Felicity*'s hull—the ship tilted forward, inch by inch.

Ebba knew with horrible certainty the ship would soon tilt over the edge. But not knowing what came next was worse; how far would they fall? Into what? Would the ship and the crew survive? The fear-laden questions raced through her mind as the ship whined, finally leaning out past the point of no return.

Felicity began to free-fall, and Ebba's gut surged from her feet to her mouth.

Ebba squeezed her eyes shut as the wind tore past her, whipping her dreads in disarray. *Felicity* slanted as they fell, and soon the ship was completely vertical. They were plummeting to their doom face-first. Would *Felicity*'s bow split upon impact? Would the knotted ropes holding her fathers to the ship withstand the jolt at the bottom?

"Hold on!" she screamed, hoping some deep recess in her fathers' minds might register her warning.

Wood shrieked, air rushed through her ears, and there was a mighty crack as *Felicity* plunged into water, submerging the entire deck and its crew.

Ebba was ripped from the rigging.

She flailed under the water, thrashing for the surface. White bubbles blocked her view; her clothing and weapons dragged her down. Solid ground came up to meet her from underneath—the deck!

Her lungs threatened to explode. Black shadows began to dot her vision, just as the ship burst through out of the water in a massive roar.

Ebba was flung against the wheel before rolling back to rest at the rear of the stern.

She lay on her back, gasping for breath, too stunned to react as water poured from *Felicity*'s deck out of the scuppers.

Coughing, she rose onto all fours and peered under her arm at Stubby. Flat on his back. Still.

Clutching her right side, Ebba crawled to her father and rolled him onto his side, thumping him on his back until he coughed up water. He didn't regain consciousness, but he was breathing.

She rested against the wheel, listening as the rush of the waterfall began to fade behind them. The siren's wail had died off for now. Ebba glanced up, trying to gain her bearings.

The waterfall had dropped them into some kind of cavern. A big one, judging by the way the sound of the hammering water was echoing in the space. The current that had pushed them through the cliff passages at the top of the fall was still here. She could feel its tug under the ship.

Which meant there was no time to rest. She had no idea how long they'd be in this cavern or if there was another magical booby trap waiting ahead.

Ebba needed to move.

She groaned and rose to stand. First priority: checking on her fathers and Cosmo. Without them, there wasn't any point. She left the helm and stumbled to the mast. Plank's eyes were open, his chest rising and falling. A quick search told her he wasn't bleeding.

She staggered on to the main deck. Peg-leg was—amazingly—still standing and staring up at the waterfall, presumably where the siren sat.

Would the siren wait to see if the crew were dead, or alive before resuming her call?

Taking a wide berth around Peg-leg, Ebba hurried to the bow.

Barrels and Locks would've suffered the worst impact. Sure enough, both lay still. Locks was unconscious, his eye patch sitting askew, but breathing. Barrels, however, had a wide gash in his shoulder and was neither breathing, nor conscious. She rolled him and thumped him, like she had with Stubby, to no avail.

She listened to his chest. His ticker was still going. Just. Why wasn't he breathing? Deliberating for a brief moment, she wound up her arm and socked him in the gut.

Barrels projectile vomited across the deck.

Ebba reached over to pat him on the back as he choked.

She tore off her sash, shucking the weapons from it, and tied it tightly around his bleeding shoulder.

It would have to do.

She stared at the splintered front of the ship as she knotted the silk tight. The bowsprit was gone, explaining the intense splitting noise she'd heard upon impact.

Were they taking on water below?

Ebba hovered, unsure if she had time to search the hull.

. . . Just a quick look. Ebba jumped down to the main deck, pressing an arm into her side, and ripped open the bilge door.

She shrieked at the sight of Cosmo standing there, his eyes flooded with black. Ebba slammed the bilge door closed, wincing as a series of thuds from the other side told her the possessed servant had tumbled down the ladder.

Opening the door again, she strained her ears for any sound of water rushing below.

. . . Nothing. If there was a leak, it wasn't major . . . *yet.*

As Cosmo moved to climb the ladder once more, Ebba slammed the door, ensuring it was secure, and headed back to the helm as fast as she could. Normal Cosmo was no threat. A snarling Cosmo with black eyes was friggin' terrifying. One more unspeakable terror on top of the terror that clutched her tight in its grip.

But she couldn't think about the darkness again and the rocks.

She snapped to a standstill. Shite! The lanterns! She should've been filling the damn lanterns. But Barrels hadn't been breathing. Ebba's chest rose and fell. There wasn't even a bowsprit to hang the lanterns from anymore. The plunge from the waterfall had snapped it clean off.

Her mind spun on the verge of panic.

Grubby! She'd forgotten about him.

Her eyes searched the crow's nest. Where was—? There! Relief coursed through her. He'd been thrown over the side, but swung by the rope around his waist.

It'd have to do for now.

Ebba returned to the helm, swiping Stubby's weapons and tucking them in her own belt. She wound the two yards of free rope around his legs, so the man wouldn't be able to stand and attack her if he regained consciousness again.

She could barely hear the waterfall now, but the sudden hiss of spray ahead was as dreadful to Ebba as the siren's lament. The walls of the cavern were narrowing into the cliff passages she'd sailed through before the waterfall.

There were another two days left until the end. And she had no lanterns to guide her.

The despair in her chest widened and her hope began to dim.

To flicker.

To darken like the slick walls that would be the tomb of *Felicity*'s crew because she'd failed.

She jolted, screaming as three blaring beacons erupted before the ship, and threw up an arm to shield her face.

Nothing happened.

Eyes watering, she peered over her arm.

Ebba could make out three white lights. The glowing circles flared where the ship's bowsprit had been before, exactly where the lanterns had been placed. The beacons floated in thin air, illuminating much more of the rocky path ahead than the weak lanterns had done. Where had they come from?

Ebba whirled to look behind her at a soft chittering sound.

She stared, mouth ajar as a tiny, winged creature, *several* of them, pulled the boom back to where the sheet holding it firm had snapped just in time to stop Stubby from knifing her. . . . Then before her eyes, two creatures held the severed ends together and, with a burst of white light, fixed the sheet to hold the boom in place.

Magic.

The creatures took up position at the bow while another of the winged beings hovered in front of the wheel. The creatures at the bow chittered, and the one in front of her nodded curtly, then waved her hand in front of Ebba's face, pointing urgently to the left.

Not quite believing this wasn't an effect of being hit in the head several times, Ebba spun the wheel left. "Enough?" she croaked.

The creature chittered over her shoulder, waiting for a reply, then shook her head, pointing left again. Ebba swallowed and spun the wheel more. A minute later, *Felicity* sailed past a jagged rock extending two yards above the rolling water.

Ebba wavered on the spot, bloodied, battered, and tired from fear and lack of sleep, and the creature surged forward, slapping her several times in the face.

They'd just sailed over a magical waterfall to escape a vengeful bird stuck in a beautiful woman's body, and now tiny winged creatures were lighting the way. Ebba's mind threatened to explode with the unknown. But she blinked several times, regulating her breathing through sheer determination. No matter what Sherry or Cosmo thought, Ebba was never happier to have experience in forcing away a torrent of unanswered questions attacking her mind than in that moment. She forced the last dregs of her frenzied panic aside to focus on the task at hand.

She was going to save her fathers.

The siren's lament filled the dark cavern again and Ebba gritted her teeth, steadying herself. She tightened her grip upon the splintered spokes of *Felicity*'s helm.

And as one of the winged creatures perched on her shoulder, hope flickered within her, the tiniest bit stronger than before.

SEVENTEEN

She wasn't in her hammock. She knew because no hammock, especially not hers, had ever felt so uncomfortable in her life. That was until Ebba shifted and discovered the pain wasn't from the hammock, but from her body. She groaned deeply, unsure whether to clutch her head, or her ribs. Actually, raising her arm might be impossible right now.

"Try to stay still, Ebba-Viva," whispered a deep voice.

Locks.

Ebba was glad he was okay. She frowned. Why wouldn't he be?

Somehow she convinced her eyes to open. Focusing her blurry vision was another matter again. Finally, the sleeping quarters of *Felicity* came into view, as did the very concerned faces of five of her fathers and Cosmo.

Something didn't add up. *Darkness. Rushing water.*

"The siren," she said hollowly.

Plank nodded, his face tight. “Aye, little nymph. Do ye remember any o’ it?”

Did she remember Stubby’s black eyes and the terrible beauty of the siren hovering before her? Her eyes fell to her bandaged forearm. Did she remember the siren’s talons sinking into her flesh? The terror of falling and crashing into the unknown? The horror of thinking she might die alone, or lose her fathers? Did she remember the winged creatures who helped her?

Aye, she did. She remembered it all in vivid, horrible detail.

Ebba swallowed. “I don’t wish to speak o’ it yet,” she said quietly.

Locks’ emerald eye regarded her, though he didn’t comment. “Aye, lass. We can understand that.” He leaned over and picked up her hand, kissing the back of it. “We be here with ye now, and we’re all right. Pillage be a scant spooked and isn’t leavin’ the hold just yet, but he’ll be fine in time.”

“Where are we?” she asked, her throat burning as she forced the words out.

Cosmo appeared with a goblet of grog.

Peg-leg snatched it from him and held her head up, trickling the liquid carefully into her mouth.

“Less than an hour from Portum, but with two days of repairs to make before we can set sail again,” answered Barrels. “You got us through, my dear. None of us recall anything after the morning of the second day. Not until we woke on the other side of Syraness, bloodied and confused, yesterday morning.”

“Ye were still behind the helm,” Grubby’s voice cracked.

Locks gripped his shoulder and turned back to her. “Ye were at that, lass. Ye wouldn’t speak. Ye just stared ahead, adjustin’ the helm as needed. Ye clutched to the wheel so tight, it took four o’ us to remove yer hands from it.”

Ebba's eyes filled as she stared down at her bandaged fingers and palms.

"Took a while to get all the splinters out," Plank said softly. "As soon as we took ye from the helm, ye collapsed."

Peg-leg sniffed, blinking furiously. "And no wonder, awake three nights and two days straight, workin' a ship by herself through who knows what. No food or drink in her." He cut off and busied himself retying her bandage.

That wasn't strictly true. The tiny glowing creatures had brought her some grog.

A tear dripped down her face, rolling down her neck. Grubby caught it on his finger and kissed her cheek.

"Where's Stubby?" she asked.

Plank avoided her eyes. "Stubby's. . . ."

"He's okay?" she blurted.

"Aye, Ebba. He's fine and well."

She crumpled in relief.

"Considerin' the bruises on his noggin'," Plank finished. "He's makin' repairs on the ship. Ye know him. He's in a tizz because *Felicity* be banged up."

She grimaced. "How much damage?"

"Gouges down the starboard side." Peg-leg ticked off on his hand. "Few minor leaks in the hull. Torn sails and riggin'. The helm will need to be replaced. And the bowsprit looks like it ripped right off."

"That happened when we fell down the waterfall," Ebba forced herself to admit as her mind catapulted back to the dark free fall.

Cosmo broke the stunned silence. "*A waterfall?*"

Ebba looked at him squarely, noting the cut on his chin. "The ship hit the water straight on her head," she whispered. "The whole ship went under for a few seconds."

"Lass," Stubby said quietly. "Many a ship has sailed through Syraness. And none have ever mentioned a waterfall."

"Did they mention a siren?" Plank countered.

A shiver wracked through her and Ebba jerked her head to Barrels' shoulder. "That's how ye got that cut on yer shoulder. Ye weren't breathin' after we hit the bottom of the waterfall; neither was Stubby." Her voice stuttered to a halt.

Peg-leg sniffed again behind her.

Locks lay a heavy hand on her shoulder and she looked into his eye. Without a word, he lifted the bottom of his shirt to reveal the worst rope burn Ebba had ever seen. The skin was beyond rubbed raw; it appeared as though blood had poured freely from the wound encircling his waist, and likely his back. Not only that, ugly purple bruises spanned a hand-width either side of where the rope had sat.

He dropped his shirt. "I can't imagine what kind o' animals we turned into, lass. Ye faced the darkness in Syraness, and ye brought us through the other side. None o' us can imagine what ye went through, but ye have our gratitude, Ebba-Viva, for not givin' in to the evil singing bitch."

Ebba attempted a smile, but winced as her top lip cracked.

Locks dashed a finger under his blazing eye. "Don't speak o' it until ye be well and ready. We'll be here when ye wish to. *If* ye wish to. Ye know we won't make a fuss." He squeezed her wrist just above the bandages and muttered something about going to help Stubby.

The others moved away, each adding a stroke of the hair and kiss of the forehead or cheek. By the end, Ebba's eyes burned with suppressed tears.

"Little nymph?" Plank called back.

She lolled her head to the side to see him.

"Stubby be feelin' pretty guilty right now. Didn't take much to put two and two together, with yer black eye and him stripped o' weapons and trussed up like a pork roast. We don't expect ye out on deck until ye're ready, but a kind word when he makes it down to see ye wouldn't go amiss."

Ebba stared after him as he climbed the ladder.

One person remained.

He spoke softly from her other side, "I can leave you alone to rest, if you wish."

Fear, still ice-cold, stirred deep within her. "Alone?" she asked. "Nay, I don't wish to be alone, Cosmo."

"Thank goodness, because I really do flop around like a fish on deck."

His comment startled a laugh from her. She clutched at her ribs in agony and turned to face him.

Cosmo grimaced, appearing stricken. "I take it I shouldn't attempt to make you laugh."

Ebba breathed through the cloud of pain. "Nay, thank ye. Not for another week at least." She smiled to take the sting from her words.

Cosmo shifted his stool closer to the post by her feet, and leaned back against the post, watching her. "To tell you the truth, I have learned several things in the last few days. Though I highly doubt your fathers would have asked for my help had you been fit and . . . well, conscious."

She blinked sleepily. "Poor Cosmo. What did they make ye do?"

"They gave me a few things to choose from. After seeing you scuttle up the ropes with such ease, I elected to climb the riggings."

She snorted softly.

"I quickly came to understand that I have a crippling—and previously untested—fear of climbing ropes while at sea. The ropes cut into my feet for starters. I fear you may be correct about my softness. The farther up I got, the harder it was to hold my body to the ropes. Not to mention the pitch of the ship. I went up about two yards and came back down, swearing I'd never be so foolish again."

Ebba chuckled under her breath, painfully.

"After that, I attempted to help repair the sail and was banished by Grubby himself."

"Grubby couldn't banish plankton," she said, disbelieving.

Cosmo shrugged, a small smile playing on his lips. "Yes, well. He did so with many a pat on the shoulder, but banish me he did."

Ebba pressed a hand to her side and gave in to laughter. Nothing had ever hurt so much, nor felt so good. She gasped as the amusement shaking her body dissipated. "We might make a pirate o' ye yet."

A shadow flickered through his amber eyes. "If we had more time, perhaps you could, but even with two days lost to patch *Felicity* up, we'll reach the treasure not long after. Then it won't be long until your crew deposit me at Kentro."

"So ye'll return to Exosia and find more slave-lubber work? Ye could always stay here with us."

He stared past her to the inside of the ship's hull and sighed heavily. "Unfortunately, I must return."

"Ye have family?"

"Two sisters, and a father who needs me, though he'll never admit it."

Disappointment twanged within her, yet she couldn't argue with Cosmo's decision. Family came first. "I'm sure he misses ye."

Cosmo drew to his feet and leaned over to right her tattered woolen blanket. "Perhaps, though he has not wielded truth in his hands for a long time. I'll leave you to rest, Ebba-Viva. And not stir you up with any more laughter, or use you as an excuse to avoid your terrifying fathers."

Locks must have put something into the grog she drank. Suddenly, she was extremely comfortable.

Ebba snuggled deeper into the hammock. "They ain't terrifying, Cosmo. It's naught but smoke and airs." She sighed. "Just smoke and airs."

"Sleep well, Mistress Fairisles," he said.

Warm lips pressed against her forehead as she surrendered to sleep.

EBBA PULLED HERSELF UP, using the side of the hammock as leverage. Her battered body ached, made worse for all the lying about, she was sure. She'd slept for two days after they pried her from the helm, and another day must have passed since she woke yesterday.

In slow movements—because she couldn't manage anything else—Ebba changed into her last set of clean clothes. She reached behind to run a hand down the strands of beads in her dreads, lingering on them with an odd heaviness in her chest. Her fingers trailed over the new strand containing two beads, and she twisted them both.

Ebba still had her fathers. She still had her beads. *Felicity* still had her figurehead. Everything else would be okay.

She released a shaky breath, listening to the shouts and calls of her fathers above.

Hobbling to the hold, she chewed carefully on some slices of mango Peg-leg had arranged in a smiley face for her as though she was five years old. The gesture brought a small smile to her face, though, so maybe part of her was five and always would be five. The rest of her felt unaccountably old after Syraness.

Ebba downed three goblets of the watered-down grog to take the edge off her thirst.

Making it up the ladder took longer than she liked, but eventually Ebba pushed open the bilge door and blinked into the stark brightness of the cloudless sky. Her heart squeezed tight at the sight of the sun.

"I forgot to tell ye," Plank called from the bulwark. "We passed some wind sprites the day after Syraness."

Ebba crossed the deck to him. The sea's calm had returned, as had the tropical, aqua blue she was accustomed to.

"What're wind sprites?" she asked.

"Little white, winged creatures they were. Flittered around the bilge door for an age. We didn't dare to draw close to them, though they seemed harmless enough."

Her tiny helpers had a name. "What be the legends o' them, Plank?"

Plank pressed his lips together for a moment. "All I know is they haunt places where the sea has claimed many lives."

Ebba frowned. That didn't seem to fit with the creatures she'd seen. They'd saved *Felicity*.

"I don't think that be true," she said. "I think they linger in those places in the hopes they can be helpin' people against dark creatures."

Plank glanced at her. "Aye, little nymph. Ye may be right at that. Ye may be right."

Though the thought of peering out across an endless, *rock-less* sea beckoned her to the crow's nest, the rigging was out of the question with her injuries. Ebba held up a hand to her eyes and scanned the sparkling ocean from the deck instead.

A darting movement caught her eye, and she watched as Stubby ducked behind the helm.

Plank shook his head before busying himself.

Crossing the deck, Ebba stared down at Stubby's light-gray curls. He was focused intently on the hammer in his hand, studiously ignoring her. Without a word, she bent and wrapped both her arms around his stomach, careful to avoid the rope burn and bruises she knew would be there.

"I love ye, Stubby," she said.

A choking noise passed over her head, and his arms rose to encircle her. "I love ye, too, my Ebba-Viva. And I'm so stinkin' sorry to have hurt ye."

A lump rose in her throat. "Ye didn't hurt me, Stubby," she lied glibly. "As soon as yer eyes went black, I took yer weapons and wrapped ye in rope, knowin' ye weren't in yer right mind."

The form in her arms stilled. "Did ye? But what about yer eye?"

She pulled her head back and looked into his soft eyes. *His* eyes—no black remained. The monster in the siren's nest was a person possessed by a twisted creature. Stubby couldn't be blamed for his actions then. The fact he'd hurt her would eat away at him inside. Her decision to tell her fathers about Pockmark's plunder had caused enough harm without adding that to the list.

"It happened when we fell over the waterfall and hit the water." She shifted her eyes to an oar leaning against the stern. "The butt of an oar whacked me one, I think. Hard to know, it all happened so quick-like."

Stubby lifted an arm and rubbed his face. "I think it caught me, too." He rubbed the back of his head. "And somethin' else, by the feel."

She kissed his cheek. "Aye, the boom sprang free. So stop tryin' to hide from me; this ship be far too small for that."

Stubby shooed her away, eyes glistening.

Cosmo swabbed the deck alongside Grubby, and Ebba settled atop a barrel, watching everyone go about their work. A part of her couldn't believe they were all here, alive and in one piece. She just had to keep it that way.

"Plank," she called. "How far is *Malice* behind us now?" They'd anchored for two days to make repairs, after all.

"Two days, if we be lucky," he replied after a moment.

Ebba's chest tightened. "And if we ain't?"

"If they've had a fair wind, *Malice* could only be a day away."

EIGHTEEN

"Portum ahoy," she yelled from the crow's nest, clutching her side. Climbing up here had taken a while, but the pain was worth the few hours of solitude as the final repairs were made and they set sail again.

She waited for a tendril of excitement to find her as it had in the past, but if the emotion was there, the fog of foreboding surrounding her was too thick to penetrate.

Ebba edged over the side of the crow's nest, feet searching for the rigging below. Locks said the pain in her ribs would take a few weeks to go away. Certainly felt like it. She reached the bottom, and relief flooded through her torso as she lowered her arms.

"Do ye need somethin', Ebba?" Stubby asked.

Peg-leg popped his head around the mast. "I can get it."

"I'm headed down to the hold." Plank patted the air above her head, not quite touching her as he passed. "I'll get ye a snack."

Peg-leg and Stubby scowled at him and turned back to their work.

Ebba sighed, catching Cosmo's eye as he sat reading a book on deck, an unconcealed grin on his face.

"I think they'll be doing that for a while yet," he said, warm eyes glinting.

Ebba groaned, cutting off the sound when Stubby threw her a concerned glance.

"A tad overprotective, aren't they?" Cosmo observed.

Aye. Far more than the average seventeen-year-old, but maybe Sherry was right and they were just six times as protective as one father would be. She shrugged. "Dunno. I guess. That's just how parents are s'posed to be, mayhaps."

A tinge of hurt entered Cosmo's amber eyes. He stared down at his book—one of Barrels', she assumed. A curious smile lifted the corner of his mouth, and he raised his head to look at her. "You know, Ebba-Viva, just when I decide you're the most light-hearted, carefree pirate in the Free Seas, you come out with a bit of age-old wisdom."

She snorted, though the compliment sent a foreign spark through her chest. "What seaweed are ye smokin', Cosmo?" She heckled Plank, who'd returned from the bilge, "Oi, Plank, Cosmo was just callin' me wise!"

Plank's eyes narrowed on Cosmo. "Did he?"

Cosmo stuttered, "Yes. Your crew have taught her much about the seas and sailing, that I-I. . . ."

Ebba cast him a curious glance. "That ain't what we were talkin' o'."

Plank didn't take his eyes off the younger man. Without another word, Cosmo became suddenly occupied by his book and wandered away.

Ebba followed Plank. "Why are ye scarin' him off?" she asked. "I've never had a friend afore." She liked Cosmo. In fact, she could still feel exactly where he'd pressed a kiss to her forehead the other day. Ebba wasn't quite sure what to do with that knowledge.

"We're yer friends," he answered.

"One my age."

"Aye, Ebba. Except ye're a beautiful young wom—uh, pirate."

The woman-female subject was cropping up far too much of late. Fear twisted her gut. Should she be worried? "What's yer point, matey?"

Plank met her gaze and then quailed. "No point."

Silently, Ebba could acknowledge what he was trying to say. Plank meant that Cosmo might want more than friendship. Ebba wasn't clueless. They'd left her at a *brothel* when they abandoned her—some things couldn't be unseen or forgotten.

Sure, Cosmo was attractive; she liked his amber eyes, and enjoyed spending time with him. But he couldn't take anything more than she was willing to give, and Ebba wasn't willing to return a deeper regard. She loved being a pirate and sailing the seas. She didn't just do those things out of fear her fathers would leave again. Ebba was too busy for things like *regard.* And even after recent happenings, and especially after the uncomfortable regularity of the current subject, she couldn't see her status changing.

Ebba watched Plank curiously.

When they docked, multitudes of women threw themselves at him and got no response. It wasn't that Plank didn't like the female attention; it was more that he didn't see them at all. Ladon's words on the mountain of Neos came back to her, the ones about the pirate murdering Plank's wife. For the first time, Ebba wondered if his avoidance of women was more purposeful than she'd realized.

Their days after defeating Ladon hadn't exactly allowed time for Ebba to ask who Mutinous Cannon was, and what he meant to her fathers. She'd never seen her fathers so vacant as when they heard Ladon's final, cruel riddle. Not even when they'd heard the siren's song. The siren turned them into monsters, but when Ladon had taunted them, it was like they'd each had to fight a demon only they could see.

Honestly, fear stopped her. Fear over what they'd tell her. And fear because if she defied the second ship law to ask her fathers *why,* then that opened the door for them to ask her questions. Ebba was realizing there were a whole heap of questions about herself that she didn't have answers to. *One* day she'd ask her fathers about Mutinous Cannon, but not today. At least not until Syraness was a bad memory—which it didn't seem in a hurry to be.

The distance between *Felicity* and Portum narrowed, and soon *Felicity* was carrying them around the shores of the long, flat island.

Stubby directed them into a shallow cove at the northern end. "We'll be screened from other ships here," he said.

No one answered, knowing he referred to *Malice*.

Ebba crossed to the rowboat to help lower it, but Grubby rushed in front of her and took her usual place with a smile and a pat.

Glaring Cosmo's way at his obvious amusement, she sat out of the way and waited for the boat to lower.

"Ye sure ye'd not prefer to stay aboard?" Locks asked gently.

"Nay," she answered. They'd nearly died enough times getting to this treasure. A sea of manta rays couldn't keep her from it now, even though they were fierce bad luck.

Locks backed away, arms raised defensively.

After a small debate, the whole crew decided to go. Only Pockmark and his crew would be in this part of the Free Seas, and *Malice* was two days behind them.

"Damn rays." Locks pushed a manta ray away with the end of the oar as they settled into the rowboat.

Ebba's eyes fell on the ray and her scalp prickled.

Doesn't mean anything. Just a harmless manta ray.

They heaved to the shore and everyone leaped out when the bottom scraped on the shingled beach—except Barrels, who didn't like getting his buckled shoes wet. Ebba stayed in this time, too, waiting as Locks tethered the rowboat to a large rock. She was as likely to make a fool of herself leaping out as not with injured ribs.

Cosmo took her elbow and helped her step out onto a rock.

Peg-leg snickered as Barrels jumped out and landed straight in a shallow rock pool. Ebba grinned as well, and then set her eyes upon Portum.

Rocky coastline met her searching gaze; ten paces of the shingled shore were exposed. The shallow bay was bordered by a crescent of solid rock taller than Plank, and it appeared as though the waves and saltwater had taken large chunks of the rock away over the years.

"The cave be on the far northern side," Stubby said, voice grim. His face screwed up. Clearly, he was remembering eating the mountain apple.

Locks studied the island. "It ain't big. I think we should split in two. One goes on land, and one goes around the shore."

Ebba stiffened. She didn't like that idea.

"It be this way," Grubby said suddenly.

The crew stared at him mutely. He pointed along the shoreline—north.

Stubby and Barrels exchanged a long look.

"And how are ye knowin' that, Grubs?" Stubby asked in a neutral voice.

Grubby stared at his booted foot. The sole was coming away at the toe and water seeped in. He shrugged. "I dunno. But it be that way."

He pointed north again.

Peg-leg cursed under his breath. "Well, seems we'll be followin' Grubby's nose."

Barrels stared at Grubby's foot in the water. "Or his toe."

Cosmo drew close, whispering in her ear, "You're seriously following him? Just like that?"

"'Course. He says he knows, then he knows," she replied, checking her pistols were in place. Grubby could swim as fast as a dolphin. He had an affinity for water that their crew trusted implicitly, even if he wasn't all there in other aspects. And sure, his *toe* had never acted as a navigational tool, and maybe he professed to speak to marine life, but she also knew it wouldn't occur to her father to say he knew the way unless he actually did.

"But *how* does he know?"

Stubby laughed. "Exosian folk. Always questionin' everythin'."

"Some things just are," Locks explained. "Knowin' why doesn't change that Grub's toe knows where to go, does it? Why waste time when ye can't possibly find a reason for it?"

Cosmo didn't appear convinced. He turned to Barrels. "Doesn't this come across as odd to you?"

The crew muffled snickers.

Barrels' face turned pink. "Why yes, Cosmo. I certainly used to question these kinds of things. But I've found that the reason often turns up in time. Life at sea—" He paused as though searching for the right words. "You begin to understand not everything has a logical answer."

"Esp'cially the things we've seen in the last week," Ebba added.

Cosmo frowned. "I haven't seen anything."

Ebba stilled. "What about Ladon and the siren?"

"I wasn't there for Ladon, and apparently not myself for the second. I'm sure something did happen, though—I had a lump on my head, after all. And then your crew said the wind sprites were on deck, but I was—"

"Out with the fairies," supplied Locks.

Ebba faced Cosmo, her gaze narrowing. "Ye don't believe any o' it happened?"

Cosmo avoided her eyes. "That's not what I'm saying. Just that I haven't seen these things myself."

She heard the lie in his voice. Blood flooded into her face. She wasn't making the siren up! She gave him a dark scowl, but tempered her urge to whack him around the noggin' by remembering he was ignorant about most important things. "Ye think I made up fallin' down a waterfall and the siren? Ye don't think we saw a lizard-beast with snakes around its neck? How did we know where to find the treasure *Malice* is after if Stubby didn't eat the magic apple? And how did the bowsprit snap clean off? Ye think *I* did that?"

He took a step back and lowered his voice. "Ebba, I'm not saying I don't believe you."

"It sure be soundin' that way," she muttered, stalking ahead to join Grubby and his toe at the fore.

"Best leave her for now. Her temper is quick, but quickly forgotten," Barrels said behind her.

"I didn't mean—"

Peg-leg interrupted. "Aye, lad, ye did. But, like we said, some folk can't believe until they be seein'. And ye be one o' them."

They trudged around three small coves until, rounding a fourth jutting point, they spotted a rocky outcrop extending straight north. The tip slowly tapered off into the ocean.

“That be the northern end o’ Portum, lads,” Stubby announced.

“Aye,” Ebba echoed with the others.

Cosmo came up beside her, searching her face.

She knew his comment had only affected her so much because she hadn’t fully gotten her head around Syraness yet. But someone doubting what she’d gone through *had* set off her temper.

Ebba let out a breath and flashed a small smile at him.

He smiled back, squeezing her hand briefly. She frowned at the tingling in her fingers afterward.

Grubby kept walking, head down and one foot in the ocean at all times.

They trailed after him, and watched in bafflement as he marched another fifty yards and turned abruptly to face inland. From there he strode with huge steps across the broken shell and pebbled shore to the rock wall outlining the cove.

Ebba jogged in his wake, craning to peer ahead. She frowned; only solid rock sat ahead. That is, it *seemed* to be solid rock, before Grubby dug at the base of the rocky cliff and revealed a small hole.

“Grubs,” she breathed. “Ye found it.”

Ebba fell to her knees to help him dig, ignoring the ache in her side.

“What is it?” Cosmo said behind her.

“Grubby found the hidden cave . . . with his toe,” Barrels echoed in a faint voice.

“’Course he did,” Plank said. “Never doubted him.”

Locks snorted.

The eight of them made quick work digging a hole at the base of the cliff. Soon the hole was large enough for a person to descend into the tunnel. Though sand concealed the entrance, none of the granules actually fell into the cave itself—a fact that had Barrels muttering to himself about the lack of science and Plank muttering about the presence of magic.

The muscles in her legs coiled as she prepared to slide down the steep sandy incline into the black rock cave.

"Wait," Plank called, catching her arm.

She stopped, glancing back.

"The tide," he nodded toward the sea. "It'll be high in an hour."

"If we don't go now, we'll have another half a day to wait until we can enter again," Barrels said.

Stubby said, "We may still be a day ahead o' *Malice* if the wind was weak on the Kentro coast, but we can't count on that. We ain't got time to wait around. We need to be in and out of the cave, smart-like."

"Nothin' could possibly go wrong with that," Locks muttered, reaching up to adjust his eye patch.

Stubby nudged Ebba aside and bent to sit on the sand, sliding down into the cave ahead of her.

She slithered down after, blinking into the dark as her eyes adjusted.

A match flared behind her, illuminating Barrels' face. He lit a lantern and passed it to Stubby, and then passed another to Locks, keeping a third for himself.

Stubby held his lantern high and the soft light of the flames within bounced off the cave walls in all directions. Quartz sparkled in the solid gray stone and a seam of rusty-colored stone traveled directly through the middle of the ceiling, pointing ahead.

"One hour," Peg-leg reminded them.

They set off.

Whatever Ebba's sentiments before entering the cave, she was relieved to find excitement flooding through her again as they hurried along the tunnel. Navigating a hidden cave with her fathers in search of a coveted treasure? This was the quest she'd longed for, but it struck her that maybe adventure went hand-in-hand with trial too. If it was all sunshine and mangoes, everyone would go embark on these kinds of quests, and then brave deeds and stories recited in the light of the full moon wouldn't hold the same weight.

"Ye're kickin' sand in my boots." Stubby scowled at her.

She straightened and slowed her pace.

The stalagmites grew thicker and longer as they moved farther into the cave's depths. Drips of water trickled from their tips, forming puddles on the rocky ground. *Felicity*'s crew squeezed between narrow spaces in the tight path.

"Hold on, mateys," called Peg-leg from near the back. He was wedged between two stalactites.

Barrels sighed. "You need to lay off the mangoes, dear fellow. Cosmo? If you push him, I'll pull."

"All right," Cosmo said in a strangled voice.

Ebba grinned at a nudge from Stubby, whose own face was red from the effort not to laugh.

Peg-leg slid free and his tight voice echoed up to them, "Not one peep from any o' ye or I'll serve charcoal for a month."

Heeding his warning, the crew resumed their hike without comment.

"It's beautiful," whispered Ebba, admiring the way the light from their lanterns caught at the shiny pieces in the gray walls.

The temperature dropped as they moved deeper, and tiny straws hung from the ceiling—the first sign of the rock growing downward into spikes.

Stubby swung his lantern. “Sumpin’ up ahead,” he mumbled. With his other hand, he drew a pistol, leaving it uncocked.

Ebba kept both hands on her pistols in readiness. After lizard-snakey-beast and bird-woman, who knew what waited for them in the depths of this cave. She peered over Stubby’s shoulder, but couldn’t see past the lantern light.

“What is it?” she asked.

“The cavern opens up. Looks like there be light.”

She inhaled sharply and tightened the grip on her pistol butts.

No one behind her—not even Cosmo— made a peep.

The cold tightened until Ebba could see her breath fogging in front of her. The high ceiling of the narrow passage slowly widened and the rocky floor smoothed and flattened.

Stubby jerked to a halt in front of her and she barely avoided colliding with him. She crept beside him.

The circular cavern was bare, but for a sole stone pedestal sitting upon a raised platform at its center. A thin beam of light illuminated the pedestal from above.

Stubby scratched his chin.

“What?” Ebba asked him.

He ignored her. “Ye ever seen a treasure arranged all nice and easy like this, lads?” he asked.

There were riches up there? The beam of light shining through the hole in the ceiling created a golden aura Ebba couldn’t see through.

“Nay.” Locks came to stand on his other side. “I reckon treasure norma’ly be buried six-foot-deep and surrounded by booby traps.”

Ebba swung her head to look at him. “Ye’ve searched for plunder afore?”

Locks let out a breath he'd held. "Aye, lass. Just once, or twice."

She narrowed her eyes. He met her gaze with an innocent expression.

Stubby glared at the pedestal as though it held a secret. "Barrels," he said. "What do ye think?"

Barrels cleared his throat from behind them. "It seems very . . . pleasantly situated. However, we must take into account the entrance to the cave was hidden. Maybe the pirates who hid this believed the treasure to be safe, tucked away in Portum as it is. Portum is a place surrounded by dangers, known of by few, and explored by fewer."

Ebba glanced at the blaring gold aura again, and then back at her fathers as she took a step forward. "It's just there," she said. "Why don't we grab it?" She very much wanted to know what *it* was after all the trouble.

Peg-leg hauled her back and shoved Cosmo forward with his other arm. "Send this one."

Cosmo's amber irises widened and he squeaked.

Ebba and the others watched him.

"Y-you can't be serious?" he said, looking around the group for a speck of mercy.

Locks hummed to himself and Cosmo took a step away from the pirate.

He *did* appear menacing with his eye patch. The light from the lantern made the splinters of emerald in his sole eye swim like fish.

The pirates closed in on the prince's servant, sealing the gaps between them.

"Ebba?" Cosmo choked. He backed away, leaping when Grubby reached out to grab him.

The pirates stopped.

Cosmo whirled around in their trap, hands raised.

Ebba caught Peg-leg's eye and couldn't hold it anymore. With a wheeze, she leaned over and slapped her hand on her thigh, gasping with laughter. Her fathers joined in, while Cosmo stood there, obviously unsure of his fate.

Barrels wiped his eyes with a handkerchief and spoke, "You know, we don't really have time to dally."

Peg-leg gave a last throaty chuckle. "Don't ye be gripin'. Ye were in on it, too."

Barrels erupted in hoots again.

"Are you sure this is the treasure?" a voice called.

Felicity's crew froze and spun to face the pedestal as one.

Cosmo stood on the raised stone circle in front of the pedestal, his brows arched in challenge. He held a cylinder in the air. The device was the color of tarnished silver. And . . . small.

That's it? Where was the chest of ancient coins and priceless gems?

"Blimey, boy. Get yerself down from there. We were only jokin'," Plank scolded him, searching the ceiling for movement.

Cosmo remained where he was.

Ebba grinned—Cosmo wasn't used to having the micky taken out of him. She heaved herself up to join him, the others close behind her. They gathered around Cosmo and stared at the object in his hand.

An odd barking sound came out of Grubby's mouth.

Ebba cast him a look. "Grubs . . . have ye been eatin' garlic cloves again? Ye know they always come back up."

Grubby shook his head, meeting her eyes fearfully.

He made the barking sound again. Ebba frowned—weirdest belch she'd ever heard. "We should get that checked out."

Locks grabbed her arm. “Did ye hear that?”

Ebba nodded. “Aye, Grubby’s—”

“Not Grubby,” he hissed. “*Listen.*”

Ebba closed her eyes and strained her ears.

A slapping sound, like a wet shirt hit on the side of a ship, was coming from the tunnel. The noise was drawing closer!

“*Malice* has found us, mateys,” Stubby breathed. “Quick. Hide!”

Ebba spun around but before she could voice her discovery, Plank beat her to it.

“There be nowhere to hide in here,” he said. “They’re comin’ from the only way out.” Plank paced around the pedestal, eyes peering in every direction.

The slapping sound grew louder and quicker, overlapping as though a hundred wet shirts slapped the ground.

What is that?

Locks shook his head; despair weighed his voice. “Nothin’ for it, lads. Too many o’ us to hide behind this platform. We keep the high ground to fight.” He drew both pistols and cocked them, aiming both barrels at the tunnel.

Grubby barked again and Plank shushed him impatiently.

Peg-leg grabbed her. “Ye need to hide, Ebba-Viva. Just down there. Take Cosmo with ye,” he said. “Ye can both make fer *Felicity*. She’ll be hard to manage, but . . . well.” He smiled. “Nothin’ ye ain’t done before, is it?”

Ebba’s eyes narrowed. “Nay, Peg-leg. I ain’t goin’ without the rest of ye. I ain’t doin’ it.” She didn’t want to be alone again. Not on Maltu. Not in Syraness. Not ever.

Peg-leg glared at Cosmo. "Take her down there," he said. "Keep her quiet."

Enraged, she drew her cutlass and dodged out of Cosmo's grip. "Ye don't think Pockmark will think to look for me when he sees the rest o' ye here? Ye big clout! Cosmo be the only one who can hide."

That seemed to stump Peg-leg.

Grubby barked again and shoved both hands over his mouth, his eyes wide.

The slapping grew louder.

Louder.

And the crew of *Malice* burst into the circular cavern.

NINETEEN

Ebba's eyes threatened to pop out of her head.

It wasn't *Malice*.

It was. . . .

"*Seals?*" said Barrels, incredulous.

Not just a couple of seals. The whiskered mammals poured into the cavern in the hundreds, slapping at the ground with their flippers. The noise was overpowering, the smell even more so. Ebba was used to the smell of fish, but hundreds of seals in one place?

Next to her, Cosmo gagged.

"I ain't never seen seals act like this," Peg-leg said beside her. "What in Davy Jones' is goin' on?"

The seals were arranging themselves in formation, and Ebba had to agree that really, *really* wasn't normal behavior. They formed four rings around the raised platform. When the last gray seal had wiggled into position in the front row, a barking sound came from the entrance.

A huge black seal stood with its chest pushed out in the tunnel entrance. The black seal barked again and the gray seals blocking his way to the platform rocked out of his way as he slowly undulated toward them.

"Did that seal just give them an order?" Stubby asked, mouth ajar.

Sure seemed that way. "Do seals norm'ly have a leader?" she asked Barrels.

He shook his head slowly, eyes fixed on the scene before him.

Locks muttered, "Shite. I've seen everythin' now."

The black seal morphed into a naked man.

Locks inhaled sharply. "*Now* I have, for sure."

Ebba gaped at the nude man, who used to be a seal. Just before. On the same spot. "Ye just turned into a man," she told him.

Peg-leg said in a firm voice, "Eyes above the waist, lass. Eyes above the waist."

The seal-man barked again and the hundreds of seals surrounding *Felicity*'s crew began to morph in a blurring of gray. Cosmo gasped beside her, stepping closer to Ebba.

"I reckon ye be seein' and believin' in magic now," she said out the corner of her mouth. Honestly, Ebba was surprised how calm *she* was, but in Syraness she'd been utterly alone. Her fathers were with her right now, and that made her brave in comparison to the dark cliffs.

"I reckon ye be right," Cosmo said quietly. Ebba wasn't even sure he realized he'd spoken pirate.

The huge seal-man waited until the last seal had changed into a human form before facing them.

"They be selkies," Plank whispered. "Seal-men."

The man below snapped his eyes to Plank. "How do you come by our name, peasant?"

Plank's mouth shut with a click. He glanced at Barrels. "It talks."

Barrels shrugged. "I'm not sure that is the most pertinent issue right now."

"I dunno," Peg-leg interjected. "It be botherin' me when the magic creatures talk. Ladon spoke like a human, too." Ebba began to nod, but stopped as the seal-man approached.

"You dare to steal what we have zealously guarded for the last seven hundred and sixty-eight years?" the creature demanded. He glared at the object clutched in Cosmo's hand.

The treasure was worth something? That was good to know. She'd had her doubts after seeing the tarnished silver cylinder, but it must boil down to something worth a whole ship full of gold for seal-man to be so worked up about it.

"We were only stealin' it, Master Selkie, because someone else, someone *worse* be comin' for it," Plank explained.

A pirate truth if she'd ever heard one.

The selkie tossed his long black hair back, and Ebba watched as it rippled down his muscled back, her cheeks heating. He was prettier than half the women she'd met, but possessed a masculinity that made it impossible to tear her eyes from his form.

She flushed anew when she noticed Cosmo watching her, a curious glint to his eyes.

"We are aware of the ship which enters our cove," the selkie snapped.

They'd seen *Felicity* drop her anchor. That meant they'd watched *Felicity*'s crew since they entered Selkie's Cove, waiting for the opportune moment to catch them in their net.

All Ebba knew about Selkie's Cove was that women having trouble conceiving would visit the waters for luck. She hadn't actually known what a selkie was. But maybe their crew should start putting a bit more consideration into why places like Syraness and Selkie's Cove were named the way they were.

The man barked again, and the beautiful men filling the cave held their hands out in front of them. A light shimmered above their palms and Ebba gasped, shielding her eyes as it intensified to a bright flare.

When she looked again, a shining silver spear sat in each selkie's hand. In unison, the men pointed their weapons toward *Felicity*'s crew. Ebba took hold of Cosmo's belt and wrenched him back to the pedestal.

"Now, now." Plank held up his hands. "I'm sure we can—"

"We shall kill you and conceal the entrance once more," the leader decided.

He raised a single hand.

. . . Grubby barked.

The selkie leader whirled to the sound, leaping up onto the pedestal in one huge, effortless jump.

He barked inquisitively. . . .

Grubby barked back.

Ebba and the others cast furtive looks at each other. Stubby cleared his throat politely.

Shouting in joyful laughter, the selkie leader pulled Grubby into a fierce hug. "Kin," he said, smiling. Disbelief settled over every occupant in the cavern—selkie and human, alike.

What? Ebba took a step back, bumping against the pedestal.

"Did the selkie just call Grubby 'kin'?" whispered Locks.

Ebba couldn't take her eyes off the selkie embracing one of her fathers.

"You're part selkie," the leader declared. "Why did you not tell me there was a selkie among you? It changes everything." He barked over his shoulder and his army banished their weapons again in another shimmer of bright light.

“I be a selkie?” Grubby asked, shaking his head as though dislodging water in his ears.

The leader regarded him carefully. “You didn’t know? Surely, even as diluted as your blood is, there would be some sign. Your father would have displayed more of our traits, again.”

Grubby’s ears lowered. “He ran off.”

The leader barked in laughter. “We do have that reputation.”

The selkie sounded almost proud of that. . . .

Grubby blinked rapidly. “I’m a selkie?”

Ebba blurted, “He’s a smart swimmer. Quicker than a shark.”

The leader sniffed. “I would certainly hope so, pirate pup.”

Who was he calling pirate pup? She bristled.

He turned back to Grubby. “How long can you hold your breath underwater?”

Grubby lifted his head, mouth slightly ajar. “I just come up when everyone else does. But I hold it real long when no one be around and I forget I should do it.”

Peg-leg let out a pained wheeze. Barrels raised his eyebrows, mouthing, ‘*He forgets to breathe.*’

“How long?” the seal-leader demanded.

Grubby snatched his cap off and twisted it in his hands. “Few hours, I guess.” He wrung the cap, his eyes wide on the selkie leader.

Ebba shared an amazed look with Plank. *Hours*? Grubby held his breath for hours? Maybe they should’ve been watching him more closely. Clearly, being hit with a mast had sloshed more of his skull grog out than they'd thought.

"And how many willing females have you impregnated in our cove?" the man asked.

Grubby face went blank.

"Gotten with child," Barrels supplied.

Grubby's face went bright red. "Oh, well. Uh. My tongue gets all twisted-like around women," he said quietly.

The leader waited.

"None," Grubby admitted. "I'm from Kentro, though."

The leader shied back in horror. Horrified shouts from the other seals filled the cavern.

"None?" the leader asked, aghast. "At all?"

"Are you sure he's selkie, Kahree?" another of the gray selkies called.

The expression on Kahree's face said he wasn't sure. "It is unusual, to be sure, and hideously embarrassing. . . ."

"He's not mine," another called out.

Grubby's face burned brighter and Ebba whacked Locks on the back of the head. He looked like he was about to explode from holding in laughter.

"I can hear ye, in my head," Grubby said, shaking like a fluttering sail. "Ye were talkin' to each other afore; that's how I found the cave."

The selkie leader's frown disappeared, and he clasped Grubby's shoulder. "That settles it. Only one who shares our blood could do so. You are certainly our descendent." He observed the rest of *Felicity*'s crew for a long moment, before gripping Grubby's shoulder again. "You are one of us. And I must say . . . your sea-fellows do not seem to follow in the typical mold of human. Even the female wench is resisting our charm."

She'd take pirate pup, but not female wench. Ebba fisted her hands and opened her mouth. Barrels reached over and pinched her lips shut.

"I shall disclose the entirety of the situation to you," the leader said wearily. "For fear of the ship that has entered our cove."

"*Felicity*?" Ebba mumbled around Barrels' fingers.

Kahree stopped and gazed at her. "Your ship? The small one?"

Ebba bristled again, but managed to keep her mouth shut.

"No," the leader said. "Another. Black with crimson sails. Much larger, and with an evilness about it that pollutes our ancient waters."

"*Malice*," Cosmo said darkly.

Kahree nodded. "A fitting name for such a dark vessel. I have not felt such malignant evil since magic was ripped from this realm and locked away behind the wall. And it is no coincidence that they are headed to Portum, I feel it. They come to this cave to take the *dynami*."

The treasure had a name. Pockmark had searched for this specific object for four years. How had *Malice*'s captain even known the *dynami* existed? Or did Pockmark believe the plunder to be gems and gold as they had?

"*Dynami*," repeated Cosmo. "Like the far Dynami Sea?"

"No, not like that. But what other name is there for the seas of this realm?"

Cosmo rubbed his head. "King Montcroix renamed the western half of the Dynami Sea after his son about twenty years ago. It's now the Caspian Sea."

The leader seemed surprised. "We have recently returned to this realm from our prison, though the *dynami* preceded us. Much has changed.

When old magic reigned, the Dynami Sea was the only name for the ocean and the wonders it hid."

"Why have you returned now?" prompted Barrels. "We've come across a few other magical creatures. You mentioned a wall." He said the words as if pained. Admitting magic existed probably *did* hurt his deep respect of books and logical things.

The selkie dropped his arm from Grubby's shoulder. "The walls that long locked immortals away from this realm steadily weakened over the centuries. Recently, the wall became too weak to contain my herd. We, possessing lesser powers than other magical creatures, found it easier to slip through the cracks than others," he replied, the other selkies stirring restlessly.

"That could be explainin' why Ladon was flickerin' in and out as he was," Plank said.

"Ladon is no kin of mine," Kahree spat. "But like the rest of us, he is separated from the majority of his powers still. There was a day when a third of our number could have handled the evil entering our territory. But the wall still contains most of our magic, and we are no match for the power I sense is pushing *Malice* to this place. That power has been back far longer than us and has had time to grow in strength. It is not a risk I am willing to take. Separated as we are from the flow of old magic, I fear to die here would be to die in truth. And to let the *dynami* fall into the wrong hands would be worse than death itself. It *was* worse than death itself." Kahree shuddered, and his face hardened as he surveyed them. "The wall will continue to weaken. Immortal creatures of greater power will return. In time, the selkie will be reunited with their full power. But how long the wall will take to crumble completely, I have little idea."

Ebba's eyes rounded. "Ye mean the wall will go altogether?"

Kahree nodded. "Magic will return in entirety. Tis only a matter of time."

The selkie watched Grubby intently. Their expressions changed—eyebrows lifted, mouths quirked, and eyes widened—as they silently spoke. As they conversed, a tear dripped from Grubby's eye, and the shaking in his body slowly receded until he was still.

"No," Kahree said out loud at last. "The *dynami* cannot stay here. I do believe this is the right course."

Grubby looked fearful, but the other seals nodded.

Kahree approached Cosmo and took the cylinder from him.

"But why?" Plank asked. "Why has magic suddenly returned? I don't understand."

The selkie shook his head. "I have no answer for you, mortal. Though I wish for one as much as your herd, for evil magic of the like I sense on the ship *Malice* was locked away for good reason. But whatever the explanation for the wall crumbling, as mere guardians the selkie are not privy to knowing it."

Shite. Ebba glanced at Plank and saw his lips were pressed together in a grim line.

Ebba shifted restlessly until Kahree handed the treasure to Grubby. "I pass the *dynami* into your care, son of our kind. You are its guardian, you and the rest of your herd. May it lend you its namesake," he said.

Ebba stared at the object in Grubby's hand. Were they daft? All of this nonsense over a silver tube with a rounded knob at one end and some swirly decorations down the side. "What does it do?" she asked.

Plank yelped behind her. "Shite, the tide."

"You must go." Kahree nodded. "Your bodies are not meant for the water."

That was an understatement. "Hold on," she blurted loudly as the selkies began to shift back into seals, and the stink of fish filled the air once more. The crew of *Felicity* hadn't come a whisker within death multiple times to still not know what the damn treasure was. "What is the *dynami*?" she called to Kahree.

Her question appeared to puzzle him greatly. "What is the *dynami*?" He repeated.

"Ebba!"

She raised her head to see the rest of her crew were already halfway to the tunnel. "Aye, that's what I said," she said urgently. "What is it?"

"But what do you mean? It's in the name." The selkie leader insisted. "The *dynami*."

"*Ebba-Viva Wobbles Fairisles.*"

Sink her. He was full of helpful answers. Her fathers shouted a third time, and Ebba swung down to the rocky floor, wincing at the pang in her ribs. "Guess we'll figure that out ourselves," she muttered, striding for the exit. Useless seal.

"Swim strong, pirate pup," the selkie leader called after her. "And swim fast."

TWENTY

"How long did it take us to get in?" Peg-leg puffed, squeezing around the rocky protrusions as quickly as his wooden pin could carry him.

Cosmo called back from the front, "Fifteen minutes or more."

Ebba's gaze fell to the swirling water around their ankles.

They hurried on, Ebba pulling Peg-leg through the tight gaps when needed. Yet soon the water had crept to their knees.

"Hurry," shouted Plank from behind her.

The water pushed against them, fighting to come in as they shoved to get out. The tide twisted around their legs, and as it rose higher to their waists, each dragging step became a struggle.

"There's light ahead," Cosmo called back, panting.

Peg-leg turned sideways to sidle through a narrow space between two thick rock spikes. He grunted, shoving a few times. His eyes widened and met Ebba's. "I be stuck again."

He pushed to get free without success. Ebba gripped his wrist and pulled with all her weight.

. . . The cook didn't budge.

"Plank! Peg-leg be stuck."

"I can see that," Plank answered from Peg-leg's other side. "I'll push him."

He rammed a few times against Peg-leg's gut as Ebba pulled.

Plank panted. "It's no good. He's jammed in there tighter than a cork in a thousand-year-old bottle o' brandy. Locks!" he shouted. "Peg-leg be stuck again."

"Yer kiddin'?"

Peg-leg thrashed to each side. "Nay! He ain't kiddin'. If ye spent less time gabbin', I'd be out already."

"If ye spent less time samplin' yer cookin', ye wouldn't be stuck," Locks replied.

Peg-leg glared at him in the dark. "It's my shirt. It's thick material."

None of them laughed this time.

The water surged over Ebba's belly button.

"All righty," said Locks. He stood on one side of Peg-leg, clutching his arm, while Ebba bent and gripped him around his good knee. Plank would push from the other side.

"Heave," grunted Locks.

There was nothing for a short moment, then the smallest shift. With a pop of a button, Peg-leg began to slide. He burst free, disappearing underwater on top of Locks.

They emerged in a spluttering splash, and Plank wasted no time sliding between the two stalactites after him.

The water was nearly to Ebba's chest now.

"Hurry," came a cry from the exit.

Locks wiped the water from his eyes and lunged for the end of the cave.

Plank gripped Peg-leg by the collar and threw him in the direction of the exit. "*Move*, ye gapin' cods."

Ebba struggled after the cook.

Their pace was tortuous. They were fifty yards from the cave's entrance, but as the water lapped to her chest, and then her neck, nothing had ever seemed so far away. Her limbs moved as though they were ten times her weight, pushing at the water to help move her body forward.

Salt water tickled the underside of her chin. "Quickly," she gasped.

Locks panted from the front. The walls closed in on them from every side. Ebba tilted her chin up to breathe in the remaining air pocket, still kicking in the direction of the exit.

"Nearly there," Locks called back. The others shouted from outside the cave.

As Locks made it out, water crept in on the remaining space. Ebba took a last breath and dropped under the surface.

Swim far, swim fast, pirate pup.

White bubbles erupted in front of her as Peg-leg kicked. Ebba wriggled after him as hard as she could against the ocean's current. It wanted to drag her back into the depths of the cave, to drown her. Her lungs burned, warning her the clock was ticking. She threw her arms out, dragging them through the water, kicking savagely, knowing Plank—behind her—had farther to swim than she.

Her lungs tightened painfully.

An arm thrust through the water and grabbed her under the arm, dragging her upright. She gasped for breath, wiping the salt water from her burning eyes to blink at Grubby. She whirled to look behind her.

All seven of them waited, standing in the waist deep water outside the cove. The shingled beach was long gone.

"Plank ain't comin'," Ebba whispered. "He's not comin'!"

Without a word, Grubby dove into the water.

She started after him, but Stubby pulled her back. "Grubby can be holdin' his breath, lass."

Her shoulders sagged. "Aye, that's right."

Not long passed before Grubby reappeared with an unconscious Plank.

"He ain't breathin'," Grubby muttered, dragging him through the water.

Ebba swished toward him. "Here, this is what I did for Barrels when he weren't breathin'."

She wound up her arm and socked Plank in the gut. He contorted in the water, coughing up a few goblets full of salt water. Stubby and Grubby held the pale-faced pirate up between them.

"That solves one mystery," Barrels said, rubbing the space under his ribs.

Ebba folded her arms, and shrugged, saying, "It works."

Hands on his knees, Peg-leg panted, "Come on. We've got to be goin'."

Their spluttering crew waded back around the cove in a line, with Cosmo at the fore. Upon reaching the jutting tip of the current cove, Cosmo turned back and gasped. His amber eyes were frozen on something in the distance. His usual regal bearing was something much different, vulnerable and unsure.

"What?" Locks asked.

Cosmo lifted an arm and pointed, swallowing hard. "*Malice*."

Breath quickening, Ebba searched the sea north of Portum and inhaled sharply. He was right. She'd recognize the crimson sails of the triple masted ship anywhere.

Peg-leg cursed under his breath.

"It's several hours off, yet," Stubby said tersely. "We have a faster ship. We can—"

Ebba squinted. "What're they doin'? It looks like they're furlin' their sails."

Locks gave a heavy sigh. "They'll be anchorin' at the soddin' bottle-neck out of the cove to block the way, lass. Pockmark knows *Felicity* has him for speed."

"He ain't that smart," said Stubby. "It's that Jagger son o' a bastard."

"He ain't goin' to race us—he's goin' to tear us apart with his cannons," Locks continued.

Cosmo said, "We can go back through Syraness. We'd have go north-east, closer to *Malice*, but not past them."

Ebba's eyes rounded as her heart set off at seventeen knots an hour. "I'm not goin' back through there again."

"Didn't ye say there was a waterfall?" Locks screwed up his face. "Not sure how much luck we'd have goin' up that."

They hadn't entered through the top of the cove, near Kentro, but now it was the only way out. *Shite.*

Plank straightened, shaking off Stubby and Grubby. "Well, this much be true. We need to get back to *Felicity* afore this tide comes in any higher."

"And then what?" asked Ebba. They had the treasure; they couldn't let the *dynami* fall into *Malice*'s hands, especially when that meant they'd all be dead.

Plank paused. "And then, little nymph, we see if there be any way to get out o' this mess with our lives."

"THIS TRIP HAS BEEN one misfortune after the next," Stubby muttered as they rowed back to *Felicity*. Pillage had finally left the hold and now yowled to them from the starboard bulwark, no doubt hastening Barrels' return.

"I don't know," Barrels said quietly. "Grubby found where he came from. That was a great bit of fortune."

Grubby's face turned a rosy pink. He shook his head, brows raised in bafflement.

"Ye have a family of seal-men, Grubs," Ebba said, nudging him.

A frown appeared. No doubt finding out he was part seal was a lot to take in.

"I'm going to swim back to the ship," he declared. With that, he dove into the depths and disappeared.

"Grubby with selkie blood in him. Never saw that comin'." Plank rubbed at his light stubble, taking up an oar.

Ebba hummed in agreement with the others. "I ain't sure my skull knows what to do with that inform'tion after the last two weeks."

"Aye, lass," Peg-leg muttered. "Mine either."

They were quiet as they rowed back to *Felicity* which was bobbing in the waters just as they left her. What if their crew had decided to wait until the next tide to enter the cave? *Malice* could have captured them already. Ebba shivered in her wet clothes, despite the warm temperature.

Stubby and Barrels' whispered conversation caught her attention.

"Aye," Stubby was saying, "but there's nothin' here for us to eat. Ye can see it. All sparse woodland and salt. Nothin' edible be on that island."

"I'm at a loss then, my friend," Barrels said wearily. "Syraness and the whirlpool forms a wall to the east. Rocks lay to the west and south. The only way out is north, out of the cove to Kentro. *Malice* will simply wait at the bottleneck into the cove until we starve if we remain on Portum."

The rowboat bumped gently against *Felicity*'s side. Ebba latched onto the rope ladder and hauled herself up and over the bulwark.

When everyone was on deck and the rowboat raised and tucked into its usual spot, *Felicity*'s crew gathered in a circle, a white-faced Cosmo huddled between Peg-leg and Locks.

Ebba licked her lips. "So, what do we do?"

From what she'd overheard, they were trapped here. That they'd come so far for *Malice* to swoop in and take the treasure after all didn't seem fair. And Pockmark wouldn't just stop at taking the *dynami.* Not after searching for it for so long.

Blimey. She passed a hand over her face. This adventure had turned into an absolute mess. When she'd convinced her fathers to go after the treasure instead of *Malice*, she'd never intended for this to happen. Maybe her intentions had been mostly centered around protecting her crew, but a part of her had yearned for an adventure. Deep down, she'd wanted to show *Malice* who they were messing with. Those urges for reputation, glory, and excitement were the cause of the heavy guilt smoldering in her chest. A single slip of the tongue and now all their lives were at risk. Such was her guilt that Ebba was now uncertain if the slip had been a slip at all.

The only way out of the mess was to get past *Malice.*

. . . *Malice,* with cannons and top guns, and a crew of one hundred.

Before, she'd been envious of *Malice.* Presently, she was just afraid of what the sleek ship and its cruel crew could do to her crew and Cosmo. Ebba stared around the circle of her fathers. Which one would she lose? Or would it be two, or three? Would all of them perish?

How could Ebba possibly live with herself if that happened? A lump rose in her throat. She couldn't bear to be parted from any of them. Never had been able to, and never would be.

Stubby sighed. "I have a plan, my hearties." He stared over *Felicity*'s deck out to sea, to the east, and then turned back to the crew. "I want to go through Charybdis."

TWENTY-ONE

"Ye . . .what?" Ebba stared at Stubby.

They all did.

It was completely nuts. It would never work. It. . . .

"I want to go through the whirlpool. If we can't go through the cliffs, and *Malice* be blockin' the entrance to the cove, the whirlpool be the only other way. We use the very outside ring to circle around to the o'posite side. We'll come out a day's sail from Zol."

Plank stood abruptly. "There be much wrong with that plan."

Even Stubby seemed unsure and it was *his* idea. "Ye know as well as I do, *Felicity* can close-haul better than any other. We stick to the outside o' the whirlpool. Close enough to take its power, but not be sucked into oblivion."

Her fathers fell silent.

Ebba gazed around the circle. Were they serious?

Her fathers were good sailors. They knew their stuff when it came to the business. But this? In all Ebba's life, aside from the last two weeks, they'd never done anything bordering on dangerous. They were thinking like pirates half their age and, well . . . pirates who were actually real, adventurous pirates who didn't steal-trade fruits and vegetables for a living. She chewed on her lip.

"It'll take all of us to get her bow pointed out once we're in," Plank mused.

Peg-leg nodded. "And no small amount of luck." His eyes fell on her. "What about Ebba? It'll be right risky."

"Better to risk the whirlpool than let Pockmark get ahold o' her," Stubby said. "Ye saw what he did to her for nothin' more than being in the alley. What d'ye think he'll do to her now?"

The six glanced between each other.

"If this be our best chance, then we're doin' it," Ebba said, folding her arms. "Ye can't be worryin' about me."

Barrels surveyed her and nodded quickly. "We know, my dear. But we'll always worry about your safety."

"I know, Barrels." She tilted her chin. "But I ain't a child anymore. Ye know I can do whatever needs doin'."

All six of her fathers studied her.

Stubby gripped her shoulder. "Aye, we do at that."

"It's settled, then," Locks said with a sigh.

Ebba jerked as her fathers disbanded, each hustling away without another word. She watched as Peg-leg began to lash down loose objects on the main deck. Plank unfurled the mainsail. Grubby scuttled up the rigging to scout ahead. Barrels and Stubby weighed anchor, and Locks checked the sheets and winches for strength.

"They mean to take us around this Charybdis, I gather," Cosmo said from behind her.

They hadn't spoken enough about the actual plan. Ebba stared around the deck of her busy fathers, still in some state of shock over what they intended to do. "Aye. . . ."

"What exactly is it? Charybdis?"

"The whirlpool I was tellin' ye about," she said, glancing back in surprise. "The one we avoided on the way here. It has a current so powerful I've heard it can shake ships apart."

Cosmo paled. "Yer fathers know what they're doin', though?"

Ebba frowned. He was speaking pirate again. "We've never done anythin' like it afore."

Cosmo took a deep breath and touched her hand. "Okay, then I shall have to put faith in you. You got us through Syraness, away from the siren—"

"Ye believe in the siren now?" Ebba asked tightly.

Cosmo's eyes lost focus. "I'll believe anything after seeing seals turn into men."

Ebba chuckled, the tension between them dissipating. "Aye, that was somethin', weren't it?"

"My friends back home would think me mad if I told them."

"Why would they think that, if they trusted ye and knew ye to be honest?"

Cosmo shrugged and pulled at his yellowed tunic. His smooth skin had begun to tan in places as he slowly toughened up. Maybe he wouldn't be soft forever.

"Things are just different where I come from," he said heavily. "As one of your fathers said, we are people who cannot believe without seeing. To give fancy to your imagination is seen as childish."

"I be thinkin' a lot of things in this realm are seen as childish," Ebba said sadly.

They fell silent, watching the six pirates rushing about the deck as *Felicity* lurched to life.

Ebba stared with unseeing eyes, not voicing her doubts to the nervous Cosmo beside her. But she didn't know if her fathers could pull this off.

And she didn't know if they'd make it out of Charybdis alive.

THEY SAILED *FELICITY* EAST—AS if heading back into Syraness. But soon, they would alter their course to sail toward what sat immediately south of it—Charybdis.

In the distance, the crimson sails of *Malice* had been hoisted, and the schooner was lurching closer, into wider waters. Pockmark would want to cut them off from re-entering the cliff passage. Little did he know that wasn't their plan at all.

Plank blew a breath out. "I hope *Felicity* holds true."

Stubby replied, "We just need her to keep it together until we be out of Charybdis. Zol ain't far after that."

"Aye," Plank said.

Felicity was pulled forward, making the crew hush. The tug was palpable, and it didn't let up; it began to grow.

"The whirlpool's current," Ebba gasped.

Peg-leg strode to her. "Ebba, we'll be tiltin' something fierce. Show Cosmo what to do, smart-like."

He bent down to scoop up Pillage who swiped at him, hissing. Her father bellowed, jerking his finger back. He scowled at the feline and then inspected his finger. "Ye drew blood, ye shitey furball. Barrels!" he yelled. "Get yer cat below deck before I chuck him in the whirlpool myself."

Insides twisting, she turned to Cosmo. "We've sailed pretty flat for the most part, so far. Ye recall our tiltin' in Syraness? Afore your eyes went black, and I pushed ye down the ladder by accident?"

He reached for his forehead. "You did what?"

"It'll be worse than that bobbin'. Ye'll need to hold on to the ship's side here, the bulwark, or ye'll slide over the deck and be lost to Davy Jones."

His eyes popped. "It will be that bad?"

Ebba met his amber eyes. "I have no idea how bad. More tilt than even I've been on." Her eyes fell on his hands. He held the treasure. *Dynami*, the selkie had called it.

Holding out her hand for it, she said, "Give me that—ye'll need both hands and both legs."

"Should I—I don't know. Tie myself to the ship?"

"Nope. That's no good if ye've got to scramble across to the other side when the tilt changes. I'll let ye know if ye need to do that. Listen out for me."

Cosmo passed over the *dynami* and Ebba tucked it into her belt, tightening the belt another few notches. No way was she losing the blasted treasure now. Ebba glanced out over the port side at *Malice.* They'd realized where *Felicity* was going. They were lowering their crimson sails again, coming deeper into the cove than before, but there was no way the black ship would get close to the whirlpool.

Pockmark would just be waiting to ensure they perished to the oblivion.

Felicity lurched forward again with a terrible creak.

"Did you feel that?" Cosmo breathed.

"Aye."

The waves slapped at *Felicity*'s sides. There was another pitching pull under the ship. Spray careening over the deck, water rolled across the wood by the sudden gale rising out of nowhere.

Ebba tugged Cosmo to the corner of the bilge and demonstrated. "Ye hold on here. Quick now." She held his gaze. "Ye hold on for yer life, do ye promise? Don't take a hand off. Not for a moment, even if it seems calm."

He wedged a foot against the bilge wall and laid one arm over the bulwark, with the other underneath as she'd just showed him. He gazed across at her. "Don't worry about me, just worry about yourself. Please."

She smiled grimly and hurried to join Plank. They checked the sheets, and Ebba's legs adjusted as the ship tilted violently.

"Ye ready?" Plank asked with a grin.

"Aye?" she said, in some confusion at his expression. What was he grinning about? A quick glance around her fathers showed Ebba he wasn't the only one grinning. They appeared almost savage as the wind churned, whacking at their shirts and sending their hair in all directions. If she had to venture a guess, she'd say they were *enjoying* this. . . .

They appeared the epitome of pirates as *Felicity* careened closer to the whirlpool. And Ebba knew that if others could see her fathers right now, they'd be forced to agree.

She shook her head, smiling, and quickly tied her dreads back.

The tow underneath doubled, nearly sending Ebba flying. Plank grabbed her. "Ye'll be needin' those sea-legs to help me with these sails, little nymph."

Ebba planted her feet and nodded.

"Hoist the sail," he said.

She heaved alongside him with all her might. The wind caught at the sail and *Felicity* pitched to the starboard side, tilting to the water.

She held her position against the bulwark—just—and adjusted her grip on the rope, lips pressed together.

"We be goin' 'round the outer ring of the whirlpool now, lads!" yelled Stubby across deck from the helm. "We want to exit at this exact point on the opposite side."

That would see them out of Selkie's Cove and on the other side, close to Zol.

If this worked.

Stubby, Barrels, and Grubby stood to one side of the helm, both hands gripped around a spoke each, leaning back and using their entire weight to hold *Felicity* against the sucking current. Locks clutched to the mast with Peg-leg.

"Hold the sails there," Plank puffed to her, holding on to the same rope, farther up.

She held the rope tight with both hands, her feet wide, left leg wedged against the ship's side.

Felicity moved in a wide arc of doom, thrown forward by the current and wind until she flew through the pulling waters. They continued around the outer ring of Charybdis, and Ebba glimpsed the black ocean beneath, so extreme was their tilt to the starboard side.

She gasped at the dark maelstrom of the whirlpool in the distance. Looking across, the hole at the center seemed to extend as far as she could see, and the force of it tore their ship through the water faster than Ebba had ever experienced.

The gust cut at her eyes, making water stream from them in a steady torrent. Waves splashed against *Felicity*'s hull, crashing over the side and into her face. The only sound making any sense was that of the mast straining. The urge to look over her shoulder and check on Cosmo was nearly overwhelming, but she wasn't entirely sure she could without sacrificing her position jammed against the bulwark. She'd have to trust he could keep himself alive.

Her three fathers strained at the slipping wheel.

"We're comin' up on the Zol side, lads. Quickly!" Stubby yelled, peering over the helm. "We're goin' to set *Felicity*'s bow across wind."

"Keep a way-on to maintain speed!" Plank shouted back. Then to her, he instructed, "Get ready to run."

"Get ready to run to the other side, Cosmo," she yelled in the servant's direction. "As fast as ye can." She heard his call of 'yes' with no small amount of relief.

Each of them looked up, tense, waiting for the moment the mainsail would catch the incoming squall. The second it did, the boom would careen across deck and *Felicity* would tilt from starboard to port. They'd need to sprint across deck as the tilt reversed, or perish to the black waters.

"The current's too strong to point us away from the eye," Barrels bellowed. "We're not going to make it."

Even with his, Grubby's, and Stubby's combined strength, they hadn't managed to budge the ship's nose to point outwards.

"Blast it to Davy Jones'," Stubby shouted, pulling hard on the wheel.

Ebba moved to help her three fathers, but Plank stopped her with a hand on the shoulder. She looked at him in question.

"Too late, little nymph" he called. "We missed our moment to get out. We risk goin' into the cliffs if we exit now. We're movin' too fast."

"We have to go around again," Peg-leg yelled.

"Nay," Stubby answered. "It be too strong. We have to get out after the cliffs. If we enter the second ring o' the whirlpool, we won't be able to get out."

But if they completed a full circle and exited after the cliffs, they'd end up back in Selkie's Cove where *Malice* would still be anchored and waiting. . . .

"*Malice* be there," she reminded them, eyes wide.

Locks bellowed over the wind, "How much speed do ye think Charbydis has given us?"

Her six fathers stared at each other as she glanced between them in confusion. What did Locks mean?

"Let's do it," Peg-leg shouted.

Do what?

Plank turned to her, wind whipping at his raven curls. "We be movin' on to plan B. Be ready to lower the sail with me as soon as the others get the ship facing outward. We'll be blitzin' past *Malice* with the extra speed."

Blitzing past Malice? Her heartbeat thundered in her ears. "I don't understand."

"Imagine a rock in a stockin' that you whip in circles over yer head and let go," Plank said urgently.

That was plan B? Would that even work?

Scrambling for purchase, Ebba returned her attention to the rope in her hands.

A searing tingling sensation pulsed in her stomach and Ebba pulled experimentally, surprised when the sail above tightened almost effortlessly.

Plank reached her to lend his help, but only had time to glance at her curiously before *Felicity* surged again without warning.

Ebba cried out with the others, holding on for dear life as the ship threatened to overturn. It couldn't be possible for *Felicity* to move faster, but somehow it was happening. The mast strained above, warning her too much more would see it split. The wind pushed at her cheeks and she knew without a hair of doubt that if she lost her footing —if *any* of them lost their footing—they were goners.

Nothing could have prepared her for the raw power of Charybdis; the terror as the sea and sky blurred before her eyes.

Her stomach lurched as they swept around, and she had no idea how her fathers at the wheel would be able to tell when the time was right.

"We can't miss again," Plank roared over the chaos. "The sheets won't take it against the current and wind."

"Neither will the winches!" Stubby bellowed back.

To get out, they needed to use the wind against the current. If they couldn't point *Felicity* in the right direction, the wind and current would keep working together to push their ship into the center.

Ebba glanced over and saw Peg-leg and Locks had joined the other three pirates at the wheel.

"The cliffs are coming up," Barrels yelled.

Plank panted. "Get ready. We lower the sail after they angle the ship outward."

She nodded. Ebba trusted her fathers. She just had to focus on the task they'd given her.

"Aye," she replied, clenching her teeth. Her knuckles were white as she gripped the rope, ready to lower the sails faster than she'd ever done in her life.

"Nearly there," called Stubby.

"Here we go, lads," Locks yelled.

"Lee-o," Peg-leg boomed in a deep voice.

Felicity took a breath and began to tilt outward from the circling rings of the whirlpool.

Ebba released the sheet so quickly her hands blurred. She felt the shift in the ship as *Felicity* struggled to get her bow across the wind. But she knew immediately the change wasn't going to be enough.

She had to do something!

She half slid, half threw herself into the helm, and wrapped her hands around the only free spoke on the wheel.

A searing tingling flared at her stomach as she pulled. As with hoisting the sail, the wheel spun toward her seemingly without effort. It upset the footing of the five of her fathers holding on, and they tumbled to the ground, latching on to what they could and leaving Ebba to single-handedly point the bow in the right direction.

Peg-leg called from the mast, "That's it, lads!"

"Latch on, mateys. She's heelin' over," Plank shouted.

Ebba screamed at Cosmo, "Get ready to run to the other side."

A surging gale hit them without warning, pitching the ship from starboard to port side, and her feet left the deck. Ebba clung to the wheel with all her might, dangling from the helm as *Felicity* groaned and rolled.

"—Help the boom across—"

Shouting erupted from her fathers and Ebba clung to the wheel, desperate to keep the ship pointed away from the eye.

"—Check the sheets—"

Her knees hit the deck as the ship settled into the port tilt and stopped tossing forward and back. Ebba pulled herself up against the wheel, planting her feet, and dared to take a breath.

Glancing at her fathers, she found them staring at her.

"How did you do that?" Stubby asked. His gaze dropped to the wheel, then back to her. "Ye pointed the ship outward by yerself."

Ebba stared at her hand on the helm. The searing tingle was still present in her stomach. "I don't rightly know," she said in awe.

Plank was eyeing their projected course with a critical eye. "Nicely done."

Felicity was all but flying back out through the current. None of them spoke, waiting to see if they'd escape the whirlpool's clutches and, if they did, whether they'd have enough speed left over to soar past *Malice* as initially planned.

Stubby inched to the side to study the waters, but it wasn't long before they felt the change underneath the ship, the freedom in *Felicity*'s movement as she began to all but fly through the water.

"Five starboard!" Locks said.

She obeyed, pointing the bow toward *Malice*.

Felicity skimmed like a stone on a lake toward the narrow spot where the other ship lurked. Even more so when Plank and Grubby raised the topsail. *Felicity* brushed aside the waves as though they were pesky mosquitos.

"How quick are we goin'?" Peg-leg shouted over the tumult.

Plank's expression was nonplussed. "Faster than I've ever gone. Seventeen knots at least, I'd say."

Ebba looked between them, speechless. *Seventeen knots*. The very fastest *Felicity* usually went was twelve. *Malice* would take forever to accelerate to even half of their current speed.

Cosmo leaned into her ear. "How fast is seventeen knots?"

Ebba muttered under her breath, scrunching her face up. She had to times it by . . . she couldn't remember how much.

"We'll cross nineteen miles in an hour at that speed," Barrels supplied, taking Grubby's weapons and clothing as the pirate undressed. "It'll have us soaring past them and out of Selkie's Cove within fifteen minutes."

Ebba frowned as Grubby began to undress. "Grubs, what're ye doin'?"

Cosmo stared at *Malice*, which they were rapidly approaching. "That's fast."

Grubby now stood naked on the deck, except for his slops.

"What's goin' on?" she asked, eyes darting between her fathers.

Peg-leg clapped Grubby on the shoulder. "Ye best be off quick-like."

Grubby's face settled into determination. Without another word, he dove headfirst over the side of the ship.

Ebba rushed to the side. "Where's he goin'?"

Plank called from the mast, "Off ahead o' us to tamper with *Malice*."

Tamper, how? "What—?"

Locks came up beside her, his green eye blazing. "Were ye always that strong, like with the wheel?" he asked. "Seems a bit out o' the blue. Not that I'm complainin'."

Ebba lifted a hand to shield her eyes and look ahead at *Malice*. "Don't think so," she said. The strange searing tingle pre-empted it both times, however. With raising the sail and turning the wheel. Ebba had a strong suspicion the *dynami* was behind her new strength, but she wanted to test it again before sharing the theory with her fathers.

He looked at her, perplexed.

"*Malice* ahoy," Stubby called.

Their speed began to drop.

Holding on to the side, Ebba craned to squint ahead.

Felicity was close enough that *Malice*'s crew were visible. So was the word '*Malice*' painted on the side, in the same crimson color as the sails—at least, she assumed the word said *Malice*. It could say morons for all she knew. Those of the enemy crew not on the cannons stood ready at the top guns in their black uniforms with the red sash.

They watched *Felicity*'s skimming approach, awaiting their captain's command to fire.

"What do we do?" Ebba shouted to Peg-leg at the mast.

He gave a woeful tilt of his head. "We've done everythin' we can, lass. The rest is up to Grubby."

"Where is he?" she asked. She hated the thought of him getting hurt. It made her insides twist to the point of pain.

Something exploded from the sea at the lowest side of the ship. Water burst everywhere. And from the depths shot Grubby.

She sighed in relief.

He lay on the deck for several moments before pushing wearily to his feet. He crawled to the mast and rested against it, eyes shut.

"Ebba," Cosmo called, inching his way to her across the bulwark.

She eyed him. "Ye made it."

The servant looked exhausted.

“Just,” he said shortly. “And perhaps not for much longer. . . .” He trailed off as their bow drew alongside *Malice*’s black stern.

Though *Felicity* moved faster than ever, each yard turned into five and each second to ten, and the size of *Malice* became suddenly and painfully clear. The dark ship dwarfed them by four times.

She swallowed. They were alongside the middle of the *Malice* ship. The deep-crimson sails of the vessel blocked most of the light, casting them all in shadow. Soon the cannons would fire, straight into the hull of *Felicity*, tilted as she was.

“Any words o’ wisdom?” Cosmo whispered in a shaking voice. He definitely spoke pirate when he was scared.

She cleared her throat. “Odds are ye won’t be hit by a cannonball. Pegleg told me once that ye’re more likely to get hit by the splinters from the gun and cannon fire. So avoid those.” She tilted her head. “And the bullets.”

Ebba wasn’t sure if Cosmo answered because at that exact moment Pockmark came into view above them. The captain wore his gold-embroidered tricorn hat and his eyes were murderous.

Riot and Swindles stood to one side of him, and. . . .

“Jagger,” she hissed under her breath. “That filthy, malaria-ridden swine!”

If he hadn’t legged it back to *Malice* after guiding them to Neos Mountain, none of this would’ve happened.

“Ebba,” said Cosmo, slowly. “What are you doing?”

Ebba cocked her pistol and aimed it at Jagger, but he wasn’t even looking at her. The guide stared at Cosmo beside her, and she watched as the shock on his face hardened until hatred etched every facet and line.

She fired her pistol at him, grinning when all four of the spineless rodents up there hit the deck.

"Ebba-Viva!"

She straightened at Stubby's reprimand.

Plank was looking past her. "Hit the deck," he bellowed.

Flattening herself, Ebba dragged Cosmo down with her as the crew above them shot at *Felicity* from the deck. The tearing pace made their ship a harder target. But with at least seventy men shooting at them from above, many of the bullets hit their ship, whining as they whizzed overhead. They tore chunks out of the mast and bilge and the cedarwood splintered, exposing a lighter color underneath.

Ebba covered her ears, eyes scrunched as she tried to orient herself through the booming sounds around her. Her fathers shot back at *Malice*, standing and ducking down again. They had only two pistols each, with one shot per pistol. Their gunfire was nothing against the crew of *Malice*'s.

"Cannons ready," she heard Pockmark shriek.

She and Cosmo stared at each other in terror at the call from the other ship. She grabbed for his hand, clutching tight.

"Fire," Pockmark screamed from the other ship.

Ebba squeezed her eyes, waiting for the inevitable explosion of fifteen cannonballs. They'd only have once to fire. After that, *Felicity* would be gone.

How much damage could fifteen cannonballs do. . . ?

"Ebba," Cosmo said insistently, telling her it wasn't the first time he'd said her name.

She cracked open an eye.

"Let that be a lesson to ye, ye scurvy scupper rats," Peg-leg shouted through cupped hands. He clutched his belly, snorting with laughter.

She dropped Cosmo's hand, noting the nail marks on his palm.

"What happened?" she demanded. She peeked over the bulwark. They were past the black-and-crimson *Malice*, though a few of the crew still shot at them. "What happened?" she asked again.

"Grubby wet their gunpowder." Plank beamed, clapping Grubby on the back.

Ebba's face fell. That was what Grubby left to do?

She stomped her foot. "Ye didn't think to tell me? Ye soddin' curs. Me and Cosmo were half dead with fright."

"Ye watch yer language, Ebba-Viva Fairisles," Stubby scolded. But his grin echoed the expressions of her five other fathers. "There was hardly time to tell ye on the way."

Ebba scowled. "I be rememberin' a time or three," she said.

Plank slung an arm around her. "We're beggin' yer pardon, little nymph. Sorry to have frightened ye."

She cocked a hip out. "I'd be inclined to forget the whole thing if ye get me another bead."

He kissed her temple. "Aye, that can be arranged."

She should have asked for three.

"We made it," Peg-leg roared.

The crew of *Felicity* cheered.

Her guilt over causing mostly all of the trouble aside, she could still celebrate a triumph. Ebba cupped her hands together and shouted as loud as she could in the direction of *Malice*, "Screw ye, Pockmark. Ye butt-faced, toothless whore o' a drunk fisherman's rottin' grandfather!"

Perhaps, despite the bleak odds at many points throughout, the quest would work out okay. They had the plunder after all, not Pockmark. Whether *he'd* been hurt as much as she and her crew were while searching for the *dynami* wasn't certain, however. The dark ship was tacking to give chase, but a small smile played on her lips. There was no way *Malice* could catch up to them from a standstill. Even with the damage *Felicity* had suffered.

"Ebba," came a weak voice.

Smile still on her lips, she turned to Cosmo and her grinning celebrations screeched to an abrupt halt. Ebba stared at the blood oozing from his chest, cold horror freezing her to the spot.

TWENTY-TWO

"Locks, help," she cried, falling to her knees beside Cosmo.

Cosmo smiled weakly at her. "You warned me about the splinters."

She tore open the top laces of his tunic as Locks crouched beside her.

"Not how I imagined you undressing me for the first time," Cosmo slurred. Locks whacked him upside the head and Cosmo jolted awake again.

"Locks," Ebba scolded. "He's bleedin' heavy."

Her father located the source of the blood at the left shoulder. A wooden wedge as thick as her thumb was lodged in there.

"Aye, that's a good one," Locks said grimly.

Cosmo gasped. "Wait. Aren't you the ship's carpenter?"

Ebba drew the tunic gently down Cosmo's arm, careful not to jostle the wound. "Oh, aye," she said reassuringly. "But sometimes he doubles as the surgeon."

"Just another set of tools, lad," Locks said. "Though I'll admit my hands ain't made for the fiddly work." He poked at the wound and Cosmo turned chalk white.

Locks didn't raise his head as he spoke, "Clean rags, a needle and thread from Barrels, and a bottle o' Stubby's strongest brandy. Smart-like."

He pushed once more on the wound and Cosmo's amber eyes stopped focusing on Ebba's face and rolled back into his head. He slumped in a dead faint.

She raced below deck, hurdling the objects strewn about by their passage around Charybdis.

Stubby kept his brandy in the back of the hold and thought she didn't know about it. She trawled through the bottles, checking the tiny numbers on the side and located one that was ninety percent. Ebba tucked it under her arm, weaving around barrels and buckets and cabinets filled with their supplies.

She threw open the door to Barrels' office, rifling through his desk drawer to grab the needle and thread he used to fix his cravats.

She stopped. What else had Locks asked her for? There was a third one. She was sure of it. Her eyes fell on her stained slops. Rags! Flinging open one of the small cooking drawers, she found Peg-leg's cleaning rags.

. . . *Clean*. Her heart fell at the grimy appearance of the cloths. Minutes later and with four of Barrels' cravats tucked in her pocket, she raced back to Locks, who still knelt at Cosmo's side.

Her other fathers watched from afar, but were occupied with manning the ship and evading the danger at their stern. A quick glance told her they'd passed out of Selkie's Cove. The west end of Kentro loomed in the distance.

Locks took the brandy she offered, staring at the label, and sniggered loudly. He stared at the cravats in her clenched fist and sniggered again. Taking the needle and thread, he popped the cork of the bottle and poured the brandy over the needles, thread, and his hands, taking a long swig himself.

He passed the needle to her. “Only touch the blunt end, mind.”

She took it gingerly.

Locks sighed and wiped his hands on his dirty slops. “Now that I be a‘hygiened,” he said. He leaned over and yanked the wedge out of Cosmo’s shoulder.

Ebba jerked at the suddenness of it and Cosmo bucked from the pain, but remained unconscious.

“Better out than in,” Locks said pleasantly.

She swallowed back bile at the blood and tissue hanging from the wedge and made no answer.

Locks pressed three of the cravat rags against the wound for a full five minutes. “Brandy,” he said.

She passed it to him.

“Dreadful waste o’ brandy,” he whispered to himself, before lifting the rags and pouring a stream of the alcohol into the gaping wound.

Locks pressed the rags down again. “Pass that needle now, lass.”

She held out the threaded needle to him and took over pressing on the rags to stop the bleeding.

“Up with the rags,” her father instructed.

She lifted the rags away and watched in morbid fascination as Locks dug the needle into Cosmo’s skin. Wooziness struck her and Ebba drew in shallow breaths through her thinned nostrils. Watching wasn’t such a good idea. She turned away, peeking over the bulwark.

Malice had already fallen far behind, along with that flaming sod, Jagger. She wondered if her bullet hit him.

"Where will we go now?" she asked no one in particular.

Peg-leg replied from the mast, "*Felicity* be in bad shape. We'll stop at Kentro to make repairs."

Ebba looked at him. "Isn't that where *Malice* will expect us to go?" she asked.

"Aye. But there's nothin' for it. Grubby's, uh, selkie kin have told him of a spot they visit on Kentro shores. They said the cove is deserted, but for the occasional human female wishin' to be . . . well. . . . Anyway, the cove is hidden from the sea. And *Malice* will be too big to get into it."

Ebba sighed in relief. In a few hours they'd make it to Kentro and all of this would be over. They'd make repairs, sell the *dynami*, and head back to Zol to retire. Nothing had ever sounded better. Especially now she knew her fears about her fathers being past the age of excitement were completely unfounded. They were pirates through and through. And so was she.

Locks tied the end of his stitching off. She glanced at his work, grimacing. Cosmo would have a meaty scar. But that wasn't the worst that could happen. "Will he keep it?" Ebba asked.

Locks gathered up the bloodied rags. "Only time will tell, lass. I've seen pirates lose their limbs from less than this." He looked at Peg-leg.

Ebba blinked. "But he'll live, won't he?" she blurted.

Locks handed her the brandy, avoiding her eyes, and made for the bilge. She stared down at Cosmo—her *friend*, even if they'd only known each other a short time. Sweat beaded on his high-boned brow. She brushed back the russet hair stuck to his forehead and had a sudden, fervent wish to see his amber eyes staring at her in his intense, fascinated way.

She recalled her scathing remarks to *Malice*'s captain an hour before with a sinking heart.

It looked like Ebba celebrated too early.

She cracked her eyelids open, hearing the lap of gentle water against *Felicity*'s side.

They were drifting on anchor by the feel.

Jaw cracking, she raised her arms overhead and stretched with a loud, satisfying groan within her hammock. She guessed they'd made it to the Selkie's Cove in Kentro. Last thing she remembered, Grubby was disappearing over the side ahead of *Felicity* to guide them into the hidden space. Sometime after, she'd stumbled below deck and taken the hammock next to Cosmo to better keep an eye on him through the night.

She turned her head, only half awake, to find amber eyes staring at her.

"Sink me, Cosmo." She yawned again. "Ye creepy bugger. How long've ye stared at me for?"

Cosmo's neck reddened. Actually, his entire face seemed rather red. She'd get Locks to check if it was fever.

She swung her feet to the ground. "How do ye feel?"

He put a careful hand over the bandaged wound. "Like there's a hole in my shoulder, funnily enough." The russet-haired man gave a small laugh and winced as it jolted his injury.

"I'll get ye somethin' for the pain," she said. Where did she put that bottle of brandy? She needed to fill it with grog so Stubby didn't notice it was gone.

"Mistress Fairisles?" Cosmo said. She turned, eyebrow cocked. He blushed. "Thank you."

"What for, ye dolt?"

His eyes riveted on her face, he looked her over. What was he thinking when he stared like that, she wondered?

A soft smile curved his lips. "For an adventure."

Ebba returned his smile, uncertainly. He spoke as if he were dying. Unsure what to say, because Ebba was now of the opinion the adventure hadn't been worth the treasure at all, she gave him a nod and headed for the deck.

Her fathers and Pillage lay about, lazing in the morning sun.

"What are ye all doin'?" she demanded.

"Look who's talkin'. Ye've been asleep more than twelve hours," Plank drawled. He rubbed his lower back with both hands. "My entire body aches."

Peg-leg answered his groan with one of his own. "We're getting too old for this, lads."

Peg-leg glanced away. "Aye," he replied after a beat. "My poor body can't hack it."

"I thought ye were all amazin'," she said honestly. "I never knew any of ye could sail like *that*."

Her fathers smiled quietly.

She stared at them. She'd been wrong about everything—her father's capabilities, and the grandeur of an adventure. She'd thought glory was important and had risked all their lives chasing it.

"It's not yer first adventure, is it?" Ebba asked them. She'd been content to be coddled, but now, after everything, after the mansion and Ladon and Syraness, Ebba found that had changed, too.

Stubby cleared his throat.

"Can ye. . . ?" She swallowed. "Did ye have adventures with the captain ye don't like to speak of? The one Ladon mentioned?"

Plank hung his head. "Mutinous Cannon," he said bitterly.

Locks whacked him.

"What?" Plank exploded. "We already broke our vow on Neos. No point keepin' it now."

Locks glared back at him. "There's always a reason to keep it." He looked pointedly at her.

"I didn't mean for ye to argue." She reached back and fiddled with her beads.

Stubby sighed heavily. "It's not yer fault. Talkin' o' him swabs us the wrong way, is all."

Ebba glanced around. "But why?"

"Because when we worked under him, it were a di'ferent time. And we," Stubby rubbed his chest, "we were di'ferent people. It does no good to dwell on the past." He interrupted her as she opened her mouth to ask another question. "Mutinous Cannon be dead and gone, and we be changed men. We'd all but forgotten who he was."

Peg-leg stared absently at his hands. Plank's jaw was clenched. Grubby had his eyes closed, head leaning back against the mast.

Didn't look like any of them had forgotten a single second of it.

She took Stubby's hint, however, and kept her mouth shut. They'd respected that she hadn't been ready to talk about Syraness, and it didn't look like her fathers were ready to talk about this man.

Stubby stared up at the mast, his mouth pulled down. "My ship, tattered and torn. I've got a list o' repairs the size o' the Caspian Sea."

She listened to the boatswain babble on for a while. He'd fret and yell until *Felicity* was one hundred percent ship-shape again.

"She ain't that bunged up," Peg-leg grumbled. He whacked the end of the boom to prove his point.

With an almighty crack, it splintered. A searing tingled her stomach, and Ebba lurched to catch the smaller end of the boom and held it steady so the heavy beam didn't land on Grubby's head.

Grubby scrambled out of the way.

She lowered the heavy slab of wood to the ground.

"What was that?" Locks said in wonder. "How are ye doin' these things? Ye ain't somethin' magic, too, are ye? I ain't ready for ye to turn into a seal."

Good, because she wasn't ready to be one. Ebba stared at the boom. The *dynami* was doing something to her, all right.

"It's like in the whirlpool. She hoisted the sail with the strength o' ten pirates," Plank interrupted.

Barrels added, "And pulled the wheel with the strength of twenty."

Glancing down, her eyes landed on the *dynami.* She touched it; it was warm—nearly too warm to leave her finger there.

Their eyes fell to her belt.

She glanced up at her fathers. "The *dynami.* It be warm. And it tingles my skin whenever I get strong. Kahree said that the meaning of *dynami* was in the name, but I ain't sure what he meant."

"Barrels," Plank said slowly. "What does 'dynami' mean?"

Barrels raised his brows. "Why, I would have to find a reference—I have no idea."

Ebba freed the cylinder from her belt and passed it to Plank.

He tossed it hand to hand. "It's warm."

Her six fathers passed it between them, each staring at it for a long while.

Felicity's crew eyed the silver cylinder.

Barrels cleared his throat. "Kahree did say he hoped the *dynami* would lend us its namesake, too. It must have something to do with strength."

"*That's* why that scurvy turd, Pockmark, was after it," Locks said, hotly. "He wants to be strong."

Stubby said, "All I be knowin' is I need a long slug o' my best brandy for me aching bones. I've been savin' a bottle and now seems as good a time as any to crack it open." Humming to himself, he bustled away below deck.

Unease settled heavy in her stomach as she watched him go. "Locks? Does he mean. . . ?"

"Aye, lass. I expect so."

Stubby roared a moment later. The sound echoed up from the hold. Ebba winced.

"That was the brandy we poured over Cosmo's shoulder yesterday," she said sheepishly.

The deck erupted into hoots as a purple-faced Stubby reappeared, swinging a near-empty bottle in the air.

Smiling his toothy grin, Grubby unhooked his flute from his belt and began to play. Her father was always happy, but something seemed different about him, as though a tension she hadn't seen there had disappeared. Deep down, had he worried over his differences to everyone else? She hoped he'd found some measure of peace from discovering his selkie heritage.

Ebba stomped her feet as he played. Peg-leg attempted to join in and stopped immediately with a pained expression.

The rest of her fathers clapped along.

"All right," Barrels announced, "I've got something." He clapped with the beat of Grubby's tune, and then nodded, repeating, "I've got something. I think it's good."

Peg-leg snorted. "Let's hear it then."

Barrels grinned and then sang:

There once was a lad who swam rather well
And no one thought much of it.
In a race against a shark, he won every time,
Yet no one thought much of it.

He did not rise up for a breath;
He flopped on deck, did not suspect
He was a selkie
A selkie.

Ebba threw her head back and laughed with the rest of her crew. Grubby's face colored pink as Barrels continued:

There once was a lad who knew just where to go
By dipping his toe in the water.
Prior to this, he neglected to say
He'd been hearing voices.

When young he was hit by the boom;
It's the only way he can't have known
He was a selkie
A selkie.

TWENTY-THREE

Ebba picked up a handful of Kentro sand and let the soft white grains trickle through her fingers. She'd never felt anything like it. It was so smooth when it was wet, almost like velvet. The cove here was one of the prettiest she'd ever seen. Exotic red flowers peeked out from the edges of the luscious forest at their backs, and it had a romantic, untouched feeling to it.

Felicity bobbed in shallow water to her right, wedged in a rocky indent in the cliff. A curtain of vines hung over the space. If *Malice* ever did come looking, *Felicity*'s crew would be trapped well and good, but Pockmark and his gang had passed by three days before and hadn't returned. Not by sea, anyhow.

"Beautiful, isn't it?" Cosmo said, sitting beside her, using his good arm to guide himself down. His injured arm hung in a sling around his neck.

The last edges of the sun did their best to peek above the horizon. The moon already hung high in the sky, its light catching at the calm and midnight-blue waters.

The gentle rush of the ebbing waves lulled her into a relaxed state. “Aye,” she said in a hushed voice. “It is at that.”

She rested her chin atop her drawn-up knees. “What will ye do now, Cosmo?” she asked.

His eyes shifted to the trees behind them. Beyond the trees. Did he stare toward Exosia?

“. . . Do ye miss home?” she asked.

He faced the ocean with a frown, toying with his sling. “Not nearly as much as I should.”

She tried to stay quiet, but couldn’t quite manage it. “Ye could stay with us, ye know.” She flushed. “If ye ain’t ready to go back.”

Amber eyes fixed on her face with their unsettling vibrancy.

A scuffle in the trees alerted her to the presence of others. She drew her cutlass from her side and rose to her feet, standing in front of Cosmo.

Locks and Peg-leg exited the tree line.

Peg-leg pushed a vine off his shoulder and pulled up short when he spotted them on the beach. “What’re the two o’ ye up to?” he asked suspiciously.

“Nothing,” Cosmo said quickly.

“Did ye get the supplies?” she asked, sheathing her cutlass.

Peg-leg turned slightly—though the action was unnecessary—to show her the huge pack upon his back. Locks had one just as large.

Ebba pushed through the sand to them. “Did ye get me more clothes?” More importantly, had they gotten her a new bead?

“Ye’ll have to wait and see, won’t ye?” Peg-leg said, then peered over her shoulder. “Uh-oh.”

She turned to look. Plank and Grubby were approaching from the opposite end of the beach where *Felicity* was anchored. Nothing else appeared out of place. "Uh-oh, what?"

Grubby stormed over to Locks and held out his hand. "Where is it?" he snarled.

Ebba startled at his tone and shared an awed look with Cosmo.

Grubby was *angry*.

"Now, see here." Locks took a step back as Peg-leg extracted the *dynami* from inside his jerkin. "We just wanted to see how much it were worth."

Grubby snatched the *dynami* from Peg-leg's hand.

Ebba watched the part-selkie's hands as they shook with the force of his fury. Without another word, he stalked off down the beach back to the ship.

"Ye peeved off Grubby," she said in wonder. "He didn't even pat ye."

Locks stared after their selkie crew member. "Aye, that would make his tally twice in twenty years by my count. That be right?" he asked Plank.

Plank nodded mutely.

"I be thinkin' Grubby's takin' his selkie guardian duty of the *dynami* pretty serious-like," said Peg-leg.

Cosmo got to his feet with a grimace. "Did you really ask around to see how much the *dynami* was worth? Aren't we in hiding? You don't think Pockmark will ask around the market for our whereabouts?"

Peg-leg and Locks shared a look, before Locks sighed. "We weren't about to shout out our location, lad. We decided it worth the risk since we'll be in hidin' in our home waters for a wee while now. Went to two o' our usual merchants. A waste a time, or so it turned out. They weren't knowin' what it was either. They both said about the same thing."

Ebba leaned forward.

"It's worthless. Mayhaps only worth a couple o' silver coins."

"That's it?" she croaked. *Two silver coins?*

Locks added, "We took it to a blacksmith right at the end and tried to get it boiled down. He worked the forge until it were white-hot. But the *dynami* just sat there in the middle—didn't melt, didn't change, or nothin'."

"Ye tried to melt it?" Plank asked incredulously. "Ye better hope Grubs doesn't hear that."

Peg-leg shrugged. "Mighta got carried away after the two silver coins news."

Ebba clenched her jaw. "We did all that stuff for nothin'?" It wasn't enough that she regretted starting this whole thing—now the treasure was worthless and they *still* wouldn't be able to retire and be safe from *Malice*?

"It wasn't for nothin', little nymph. We found out that magic will be returnin', after all," Plank said gently. Then he scowled. "But not why."

She didn't care about sodding magic. It could go to Davy Jones. Ebba ignored the reaching hands of the others and stalked off after Grubby.

They shouted after her, but disappointment rested heavy in her bones.

Grubby had stopped ahead, likely alerted to her mood by the shouts. He passed her the *dynami* when she reached his side.

She stared down at the hunk of junk, and sniffed long and hard. "I just feel respons'ble for all the trouble, is all."

Grubby wrapped an arm around her, smiling his toothless grin. She wiped a hand over her face and leaned her head against his shoulder. Grubby always made her feel better. He never judged her, or told her off.

"We'll be okay, Ebba," he said. "We have the *dynami*."

"But Grubs," she said. "Super strength won't help us any. The *dynami* ain't worth nothin'. We can't retire to Zol with what we have." Never had the isolated and safe shores of their Zol hideaway seemed so inviting as they did now. For all her professions to the opposite, now she felt that she could stay there forever, tucked away.

"*Malice* will be huntin' us. All our plans are ruined because o' me," she whispered.

What point was having a big ship like *Malice,* and a life of adventure, if everyone you loved was dead and gone? What was the point of exacting revenge on another crew? Her fathers made her happy, *Felicity* made her happy—and if having those meant she had to give up other pirate things, Ebba could do that.

Except that realization had come too late. Now they'd be in danger for the rest of their days. The adventure had no end in sight, and Ebba wished she could be transported back to that moment on Maltu when she'd entered the alley after Swindles and Riot. That choice would forever haunt her.

She dashed away a tear.

"Ye think this ain't worth the trouble?" Grubby asked her with a peculiar expression, tilting his head to the *dynami*.

Ebba glared at the tarnished silver cylinder in her hand. It had a shallow groove on one end, and intricate markings all along the side. The other end was rounded, like a doorknob.

She had no idea how having super strength solved their predicament. "Aye," she said scathingly. "It's a piece of junk."

Grubby dropped his arms from her shoulder, though not before kissing her on the temple again. "Then ye toss it right out to sea. Ye toss it out to sea and we can be done with it if ye wish."

He turned from her and made for the ship again.

Plank, Peg-leg, and Locks passed her silently. Cosmo followed their example, casting her an uncertain smile, tired circles under his eyes.

Alone on the beach, she stared down at the *dynami*.

The moonlight shone down on the object, and Ebba leaned forward, squinting at the swirling movement underneath the *dynami*'s surface. She reared back, recognizing the white-pearling undercurrent swirling below the brass. Just like the mountain apple.

She paused, recalling that Kahree had said the selkie had guarded the cylinder for over seven hundred years. Something that had to be guarded that long was precious, perhaps. But it also meant trouble.

Ebba ran her forefinger over the swirly letters running vertically down the middle of the cylinder. She assumed the word etched there was dynami. In her eyes, the *dynami* had only brought them pain, except for Grubby figuring out he was part selkie. While not so long ago she'd begged for trouble to provide some excitement to her day, now danger was the last thing she desired.

Her eyes fell on the cylinder. Ebba wanted their lives to go back to normal, even though that was no longer possible with Pockmark hunting them. But if she didn't toss the *dynami* into the water would they be even further from regaining their previous lives? Somehow, inexplicably, Ebba knew they would. If she didn't throw it away, *Felicity* would be dragged into more chaos, whether of the pirate or magical variety, simply because they were the new guardians to this *thing*.

Yet to toss away the swirling magical cylinder would be to force Grubby to break an oath to his selkie kin.

"I was sent to come and get you for dinner," called Cosmo from down the beach, making her jump. "Your fathers are too scared to come themselves."

Ebba blinked. How long had she been standing staring at the *dynam*i in her hand? And why hadn't she already thrown it?

"Are you all right?" Cosmo came up and took her free hand.

She gazed down at their intertwined hands. "Just a bit banged up and feelin' sorry for myself, but I'll be okay. I just. . . Cosmo? Did ye ever make a mistake that made ye feel life would never be the same? One ye wish more than anythin' ye could take back?"

Cosmo was silent as she watched the waves gently tumbling onto the shore.

"Yes," he said quietly. "I'm familiar with that feeling."

His voice rang with truth. Was he thinking back to his dead prince and burning ship? Or did some other past choice plague him?

"I made a right mess o' things," Ebba admitted. "I put everyone in danger."

"That makes two of us." He squeezed her hand, and she was glad the darkness hid her warm cheeks.

She slipped her hand free. "Hey, ye read books. Do ye know what 'dynami' means?"

He looked at her, eyes shadowed by the night. "It's a word from the old tongue," he said. "Yes, I know the meaning."

Ebba resisted the urge to touch her beads for comfort, but couldn't help the shiver tracking up her spine. "What does it mean then? Spit it out."

"Power," he said, shrugging his unwounded shoulder. "Dynami means power."

Power? Ebba shook her head. "What are we meant to do with power?" She had no idea. But there was a cruel captain who shouldn't have any more of it.

She looked out at the sea and tightened her grip around the blasted treasure. She couldn't break Grubby's oath to his kin. Despite the bad things that had happened while finding the *dynami*, parting with the plunder seemed like a failure on some level, if only because there was a chance the cylinder would somehow fall into Pockmark's slimy hands after their efforts.

Ebba hoped she wouldn't have reason to regret yet another decision.

Stomach clenched with nerves, she tucked the *dynami* into her belt, and resolutely turned away from the lapping waves.

She faced Cosmo, smiling broadly at him. "What's for dinner then, prince slave?"

Ebba's story continues in Stolen Princess!

ACKNOWLEDGMENTS

In your childhood, did you ever wish to read a dire pirate quest? I'm sure I can't be the only one. The concept of pirates enthrals most fantasy readers. After all, those savvy seafarers are the epitome of swashbuckling adventure and untold danger, and of intense romance and heart-plunging magical encounters.

As a teen, I wanted to read of dubious moral compasses, and of gasp-worthy high-stakes. I certainly wanted to read a series full of quirks and complexities that would suck me in for hours on end. While there were many books that helped to fill this yearning for a magical quest (thank you Deltora Quest, Protector of the Small, Harry Potter, and The Inheritance Cycle), Waikanae Library in New Zealand never did stock the pirate series I wished for. I would know. The beanbag in the young adult fantasy section was mine.

Eventually, I became an author in order to write the stories I wished to read. Apparently, wishing for the existence of books is an uncertain business without instant gratification. In late 2016, Ebba and her crew came to me in the middle of the night in what I can only describe as a cursing explosion of a pirate version of Snow White and the Seven Dwarves.

My first conversation with Ebba went along the lines of:

"An anti-hero?" I asked her. "Oh, and spoiled. Do you want anyone to like you?"

"Nay," she said. "I be a pirate, ye flamin' soft landlubber bugger."

And so it was decided.

The next month was a blur of obsessive planning, an array of felt-tip pens, A3 pages, and furious typing. The *Pirates of Felicity* took shape. The Exosian Realm with all of its hidden creatures, nooks and secrets wasn't far behind. For the better part of two years between the writing and release of other series, I would steal a guilty moment with my pirates whenever possible, lost in their antics as though I'd never left.

What I'm trying to say is that this series is entirely selfish.

Except, as I'm typing my husband has reminded me that all my books are selfish [please see reason for becoming an author]. But *this* series feels extra glorious and selfish being the first series I've written in entirety before releasing book one.

Where was I? So far I've only acknowledged my past and present self. Good start.

When writing acknowledgements, I always, always think of my husband. The extra things Scott does so that I can answer the constant knock of creativity is something I'm overwhelmingly grateful for. He has heard about these pirates for years and has always given me the utmost interest and support. His support even extended to climbing the rigging of a 17th century merchant ship while we were pitching in the middle of the sea and reporting back on how it felt. Sorry, husbutt!

To Scott, I say:

Yer beard be orange,
yer feet be cold,
yer snore be loud,

but yer heart be gold.

Next, to my swashbuckling manuscript team:

Beta Readers
Jill, Kate, Philippa, Jennifer

Editor One
Melissa Scott

Editor Two
Robin Schroffel

Proofreader
Patti Geesey and Dawn Yacovetta

Map Illustrator
Laura Diehl

Cover Designer & Illustrator
Amalia Chitulescu

What an incredible team. Readers of my acknowledgements will know that the majority of these women have been with me for years. I don't live in the same country as a single one of them. We range from the United Kingdom, to Europe, to the United States, and New Zealand. I love to travel, and it's exciting that people from all over the world help my stories to get shelf ready. Each of you helped to breathe life into my pirates. I'm so thankful for your feedback and expertise.

A special mention to Endeavour and its crew for answering my one million questions on the workings of a 17th century vessel. And to Sally for doing the same.

To my family and to my friends, thank you for asking, 'How are the pirates going?' for the last two years. Thank you for spreading the word, for being understanding of my numerous deadlines, and for coping with my vague and delirious contributions to conversation. Thank you for keeping me humble by introducing me during parties as Kelly the Arthur. In particular, a tip of the hat to Carly and Adam (for Game of Thrones Catan and Cob-loaf nights), Ash (for being a stellar someone who I'm completely at ease with) and Ellen (for thinking of me when I don't think of myself). To all of my Kiwi family and friends in New Zealand, you are probably unaware of this, but you never cease to remind me of what's important.

Thank you to my readers, and my Kelly St Clare's Barracks reader group, for being so patient with all my 'I'm writing a secret series' tweets and posts. If I have to keep a secret, I'm afraid you'll hear about it. From the bottom of my heart, words can't express what your support of my selfish stories means to me.

And finally, because I want to bring this back to me, me, me. Thank you to Childhood Kelly who lurked on the beanbag in Waikanae Library. That was our author apprenticeship, we just didn't know it. And now, here is your pirate story, you whiny bugger. Also, save your money, girl! What are you thinking buying all those clothes and shoes? If you'd learned back then, maybe I'd know how to control myself now.

Happy Reading,

ABOUT KELLY ST. CLARE

When Kelly is not reading or writing, she is lost in her latest reverie.
Books have always been magical and mysterious to her.
One day she decided to unravel this mystery and began writing.
Her works include *The Tainted Accords, Last Battle for Earth, Pirates of Felicity, Supernatural Battle,* and *The Darkest Drae*.
Kelly resides in New Zealand with her ginger-haired husband, a great group of friends, and whatever animals she can add to her horde.

Join her newsletter tribe for sneak peeks, release news, and disjointed musings at kellystclare.com/free-gifts/

ALSO BY KELLY

The Tainted Accords

Fantasy of Frost

Fantasy of Flight

Fantasy of Fire

Fantasy of Freedom

The Tainted Accords Novellas

Sin

Olandon

Rhone

Shard

Last Battle for Earth

Earth's Warrior

Rebel's Crusade

Traitor's Mandate

The Darkest Drae, Co-written with Raye Wagner

Blood Oath

Shadow Wings
Black Crown

Pirates of Felicity
Immortal Plunder
Stolen Princess
Pillars of Six
Dynami's Wrath
Veritas
Eternal Gambit
Mortal Trinity

Supernatural Battle
Vampire Towers
Blood Trial
Vampire Debt
Death Game

Werewolf Dens
Shifter Wars
Moon Claimed
Wolf Roulette

BONUS CHAPTER

STOLEN PRINCESS

Ebba slammed the bilge door behind her, ensuring her secret would remain a secret for a little while longer.

Skimming across the main deck of *Felicity*, she vaulted over the bulwark and onto the only wharf of their hidden sanctuary, Zol. The crew of *Felicity* and their tag-along, Cosmo, had been holed up on Zol for a whole month. A month of coconuts and rocking hammocks and gently lapping waves. A month of bawdy singing and laughing and ship repairs.

Ebba was ready to pull her dreadlocks out. Retirement sucked barnacles. And they pretty much spent their life sucking. She'd die if she had to be retired for too much longer—not that they had much of a choice, after everything.

Spotting Cosmo reappearing around the curve of the shore, she jogged down the pier to meet him, her various beads and adornments rattling as she did so. Cosmo was the only reason she hadn't gone up in a wisp of dullness the last few weeks.

"Oi, prince slave," she hollered in greeting.

He lifted his head and smiled wryly.

His amber eyes fixed on her with their usual intensity. His gaze had unsettled her for a good long while, and still did if she was too close to him when the orbs snapped onto her, but that was Cosmo; whatever he focused on, he focused on with riveted attention, always fascinated to learn every single thing. Ebba suspected one day his skull might explode. It couldn't be healthy to learn too much. Where did it all go? A person couldn't fit endless mangoes into a basket without them spilling out or getting squashed. But Cosmo and her father Barrels seemed to manage adding mangoes all the time, which made her think their baskets were bigger than other peoples' to begin with. A slight pain stabbed over her temple, and she put the matter aside.

She eyed Cosmo's bare chest, pleased to note the ex-servant looked harder than he used to. There were even muscles in his uninjured arm and torso. They'd saved him after *Malice* killed his master, Prince Caspian, and the entire navy crew he'd been traveling with. Suffice to say, he'd been as soft as any mainlander when they first took him in. Still was, mostly.

His fist was clamped around a dripping tunic.

"Ye haven't been washin' again, Cosmo?" she asked incredulously. "Ye just washed yesterday."

He smiled, showing perfect white teeth. "Yes, Mistress Fairisles. I wash every day."

She fell into step beside him as they made their way farther up the shore. "But why? Ye just get dirty again."

Cosmo's softness wasn't any secret. He'd grown up on Exosia, a place where they never ventured into the sun or got their hands mucky. Clearly.

His tone was dry. "I do believe that's the point."

Ebba looked at him sideways. "The point of what?"

"The point of washing each day is that you get dirty each day."

She shrugged. "The point of washin' each week is that ye get dirty each week."

Quiet laughter spilled from his lips. "As always, Mistress Fairisles, your logic makes a bizarre kind of sense."

She patted him. "Don't ye worry, Cosmo, we'll be curing ye of softness soon enough. Won't be long afore ye'll only take monthly washes, like Grubby."

Cosmo winced—a delicate wince as though he didn't wish to offend her by showing his full reaction. It was another thing she'd learned about the Exosian servant; he often muted his real response or thought for a few seconds before he spoke, as though dampening what he really believed. Seemed an odd thing to do. She couldn't remember pausing to think for more than three seconds in her life. But then, she was a pirate, and he wasn't—yet. If Ebba could convince him not to return to Exosia for another few months, he *might* get close to pirate status, but that wouldn't happen if their crew continued hiding in Zol eating coconut stew and coconut mash, and drinking coconut tea.

Cosmo rubbed his shoulder and, forgetting to mute his expression for once, grimaced.

"Shoulder painin' ye?" she asked. Six weeks ago, wooden debris caused by gunfire from *Malice* hit Cosmo in the left shoulder.

He smiled apologetically, though what in the Free Seas he felt sorry for, Ebba didn't know. "It is taking a long time to heal," he admitted. "For a while I was certain it was getting better, but. . . ."

She turned to him, searching his face. One thing about soft people: their skin was smoother than the spokes of a ship's wheel. Cosmo had a natural regal bearing to his features and posture. She was never sure whether it was that, or his russet hair, now curling slightly at the ends, which drew her eye. His amber eyes snapped to her own moss-green gaze and she blinked several times.

"But what?" Ebba prompted him. Was his shoulder getting worse?

He glanced around, probably checking for her fathers, and then lifted the hand that had been rubbing his shoulder. She peered at the exposed bronzed skin, no longer white after weeks outside, noticing a black mark. "Ye said ye'd washed."

"I did. That's what I'm talking about. I don't know what it is."

Ebba took a step closer and reached out to touch his skin. The black mark was small, only the size of half a copper coin. Five short tendrils weaved outward from the smudge like the rays of the sun . . . a very black and angry sun. Her breath caught and she glanced up at him. "What do ye think it is?"

His gaze dropped as she tilted her head to look at him. He wet his lips before answering, "I have a feeling it's nothing good."

She came to a quick decision. "We need to tell my fathers." Spinning on her heel with a crunch of the sand, Ebba stalked in the direction of the shacks around the next bend.

"Wait. Wait!" Cosmo whispered loudly. He grabbed her hand in a light hold. "I'm not sure that's a good idea. We should keep it secret. Just for now."

His mangoes were spilling out of his basket. "Why?" she demanded. "Ye've got black stuff in yer arm. They may've seen somethin' similar. And the crew of *Felicity* don't keep secrets." Though *that* wasn't strictly true. She'd learned a whole heap about her fathers in recent times that they'd never breathed a word about.

He tilted his head to where *Felicity* bobbed back on the pier. "No? You're not keeping your own secret on the ship?"

Traitorous blood crept into her cheeks. No one knew about the thing she kept hidden in the hold, and that was the way it would stay. Aye, so their crew kept secrets, but not *important* ones . . . that would bring the wrath of the rest of the crew upon them. "I don't know what yer talkin' about."

"You disappear into the bilge every day for an hour, Mistress Fairisles."

"A pirate needs their alone time, once in a while."

Amusement lit his eyes and she placed a hand on her hip, eyes narrowing.

"What're ye so afraid of telling me fathers for, anyway?" she shot.

He cast a furtive glance toward the shacks before startling, and peered down at his bare chest in sudden alarm. He shook his tunic out and shrugged into the wet linen, still stained despite his once-daily washes.

"Why're ye getting dressed?" she asked. "You'll just need to be takin' it off again to show me fathers."

He cleared his throat, muttering, and she strained to hear, catching something about *six overprotective pirate fathers*.

She shook her head and resumed her push through the sand to the shacks. "Yer a clownfish, Cosmo. That's for sure."

"I don't mind being a clownfish," he murmured. "As long as I'm still swimming by the end of the day."

They made their way around the white-sand beach and came to the first of the shacks. There were now eight. The shacks sat in small clearings their crew had formed in the coconut trees fifteen feet from the cliff face—so rocks crumbling off the cliffs didn't land on them. The eighty-foot space from the water to the bottom of the cliffs was half-filled with coconut trees which hugged the ring of sheer cliffs all the way around the inlet. Only the tunnel to the ocean outside interrupted the shore on the southern end.

"Mistress Fairisles," Cosmo said.

At his odd tone, she peered to where he pushed through the sand beside her. "What?"

His brows furrowed and he searched her face. "Don't you ever wonder why you have six fathers?"

Ebba's gaze froze on Cosmo's face before she remembered to walk and act naturally.

The truth? Since she was old enough to ask herself that question, she'd run in the opposite direction as hard as possible, and her fathers certainly hadn't pursued the subject either. It was fact that a pirate didn't need solid answers to survive—and one of their ship laws. Who cared about the why when it didn't change the reality of a situation? Knowing why a shark was chasing a person didn't change that it *was,* or that the person should swim like Davy Jones himself was coming after them. In her experience, pretending away the oddities in life had always worked and kept the crew happy.

A month ago that changed.

Their crew had returned from thwarting *Malice*, but they hadn't gone back to normal. Life wasn't quite the same. In some small, fundamental way, they were all altered, including her.

"Nay, I don't think about that," she replied to Cosmo through gritted teeth.

"I didn't mean to offend you, Mistress Fairisles," he replied, watching her closely.

She sighed. "I'm sorry. It be a sore point for me. Esp'cially after going through Syraness and everythin' with *Malice* . . . It may sound odd and un-pirate-like, but I'm wonderin' if I should be questionin' a few things here and there."

Cosmo appeared to think for a few seconds before answering. *Always thinking.* "I don't see the harm in that," he said, expression neutral.

Ebba shrugged. "Aye, well, I ain't decided on the issue."

Their run-in with Ladon had revealed a few things about her fathers' past, previously concealed. Despite her new understanding that some things were bad enough to not want to discuss them, Ebba had since caught herself wanting to ask questions she'd never wanted to ask. Ebba-Viva Wobbles Fairisles, born-and-raised pirate of the Free Seas, was *considering* that she should stop pretending about a few things. Like why she had six pirate fathers . . . amongst several other large issues, like the presence of magic.

"I'm sorry for prying," Cosmo said. "We can talk of something else if you prefer. Until you've come to a decision. If that happens, I hope you know that I'm happy to listen and talk."

Ebba exhaled slowly and nodded, relieved the prince slave had backed off.

She picked up her pace as murmuring voices drew her to the third shack down the row and put the conversation with Cosmo aside for the time being—or maybe forever if she could manage it. The odds were fifty-fifty.

"Ye're not just *puttin' up a shelf*, Barrels," an exasperated Plank was doing his best to explain. "It will be a perm'nent fixture of the place. And it's got to be matchin' the other shacks yet suit the other furniture and general feel of the room."

Ebba groaned loudly and Cosmo nudged her arm, grinning.

Stubby and Locks had fortified the temporary shacks, and then Plank had entered interior decoration mode. Usually, Ebba loved accessorizing and mixing and matching textures and materials, but her enthusiasm for the project had died right alongside her eagerness to stay on Zol for the rest of her life. Somewhere in the second week.

"Plank, dear fellow," replied Barrels, "I do not care where the shelf goes as long as I have somewhere to put my books."

She and Cosmo halted in the doorway.

Each crew member of *Felicity* had their own shack made of wooden slats. Woven tree leaves formed the flooring atop the sandy ground, and a bed pallet sat against the far wall. On the right wall hung a picture of Ebba that her fathers had someone paint ten years before. Her eight-year-old self was scowling at the painter, but all six of them had shed tears and bought a copy all the same.

Barrels strode to the left side of the shack and held a sawn-off plank against a different spot.

Plank rubbed his forehead, looking around in desperation. He caught sight of the pair of them in the doorway. “Ebba! Perfect. Come and tell Barrels where the shelf needs to be.”

Ebba shoved her beaded dreadlocks out of the way and scanned the room. She pointed to a space above the bed. “It’s got to go there.”

Plank whirled back to Barrels in triumph. “See. I was tellin’ ye that.”

Barrels pushed up his spectacles and smoothed a wisp of peppered hair back into the black leather thong he always wore. All of her fathers had gray or white hair, aside from Plank, who—though not the youngest of her fathers—possessed a full head of raven black curls.

Cosmo crossed his arms. “But what if the shelf falls on his head as he sleeps?”

“Ha!” Barrels said, coming over to clap him on the back. “That’s what I said.”

He and Plank faced off, neither willing to budge on the matter. She was glad Grubby wasn’t here. Confrontation made the youngest of her fathers extremely nervous.

Ebba cleared her throat after a glance at Cosmo. “So,” she drew out, “Cosmo’s got a black sun in his arm.”

Cosmo glanced at his shoulder at her comment, the wrinkle on his brow clearing as he inspected the shape of the mark. “Huh, it does look like a sun.”

Barrels and Plank slowly turned from each other to pin their full attention on the younger man.

"Does he now?" Plank asked, taking a few predatory steps. "And how do ye be knowin' about that, Ebba?"

Cosmo began to stutter, but Ebba spoke over him. "Why, I saw it after he'd washed, of course."

"W-what she means is—"

A voice bellowed from outside. "Lunch be up!"

Cosmo bolted out the door.

Ebba went before her fathers. "Ye should take a look at it, the pair of ye. I've never seen anythin' of the like."

"Ye'd think with how much he be washin', he wouldn't have a grubby spot left," Plank mused.

Ebba nodded. "That be my exact thought, too. So why is it there?"

"Maybe he doesn't wash right. Maybe that's why he needs to do it so often."

They approached the fire pit in front of the middle shack and Barrels sniffed the air. He blanched and without bothering to sniff the air themselves, Ebba and Plank reversed their direction without hesitation, gapping it back the way they came.

"Oi, you lot. I said lunch be up," Peg-leg roared.

Ebba eyed the light sweat on Plank's forehead as he turned back with slumped shoulders and ventured to sniff the air. He gagged. "Seaweed babies with shark's teeth, we can't leave now. He's seen us. He'll get in one of his moods."

"He's already in a mood," Barrels argued. "We haven't had fresh vegetables in weeks."

Ebba grimaced. When Peg-leg was upset or angry, it showed in his cooking. Meals had grown steadily worse in the last two weeks, taking a sudden dive three days ago when the last of the bananas were eaten. Peg-leg strongly believed in a balanced and nutritious diet. The garden he'd planted a couple of months ago wasn't ready to harvest, and the supplies they'd brought with them from Kentro were now gone. Peg-leg grew angrier by the day and his meals worse.

Ebba sniffed and reared back. "It be fish stew again."

"Shite," Plank cursed.

"That's one coin to the curse jar," Barrels quipped.

"What? For shite? That ain't a cuss word."

"Two coins."

Ebba listened to their bickering with one ear and watched Cosmo's expression as he sat on a log around the fire pit and took a bowl of fish stew from the bald-headed Peg-leg. He seemed to sway where he sat for a few seconds before quailing under Peg-leg's watching eye and bringing a spoon of the stuff to his lips.

"He ain't gonna do it, is he?" she whispered.

Peg-leg loomed over the top of the servant boy, hands on rotund hips and scowl firmly in place.

Cosmo shoved the spoon of stew in his mouth. He quickly chewed, smiling at Peg-leg after swallowing. Her father withdrew and the young man turned ashen.

Plank clucked sympathetically.

"I said, *lunch be up*!" Peg-leg yelled, slamming a lid on the large caldron and stamping his wooden peg in the sand.

"That's where ye get yer temper," Plank said to her grimly.

Ebba rolled her eyes. "Aye, and what do I get from ye?"

Barrels was quick to answer. "Short attention span."

Aye, she might've gotten the worst parts of each of her six fathers, but she'd probably got the best parts of them too. It all evened out, in her opinion.

The three of them took seats on the large logs bordering the fire pit. Ebba spotted Stubby, Grubby, and Locks approaching through the trees. She caught Stubby's eye and drew a finger across her throat, shaking her head.

They were gone within seconds.

"Aft'noon, Peg-leg," Ebba said pleasantly. He shot her a beaming smile as he passed two wooden bowls filled to the brim to Plank and Barrels.

Ebba ran to the pot. "Here, let me do that for ye," she said. "Ye've been on yer feet all mornin'."

He smiled at her again and sat on a log with a loud sigh. "That I have, Ebba-Viva. And no thanks I get from anyone else for the work I do. With hardly any ingr'dients. In *terrible* conditions."

Ebba made a soothing clucking noise and tipped the tiniest amount of fish stew into her bowl. "Well, we have somethin' to share with you," she said brightly. "Cosmo has a black mark on his wounded shoulder. Do ye think there be a spider inside his body, crawlin' around?"

Behind her, Cosmo gagged.

She put the lid on the pot and made her way to the far side, so Peg-leg wouldn't see the contents of her bowl.

"And just how do ye be knowin' what his shoulder looks like, Ebba-Viva?" Peg-leg asked darkly.

Why were their sails in a knot about her seeing his shoulder? They should know she was a pirate who had no time for dalliances around her career goals.

Barrels sniffed the fish stew, jerked violently, and rushed to say, "How about you show us the mark, Cosmo?" Barrels waited until Peg-leg stood and approached the young man before placing his bowl to the side with some haste.

Ebba poured her stew behind the log and covered it with sand, seeing Plank do the same. They grinned at each other.

Cosmo removed his tunic and stood hunched under the scrutiny of her fathers. Ebba squeezed into their midst and ran a gentle finger over the black mark. Cosmo shuddered.

"See?" she said to her fathers.

Plank grabbed her hand and pulled her back. "We be seein' just fine, little nymph. Don't be touchin' men. They have diseases the eye can't be seein'."

She rolled her eyes at him but couldn't help eyeing Cosmo askance. Guess a person could never be too safe. . . .

Barrels peered over the top of his spectacles. "Over six weeks have passed since you sustained the injury. If it was going to become infected it would've done so long before now."

Peg-leg glanced at his own wooden leg. "Aye, that be a certainty. It ain't an infection."

"Not a normal one, anyway," Plank said, tapping his mouth.

Cosmo swung to look at him. "What do you mean?"

Plank walked around the fire pit, hands clasped behind his back. He took his time answering and Peg-leg groaned as it became obvious to all the answer wasn't going to be quick. Plank was the storyteller of their crew and enjoyed building drama and suspense. That wouldn't be a problem, and *Ebba* certainly didn't mind his tales, but his stories were usually long-winded, which the others took objection to. Even she had to agree the weird, ominous voice Plank adopted when he told stories was a little strange. After the recent happenings, however, where a number of his stories had turned out to be partially true, Ebba now took particular interest in his recounts of mythical creatures and old magic.

"Cosmo was hit by a splinter from the gunfire," Plank said in a deep, slow voice. "Not a bullet from any gun, but one from *Malice*."

Ebba stared at him.

He put his hands palm up, reverting to his normal voice. "We know there be somethin' wrong with Pockmark and their crew. There's no knowin' what they put in their gunpowder, and the like."

"Seems far-fetched," Barrels said, clearing his throat.

Peg-leg snorted. "Just a wee bit."

Plank's face turned stony.

"The mark is growing bigger," Cosmo said quietly, breaking the tension.

A coconut thudded to the ground in the distance as they all turned to look at him.

"It is?" Ebba asked.

His eyes dulled. "It started as a pinprick about two weeks ago, and I didn't notice it at first, but now I'm sure. It's getting larger. Fast."

Peg-leg hobbled over and smacked him upside the head. "Why did ye not tell us that, boy?"

Cosmo put a hand over his mouth and swallowed several times. The cook narrowed his eyes on him and Cosmo forced a smile, no doubt swallowing back the fish stew that had risen in his gullet. Ebba snickered.

"I didn't want to bother you with it. We're already in danger," Cosmo confessed in a thin voice, still struggling to keep the stew down. "I had rather hoped it would go away by itself."

Peg-leg scratched his rear. "Aye, boy. Ye'll soon learn that nothin' goes away just because ye wish it to. Believe me." The crew and Cosmo looked down to where Peg-leg continued to scratch.

". . . What are we goin' to do?" Ebba asked, nose wrinkled.

Plank shrugged. "I don't know what we can be doin' about it, little nymph. We don't even know what 'it' is."

"Maybe we should go and find us a medicine person," she blurted, seeing her chance to escape Zol. "It's the least we can do for Cosmo. He's nearly part of the crew."

Barrels shook his head. "*Malice* and every other pirate ship between Kentro and Maltu will be on the lookout for us. We cannot risk venturing out into the open sea."

"We'll need to go out sooner or later," Ebba shot, folding her arms. "We've run out of fruit and veg'tables already. Ain't that right, Peg-leg?"

Peg-leg scowled. "That we have."

"We have plenty of food to last us a few months longer. The heat from *Malice* may've ebbed by then." Plank put in. "It may be *safer*. . . ." He tilted his head towards Ebba, and Barrels and Peg-leg followed his eyes to her.

Cosmo held up his hands. "I wouldn't dream of putting Ebba in danger."

"I be fine with danger." Ebba shot daggers at her fathers and Cosmo. "Ye all seem to be forgettin' it was *me* who got us through the siren's nest."

"I'm in no doubt of that, Mistress Fairisles, but I am happy to wait and see what happens to the mark," Cosmo replied with a reassuring smile sent her way.

"A diplomatic response as always, Cosmo." Barrels slid a signet ring onto his little finger. He tended to dress fancier than the rest of them. A clean cravat was tied around his gullet and though the sand and air were warm, he wore a doublet over his tunic and had his buckled shoes on. Barrels came from Exosia, like Cosmo, except way back when. And though he could sail and shoot to match the rest of them, there were certain things he hadn't been cured of despite decades spent aboard ships. Fanciness and reading being two of them.

Peg-leg limped closer and studied the ugly black tendrils along Cosmo's arm. "I don't know, m'hearties. It be lookin' vicious-like. I'd hate for the lad to lose a limb over somethin' like this, if we can help it." The sorrow in his voice was clear, and no one could doubt he was remembering losing his own limb. He'd never truly gotten over it, though it happened well before Ebba was born. Peg-leg used to climb the riggings, embracing the challenge of the heights on a moving ship. Ebba loved the feel of swaying high above the ocean, and couldn't imagine if one day that was suddenly gone. She guessed that was why her father asked her what she saw up there each day.

Of any of them, Peg-leg understood what Cosmo might lose.

Peg-leg didn't take his eyes off the black mark. "Nay, I vote we be goin' now."

"I vote we go now, too," Ebba said, heart racing. She liked to think helping Cosmo was equally important to her as leaving Zol for a change of scene.

"Well, I am the captain of the month," said Barrels. "And as such, I have three votes. I vote no. We wait a few days longer and see if the mark worsens. It may not be anything to worry about. Plank?"

"Ye're the one who wants to get to the bottom of all the magic, and ye said there be magic in Cosmo's arm," Ebba reminded Plank quickly. He and Grubby were the only ones who thought they should dig deeper into the strange occurrences of late.

Plank grimaced. "It comes down to safety, little nymph. Until we be sure the black gunk is magic and harmful-like, I ain't sure we should risk runnin' alongside *Malice*. I vote with Barrels—we wait a few days longer."

Ebba blew out a loud breath and earned a reproving look from the eldest of her fathers.

"Aye then, four votes against two, we'll do that." Peg-leg tore his eyes away from the smudge.

Cosmo shrugged his wet tunic back on, shivering.

Barrels picked up his bowl and glanced to where Plank's and Ebba's lay empty atop the log. "You two must be hungry. You almost inhaled your food. Peg-leg, I don't suppose there's enough for these two to have seconds?"

Ebba's jaw dropped open. Plank looked about the same.

Peg-leg's face flushed with pride. "Aye, ye know there's always plenty where that came from." He shot an evil glance at where Stubby, Grubby, and Locks had been working earlier that day. They were probably eating coconuts back in the trees somewhere. "Especially as *some* pirates don't see fit to join us for the meal."

He scooped a ladle full of the blackened slop into her bowl.

Ebba watched the stringy glops splash until the bowl was brimming with stew. Plank's face mirrored her own horror and the gentle sniggers from the other two reached her ears.

She took the full bowl and stared at the half-charcoal, half-watery-gray liquid mess before plastering a grin on her face for Peg-leg's sake.

The sooner they got out of Zol, the better.

www.ingramcontent.com/pod-product-compliance
Lightning Source LLC
Chambersburg PA
CBHW020933310726
48980CB00007B/754/J

* 9 7 8 0 6 4 8 3 3 4 4 1 5 *